Only a Captain Will Do

A Novel of Regency Romance

Teresa Sweeney

Courting Romance Publishing
California

Only a Captain Will Do is a work of fiction. Names, characters, places, and incidents are the products of the author's imagination or are used fictitiously. Any resemblance to actual events, locales, or persons, living or dead, is entirely coincidental.

Published in the United States by Courting Romance Publishing

ISBN 978-1-940319-04-9

First Edition

Cover Photography by Christina Brusaca
Cover Models: Nicole and Lawrence Sweeney III

By Teresa Sweeney

Always Rebecca

A Love Match, Indeed!

An Uncommon Affair

The Reluctant Viscount

Only a Captain Will Do

To my beautiful and amazing daughter Christina,
and her remarkable husband Jason.
Together they are faithful, strong, and invincible.

And to their beautiful children:
Lorenzo and Maria.

Only a Captain Will Do

Prologue

May 1800
The Duke of Aubry's Estate, Yorkshire, England,

Stephen Robson stood on the sprawling south lawn of the duke's estate next to his grace, keeping his lips pressed together to suppress his rising chuckles. The clear and sunny day was in direct contrast to the duke's stormy disapproving temper. While he wholeheartedly approved of the shenanigans he was witnessing, he had no wish to further exasperate his employer by indulging in a good belly laugh.

He had been called into service at a time when his eight-year-old daughter Christina was in his care, and with no other recourse, had to bring her along to await him in the duke's immense foyer while he did his employer's bidding. His work as the duke's solicitor took longer than the half hour expected and when he went to collect Christina, he found she was gone from where he placed her. He was not duly alarmed as Christina was not one to remain idle and usually looked for a way to amuse herself. He was sure the trinkets and pictures on display lured Christina from her perch, but when his cursory search brought no result, he knew he would need permission to wander further into the duke's ostentatious mansion to look for her. He sought help from the duke's overbearing butler, only to be informed by the supercilious servant how he did nothing without the duke's knowledge or consent.

The butler quickly made his way to the duke's study, informed his grace how Mr. Rothsborn's daughter was missing and suffered a scowl for his trouble. The duke was not pleased to be interrupted, especially by the solicitor he had already dismissed. His mind had moved on to other business and he felt quite put upon to leave matters important to him, to his country, to locate a missing girl. However, he did his duty and ordered his self-righteous butler to send the servants out to search for Christina. It was the results of the investigation that brought Stephen and the duke out of the mansion.

Stephen's spirits rose the moment he stepped outdoors and felt the warmth of the sun tempered by a gentle breeze. He had been in great need for a breath of fresh air having suffered a long confinement with the duke, but more so after Christina went missing. The refreshing climate was a stark contrast from London's atmosphere where coal fires, industry, and refuse polluted the air daily. Nature's clean and sweet fragrances instantly comforted him, especially now he knew his daughter was safe.

He took in his surroundings and was mesmerized by the majestic landscape. He had never been admitted anywhere but to the duke's study, so he viewed the property before him much as he would if he was visiting a museum. He looked for every nuance, preparing himself to discuss in kind with Christina what she had witnessed while adventuring outdoors. He would not be caught unawares and draw a *"How did you not see it, Papa?"* from her.

There were a number of cultivated flower gardens, sculpted yew and box hedges, and various flowering trees creating a lovely picture of color, texture, and design. As he slowly followed the duke, he spied a yew hedge sculpted to look like a stag deer pushing through a boxed hedge. He knew it would be one of the things Christina would recall to him.

His inspection took in the workers and their industry. One groundskeeper pushed a wheelbarrow that held either the debris he collected or the mulch he wished to distribute among the plants. Another gardener hunched over a bed of flowers pulling off dead petals and cutting back stems to clean up the plot, while another worker stood stock straight, like the trunk of a tree, to clip the sprouting shoots off a hedge.

He stopped his gazing when he realized how far behind the duke he fell and quickened his step to catch up with his blond-haired aristocratic employer. His grace, with his stiff posture and assured stride, led the way to the smallest of his ornamental ponds. The results of the servant's search had led them both to the scene they now spied and to which they each responded differently.

Stephen's mouth stretched wide into a grin, while the corners of the duke's mouth turned down at witnessing his twelve-year-old son Jason pelt his solicitor's daughter with water. The children were laughing from splashing and soaking their bodies. They glistened like faceted diamonds from the drenching and sparkled in the sun's light.

Stephen was hard-pressed to keep his chuckles inside. He could not remember a time he wanted to laugh so hard, not even at Drury Lane where many a comedy he attended. He felt his stomach convulse and realized how soft his figure had gone from sitting at a desk most hours of the day. He was far from the brown-haired, blue-eyed Corinthian who upon entering Society had drawn the admiration of many ladies, including the lady he would call "wife." Many would still call him handsome, even with his graying hair and thickened waistline.

He watched Christina hold her own against the duke's boy who towered her in both height and age; and thought how much his late wife would have enjoyed seeing Christina splashing away, giving as good as she got in water. He was happy to see his daughter playing as should a child for Christina rarely played without restraint, living under his brother-in-law's unyielding authority. He often worried over his decision to place his daughter under Dewksbury's stern upbringing and care after his wife died, but he could not deny the viscount offered his daughter a far superior standard of living than he ever could.

He turned his attention to his frowning employer who stood a few inches taller than him. The Duke of Aubry was an impressive man, trim and strong in stature, wearing a suit that bore the mark of Weston, a renowned tailor favored by the noble who made suits to fit like a second skin. The duke was a force to be reckon and his voice immediately cowered the children, putting a stop to their water battle, freezing them in their tracks.

No one moved until the duke waved his hands at his servants who quickly brought forth white linen sheets to wrap up the children. Stephen stood quiet, watching the duke's maids escort Jason and Christina into the mansion to rooms where they could change into dry clothing. The duke did not look at him, nor speak a word, but Stephen knew to follow his grace back into the study where he would once again await his employer's command.

"My son will make his apologies to you and your daughter," stated the duke.

Stephen grinned, "Perhaps, my daughter owes you her apology, your grace."

"Nonsense, Jason is the man and responsible for the folly we witnessed. Be assured he will be appropriately punished. You will allow me to compensate you for your daughter's ruined dress."

"I wish you would not punish your son, your grace. He is still a boy susceptible to mischievous deeds. I know both their behavior lacked propriety; however, with no guests at hand, their solecism is unmarked and easily forgotten. In all honesty, knowing my daughter, the episode will make her birthday incomparable. Her behavior is extremely checked at Dewksbury Hall and I for one was quite pleased to see her enjoying herself without restraint. She does not often have the chance to be herself."

"She is a *hoyden*?"

Stephen grinned at the absurd characterization. "No, your grace, Christina is quite the opposite, very ladylike having been tutored in all that is proper by her aunt, Lady Dewksbury. However, like her mama, she can be impulsive. She has a joy for life and takes amusement in those things we take for granted: the call of a lark, the burble of a brook, the changing leaves of the seasons. She glories in nature and enjoys the freedom it provides when the strictures of Dewksbury Hall offers her so little. Master Brentwood's folly made her laugh and I would not have the boy punished for it if I may so boldly petition."

"You serve me well, Rothsborn, so I will give you this boon only because I can see the request is important to you, but only this one time. My son must not be so easily influenced to behavior which his station dictates unseemly."

"You are most magnanimous, your grace."

"I do not fault you for bringing your daughter with you, Rothsborn, since it was I who interrupted your holiday. However, I do not approve how they engaged one another's company. It was my understanding she was left where she could do no harm. You will in the future not impose her on my household."

"Of course, your grace. Now, if you give me your leave, I will collect my daughter and make my way to London to do your bidding."

Chapter One

May 1810
Miss Wainwright's School for Young Ladies

Christina watched the bustle of coaches collecting their young misses from the window seat of her room and leaned into the cool glass pane, hoping to catch a final glimpse of her friend Amanda. Her second floor window faced the gravel driveway in front of Miss Wainwright's School, a coveted suite at the institution, which Christina's aunt as trustee had the clout to settle her. Priscilla had selected Christina's room with all the authority of a board member whose wealth the school depended. Not until later would Christina learn just how unusual was her circumstance in being given a large suite when she saw the inconsequential quarters of other girls whose family owned wealth but no title.

She had no idea when she arrived at Miss Wainwright's School her aunt had moved her bedroom furniture from Dewksbury Hall to her new living quarters, so she was quite overcome when she entered her new room to see her familiar things. Her down-filled mattress bed, gilt-wood full-length cheval mirror, mahogany writing table, rose brocaded arm chair, and the Aubusson medallion carpet that had greeted her feet each morning were placed as they had been in her old room. Her new abode was like being home and the anxiety of leaving all she knew behind eased. Even the lemony-smell of her well-polished furniture and the lavender-scented bed sheets lulled her into a peaceful sleep her first night and every night thereafter.

Her forehead chilled as she peered through the window pane looking for Amanda. The sight of a departing coach with what looked like the Larksborough crest on its door made Christina jut out her bottom lip. Sad at not catching a last peek of her friend, she lifted her head away from the glass and stared sullenly at her blue-eyed reflected image. Her lips flattened in frustration after she assessed her features.

She never understood why her one-time matching curls could not lose their coil equally or how she could be at fault when one of them hung lower than the other. At least, the small braid wrapped around the coif crowning her head was still intact and could not draw any comment from the head mistress. She doubted anyone would care about her hair once she left Miss Wainwright's school. At least, she hoped.

A resounding tattoo on her chamber door broke her inspection and she quickly rose from her window seat. She straightened her plain muslin day dress and pushed her uneven curls away from her face before she bid “enter." She felt a rush of gratitude flow through her when she saw her dearest friend Amanda. She grinned and ran to greet her.

Dressed for travel, Amanda wore a luxurious crimson velveteen pelisse and bonnet trimmed in white fur. Her deep red ensemble brought out the chocolatey richness of her brown hair and eyes. She looked quite stylish and fetching, even with pouting lips and sorrowful eyes. "Papa's carriage has come for me, Christina, but I could not leave until you assure me you will attend my *come-out* ball.”

Christina released Amanda from her hug. “Your mama will not invite a simple Miss Rothsborn to attend, Lady Amanda. We have discussed this already and you must reconcile yourself. I will not be there.”

Christina gaped when Amanda glared at her and said, “I agreed to adhering to propriety in public, Christina, but I will not abide foolishness. When we are alone, simply call me Amanda."

Closing her mouth, Christina nodded at her fierce friend whose display of temper was quickly replaced with bubbling excitement. "Now, you are right, my mama would not invite Miss Rothsborn. However, she will invite the Viscount and Viscountess Dewksbury and you know my mama would not offend your aunt by not including you in the invitation, especially if you take residence in her town home."

Christina was frustrated she had to remind her friend it was her wish to live with her father. "I will not reside with my aunt, Amanda. You know I have waited years to live with my papa."

"Yes," Amanda rebutted. "I know your papa gave you into the care of your aunt and uncle after your mama died when you were two years old, but why change your circumstances now. Your uncle cannot be so dreadful. Can he?"

"He has been most generous to me, Amanda, and could have easily refused my living with him and my aunt. I told you how my uncle was in his thirties when he married my aunt, a young debutante making her *come-out*. I am sure the furthest thing from his mind was taking on a child the moment he returned from his wedding trip, especially when their tour was cut short because of my mama's death."

Amanda was too refined to interrupt, but Christina could tell by the way she bit her bottom lip Amanda had heard her story one too many times and was impatient to speak. No sooner had Christina finished talking than Amanda's words flew from her mouth. "But why must you leave his household if he is so generous? I had hopes of us enjoying the Season together."

Weary of the conversation, Christina offered, "I am done being shunned by my betters in Society, Amanda. I wish to live where I am not so harshly judged. My childhood was full of reprimands."

Amanda dropped her jaw. "You never mentioned being struck, neglected!"

Christina quickly assured Amanda. "No, never. My aunt loved me as her own and my uncle was only harsh in his words for my rambunctious ways. It was difficult to be found lacking, but my aunt insists his sternness came from not knowing how to relate to a young girl."

"Perhaps, your aunt is right, Christina, and he has waited for you to come of age. Will your aunt and uncle sponsor you and host your own ball?"

"My aunt is *enciente*, Amanda. I know she wishes to do me the honor, but my uncle forbids her engaging in anything that could cause her fret or fatigue. She is no longer a young bride and I cannot begrudge him his concern."

Amanda's voice softened in sympathy. "Is there no one else, Christina, to bring you into Society, to help you marry well?"

"While my grandparents were titled, they have left this world and their heirs have no affection for me. Besides, even if I was Lady Christina, with no dowry, what man of consequence would marry me?"

Amanda's silence only proved Christina's point of how *ton* marriages were contracted for increasing one's position, property, and wealth. She shrugged her shoulders as if it was not important, but when her friend opened her arms, Christina accepted her heartfelt hug. As much as she claimed she did not care, a part of Christina hurt because she felt singularly excluded from a world in which she was raised.

"You will come, Christina. You will receive an invitation, not addressed to your aunt, but to you and your papa. I will not relent on this request to my mama. Trust me, she will appease me for she has little patience when I am petulant."

Amanda's ardent declaration made Christina grin. She could not have wished for a better friend and cheerfully agreed, "Very well, Amanda. If I am invited, I will attend. I know my papa will generously escort me."

"When do you leave, Christina? Does Mr. Rothsborn come for you?"

"Nay, my aunt's carriage will call for me tomorrow and bring me to her town home where my papa will join us for dinner."

"Then, when you are settled you must call on me." Before they could finish their goodbyes, the entrance of Lady Margaret Wilton interrupted them.

"Really, Amanda! Miss Wainwright had me looking everywhere for you. Your footman is tapping his toes, waiting impatiently. I do not understand why you are here when you could be long gone from this wretched institution."

Lady Margaret Wilton still had a year before her own *come-out* and was already chomping at the bit to make her debut. No doubt, she would make a splash when her time came. She had title, beauty, and wealth to recommend her, though at times, she lacked grace.

"Good day to you, Margaret," greeted Amanda. "I will have you know Mama's footmen are well-trained and would never tap their toes or demonstrate any sort of emotion."

"Well," responded Margaret. "He is waiting and Miss Wainwright asked me to collect you."

"Where are your manners, Margaret? You have not greeted Christina."

Margaret grimaced at Amanda's scold. She gave Christina a steely look as though it was her manners at fault and not her own. She whined, "Come on, Amanda. There are others who wish to say their goodbyes. I am sure, Miss Rothsborn, does not wish to detain you."

With remorse, Amanda explained, "I really must go, Christina, but do not forget to call on me." She gave her friend another hug and then walked out of the room with Margaret. The door was left open, so Christina heard Margaret criticize, "Why do you bother with that girl, Amanda? She is a commoner and cannot add to your consequence."

"Margaret, you are a fool to judge Christina poorly. You should use character and not consequence as the basis to make an acquaintance. I will warn you if you wish to call me friend, then you best think before you speak ill of Christina in the future."

Feeling a bit melancholy over Amanda's departure, Christina walked over to her desk and opened her writing box. The decorated wooden slanted chest was a present from her father, given to her the day she moved into Miss Wainwright's School. Over the years, she used it religiously to write to both him and her aunt. The box contained paper, pens, a sealed bottle of ink, sealing wax, and stamp. It also contained a copy of a letter written by Jason Brentwood when he was a young midshipman. It was her most prized possession, aside from the model ship he had given her, and she liked to read it whenever her spirits needed lifting.

As the duke's solicitor, her father was often called to make copies of some of Jason's amusing letters for the duke's mother, the Dowager Duchess of Aubry. He once took the liberty of making a copy of a particular letter for Christina when it was being shared among family and friends as an anecdote. He knew Christina harbored a fond memory of the boy and would enjoy reading about Jason's escapade.

Christina removed the letter and with great care, unfolded the aging paper.

11 August, 1801

Father,

The captain is making us midshipmen write home, so I cannot take credit for remembering you. My days are filled with learning. The ship's schoolmaster teaches us our mathematics and navigation in the morning and then throughout the day we are put to task by the boatswain to learn the skills that will make our career. I have mastered several knots and use them in a number of jobs I am put to do. We are kept busy from morning to night, but the captain will probably write and tell you we have been getting into mischief.

I must defend myself and say my honor was at stake. The Brentwoods are no cowards, so when I was challenged to climb the shrouds to the masthead, I did the deed. I took to the ropes like a monkey and soon found myself perched high above the deck. The view was incredible. I could see for miles the power and splendor of the ocean. I dare say, the captain would not have learned of my ascent if a large swell had not unbalanced me from my roost. I would have plummeted to my death if not for the grace of God's hands catching my legs in the ropes.

I dangled quite high, swaying to and fro above the deck and my stomach felt much like the turbulent ocean I watched from my upside down position. I prayed I would stop swinging and my legs would not unwind from its lifeline until I could secure myself. My mates called for help and every hand on deck came to my rescue, but sorrowfully not before I lost my battle with my roiling stomach. I am afraid my bravery was trumped by my opprobrium and I hope you agree my embarrassment is punishment enough for me to endure. I have promised the captain not to climb the shrouds alone until he has determined I have the skill required.

Your second son,
Jason

The letter never failed to make her admire Jason more for recalling his dangerous fall in a light-hearted manner that would make anyone grin and improve their spirit. His family would have been frightened as she had been when she first heard of his peril, but his letter had assured her of his well-being, as it must have done for his family. Over the years, she did her best to follow his career, seeking news from the Duke of Aubry by way of her father and watching for his name and ship in the papers.

She replaced the letter in her writing box and then picked up the model ship Apollo she also kept on her desk, easily recalling the scene where ten years ago he gifted her the ship and earned her admiration.

"Do not look so downcast. You cannot think I begrudge you."

Christina reminded Jason, "It was my fault his grace is angry with you."

"Nonsense, I command my own will and it was I who chose to engage in our adventure. Did I not press you into service?"

Christina's eyes widened at the realization of what he said was true. She grinned and excitedly babbled, "It was an adventure, wasn't it? Oh! Thank you, Jason, for giving me the best birthday present ever! I will remember this day always."

"I do not think a water battle is enough to mark your memory, but perhaps this will."

Christina was too embarrassed at being the cause of any discipline Jason might receive to pay attention to the model ship he carried and now held out to her. She carefully took the wooden frigate from his hands and inspected it, finally understanding why Jason marveled at it. The craftsmanship and detailing were superior to anything she had ever seen, plus she saw, the rigging and sailing were functional, making it more than just a toy boat but a true replica.

She shook her head and tried to return the model to Jason "No, I cannot accept it. His grace would not like you to gift me something so valuable."

"The Apollo is mine to do as I wish," he stated with authority while refusing to take the ship. "And I wish for you to have it to remember me. I have no need for the model because I will soon be on the real one. Do not refuse me, Christina, it is most inconsiderate of you, since doing so refuses me the opportunity to make amends for behaving ungentlemanly."

The reference to him being a gentleman reminded Christina how she was beneath him in class and needed to show proper deference. "Do not say so, my lord."

"What happened to you calling me Jason?"

"I am addressing you as I should."

Jason grinned. "You are a funny one. Well, accept the Apollo because I want you to have it and for no other reason than it pleases me."

Christina smiled. "You are sure you will not get in any more trouble?"

"Not for this."

"Will you suffer much for our water play?"

"Nothing my antics have not suffered me before. Do not worry about me. What about you? Will your father mistreat you?"

"Oh, no! He is most tolerant of me. Our time together is so rare he overlooks my disgraces with only chagrin. You need not worry for me."

"Then, you best be off before your delay causes further concern." He bowed and gallantly extolled, "It has been a pleasure meeting you, Miss Rothsborn."

Chapter Two

May 1810
Mayfair, London

Timmons, the Dewksbury butler, opened the door to admit Christina into her aunt's fashionable Grosvenor Square town home. He was a tall gangly sort of fellow and had served the Dewksbury household since she could remember. His usual stoic countenance often broke into a grin when she visited, no doubt recalling her many antics. He helped her remove her pelisse and bonnet and then when asked, informed Christina her aunt was in her room resting. Christina assured Timmons she had no wish to disturb her aunt, required nothing of the staff, and could easily make her own way to her room.

The room was refurbished for her use when she came of an age to leave the nursery. The walls were covered in verdant silk and framed with giltwood moldings. The Chippendale furniture that belonged to the room remained, but was reupholstered in rose silk brocade with green braid trimmings. The same fine material was used to make matching valences, counterpanes, and curtains. A rich and colorful Aubusson carpet, reminiscent of an English rose garden, lay on the floor to finish the luxurious room. Christina always felt like an impostor living among such richness, but never confided anything but appreciation to her aunt for her generosity. She would no longer live here during the Season. After dinner she would leave with her father and never have to worry about being accused of living above her station again.

All her life, she overheard the *haute ton* question her aunt's wisdom in raising Christina as a child of consequence. She first understood the difference in her station when she was scolded for not showing due reverence to a girl the same age as herself. The reprimand affected her greatly and the memory helped her to remember her place in society.

Christina looked at the room and exhaled a deep breath that swooshed much like the north wind. She felt a profound relief to know she could leave the fashionable residence of her aunt without regret, and while she had never concerned herself with budget or household management, she would rise to the task if it meant she could live with her papa. In preparation, he had moved out of his gentleman's residence and leased a respectable town home in Bedford Square. Named after the Duke of Bedford for whose property the buildings were constructed and for whom rents were collected, the square was desirable to many in the legal profession for its proximity to Lincoln Fields. The address was considered most respectable as Lord Chancellor Eldon lived at No.6, as did those judges and lawyers who were at the top of their profession.

Christina shrugged off her reflections and quickly saw to her toilette, washing her hands and face with the warm pitcher of water recently placed on the mahogany console in her room. She smoothed the stray hairs of her golden coiffure, secured pins, and then checked her appearance in the full cheval mirror before she descended the stairs to await her family in the Dewksbury drawing room.

No sooner had Christina taken a seat at one of the bay windows facing Grosvenor Square than she spied her father bounding up the front steps. She practically leapt to her feet in anticipation to greet him. She heard his gentle voice telling Timmons he need not be announced and as soon as he entered the room, Christina rushed to welcome him.

"Christina, my love, it is so good to see you."

"I am glad to see you too, Papa. I trust all is well and I will be returning home with you."

Stephen Rothsborn smiled at his daughter. "You need have no fear, Christina. You have kept your end of the bargain, minding your aunt and excelling at school. I am thrilled you will be residing with me, though I see no advantage for you. Your change in circumstance will be severe. Are you sure this is still your desire to reside with me?"

"Yes."

He warned, "You understand your position in society will no longer be elevated, Christina. Your connection to Dewksbury will be diminished by living with me."

"Yes, I know, Papa. I am well aware of the advantages I had under uncle's guardianship and should I forget, the elevated society to which you refer, have always been ill-mannered enough to inform me." She continued after releasing a deep breath, "I want to be where I belong with no need to explain my circumstances."

Stephen looked at his downcast daughter with feeling. "Forgive me, Christina, for choosing unwisely so many years ago."

"There is nothing to forgive, Papa. I had an exceptional upbringing and because of you, have the grace, education, and confidence to hold my own among my betters. I may not be titled, but in my manners I feel the equal of any debutante."

He hugged her. "That you are, my love. No father could be prouder."

The Viscountess Dewksbury witnessed the loving scene when she entered her drawing room and said, "I do hope you have saved some of that affection for your dear aunt, Christina."

Christina laughed and disengaged herself from her father. She opened her arms to her aunt and when they embraced, she kissed her aunt's cheek. She immediately felt the remnants of tears. Concerned, she pulled away and asked, “What is it Aunt? Are you ill?”

Priscilla waved her hand in denial, “No, no, just a little sentimental. Nothing for you to worry about.”

Timmons entered before Christina could pursue her concerns further and announced dinner was served. She was surprised to see her aunt take her father’s arm and asked, “Is uncle not to dine with us, Aunt?”

"No, he is taking his meal at his club this evening.”

Christina followed her aunt and father into the dining room and took her seat, thinking it quite odd of her uncle to eat apart from his wife. She waited until the servants removed the first serving before remarking, “It is uncommon for uncle to absent himself from your company at dinner, Aunt. If I did not know better, I might think he found our company lacking.”

Stephen nearly choked on the sip of wine he had taken. He blotted his lips and was about to reprimand his daughter for her rude remark when his sister-in-law intervened.

“Do not scold her, Brother. She is perceptive and knows me too well not to notice I am not myself.” She told her niece, “You must not think ill of your uncle, Christina. The fault is mine. He feared his presence would only aggravate me further, so he left to dine at his club.”

“Since Uncle has always granted your every wish except one, then, I have to surmise I am the root of your displeasure with him.” Christina waited for her aunt to confirm or deny her speculation. She raised one eyebrow to prod her along, as her uncle often did to get his wife to confess. She knew her effort was futile when her father dabbed his *serviette* against his mouth to mask a chuckle. She was trying to think of another stratagem to get her aunt to confide her burden when she heard her father solemnly ask, "Is she correct Priscilla, has Christina in some way caused friction between you and Dewksbury?"

"He will not relent, Stephen. I have pleaded and still he refuses me the honor of sponsoring my niece into Society. I feel I have miserably failed my dear sister. He says if I continue to harangue him, he will close up the house and take me home. Then, I will be completely useless to Christina." She turned again to her niece and cried, "I am so sorry, Christina."

Christina pushed herself from the table to stand and made her way over to her aunt. She gave her a hug hoping to make her feel better. "Do not fret so, Aunt. It cannot be good for you and no doubt is the reason behind uncle's diligence in removing himself this evening. However, I expect he is further vexing you with his absence."

Priscilla whose head hung in sadness, looked up to acknowledge the truth of her niece's statement. Christina continued, "You have not failed me, but given me every benefit."

"But, how will you make a good marriage if you are not properly introduced into Society with a ball?"

Christina did not want to remind her Aunt Priscilla how a woman without a dowry rarely contracted an advantageous marriage. Instead, she put on her brightest smile and assured her, "Love will find me as it did my parents."

Stephen Rothsborn smiled at his daughter and stood to walk Christina back to her seat. He professed, "My greatest wish is to see you happy, Christina, and I can think of no better way than to open your heart to love."

The tension in the room diminished and they all turned their heads when they heard the servants enter with the second serving. She realized Timmons had kept the footmen away to protect the privacy of his lordship's household. She was glad there would be no gossip or pity concerning a certain niece who had nothing better to recommend her than a titled aunt.

"So," Christina suggested, "Shall we put Uncle out of his grief and send him a note to come home?"

Priscilla called for pen and paper and then had a footman dispatched to deliver her message to Dewksbury at his club on St. James Street. Christina guessed her aunt informed her uncle dinner would be held until he arrived for the servants were removing her untouched second course plate. It seemed only minutes later, but in truth, a half hour must have passed when her uncle arrived and the second course serving of succulent roasted duck was placed before her again.

Her uncle looked quite pleased to take his seat at the head of the table; especially with her aunt beaming at him. Christina could not help but tease him. "I am glad you could join us, Uncle."

Viscount Dewksbury smiled at his impudent niece and distracted any attention to his person by asking her, "Well, Christina, have you left any more damages at Miss Wainwright's School needing restitution?"

Stephen guffawed and quickly subdued his laughter while he listened to his daughter's outcry.

"Unfair, Uncle! How was I to know the stick had a mind of its own."

One of Christina's classmates, Evelyn Stone, the school's charity student, returned from a holiday with a stick her older brother gave her from one of his many travels. He was part of a crew of merchantmen who traveled afar. While anchored at Botany Bay, he traveled inland at New South Wales and came across some natives eager to trade. He walked away with an angled stick the natives said they used in hunting and gifted the thing to his sister while narrating some of his travels. Evelyn brought the stick to school as evidence her brother had seen the world and Christina's curiosity drove her to inquire how the stick worked as a weapon. In response, Evelyn shrugged her shoulders, so Christina suggested they venture outdoors onto the lawn and experiment with it.

The stick was curved and flattened with designs painted on it. Christina thought it looked like a toy and asked Evelyn to stand at a distance to catch the stick when she threw it to her. Evelyn refused, reminding Christina the stick was used to kill animals. Her remark made Christina wonder if the stick was filled with gun powder and could explode upon impact. The idea immediately made her feel duty-bound to protect her friend by disarming the weapon.

Christina looked for a safe place to detonate the stick. The open area where the young ladies took their leisure was surrounded on all sides by the wings of the multi-storied school. The first floor contained the kitchen, the dining room, the library, the matron's office, and the classrooms; the students' living quarters were situated on the second floor and the servants resided in the attic. The girls' windows either faced into the quad or out to the neighboring properties.

The quad was used as a retreat from study where the girls could find shade under an ancient stout oak tree, lounge on the marble stone benches, or exercise by walking the perimeter of the lush lawn. Running was not permitted, nor any activity considered to be a manly pursuit.

Christina determined the two familiar large stone benches in the center of the quad were the perfect targets to disarm the stick. Her heartbeat quickened as she considered the danger. All her senses were on alert and she felt the brisk wind press her dress against her body and flutter the hair left unprotected by her bonnet. An errant blond strand tickled her ear and she frustratingly rubbed it and ended up pushing her straw hat off the crown of her head. She was annoyed her excitement was making her clumsy, so as she fixed her bonnet, she took and exhaled a deep breath to settle her nerves. With

Evelyn at arm's length by her side, she grasped the flattened stick by one rounded end, pointed the other end in the direction of the benches, and like a catapult, thrust the stick towards her target.

The stick flew high. Christina gaped as Evelyn cried out in alarm when the wooden weapon missed its target. Evelyn's scream drew attention and Christina saw a number of classmates grouping together to cry out in chorus. One girl started to walk towards them and Christina extended her arm towards her in a halting manner. She had no wish to place anyone else in danger.

They all watched the stick spin and revolve in flight until it followed an arc that brought it back to where Christina and Evelyn stood. With no other recourse, Christina shoved the frozen Evelyn to the ground and fell on top of her. The stick flew over them and shattered one of the school's window panes.

The noise of the crash and the girls incessant cries brought the headmistress and every other adult to see what had happened. Before they even inquired to the person responsible, all the young ladies, even Evelyn, pointed their accusing fingers at Christina.

Letters were sent home to parents. Christina was blamed for encouraging unladylike manners and sent to her room without benefit of supper.

Chapter Three

Christina had not considered where she would be sleeping until she entered her new home at Bedford Square and her father escorted her to a closed door. Unknown to her, Priscilla had commissioned laborers to pack, cart, and transport Christina's furniture and goods to her new residence. The workers had stood outside Miss Wainwright's School until Christina exited and entered the Dewksbury coach. They watched it rumble away to Grosvenor Square before they entered the establishment to do their job. Like before, Priscilla wanted to make her niece's transition to her new living quarters at Bedford Square as smooth and comfortable as possible, and with her brother-in-law's consent, had ordered her servants to await and receive Christina's goods, and then to organize them to her specific instructions.

Christina stood before the closed door and sensed her father's anxiety. She was sure he worried she might be disappointed and prepared herself to show her gratitude in an effusive way. She took the door knob in hand and slowly turned and pushed open the door. Before she could extol her appreciation, she spied the furniture she had called her own for so many years arranged to perfection in her new bedroom. Even the Apollo and her writing box were carefully placed where she had always kept them on her desk. Her eyes welled up and her father pulled her into a tight embrace. His fierce hug forced her to tilt her head back to see him. His wide grin made her laugh. She realized her emotional display pleased him more than any string of grateful platitudes.

She kissed her father's cheek when he told her she looked tired and bid him good night. He left, closing the door behind him. Exhausted, Christina quickly changed into her fine cotton night dress trimmed in lace and completed her ablutions. She sighed when she slid under her bed covers and fell asleep.

A ray of sunlight nudged her awake the next morning and she quickly stretched out her limbs to start her day. She was no longer a child to be looked after, but a capable adult and she was determined to be of service to her father. She bounced out of bed and saw to her own needs, dressed and organized her clothes, before she left her room to investigate her new home. She met the staff and took inventory of all she saw. As the day passed, the costs her father expended to have her live with him became evident and an overwhelming sense of guilt afflicted her.

Aside from the town home lease itself, there was the cost of staff, furnishings, linen, dishes, cutlery, food, and all the other things necessary for maintaining a household that her father never would have purchased while living in a furnished bachelor apartment. He had always availed himself of the apartment services when he needed cleaning and ate his meals at his club. His life was unencumbered and Christina's mind weighed heavy with the realization of how much her father gave up to have her live with him. She had wanted her company to be of comfort and benefit to him, but now she wondered if her presence was more burden than pleasure.

She knew the deed was done and even returning to her aunt's home would not recapture the money he spent, so she decided to be a helpmeet by reviewing the household accounts to see where changes could be made to reduce expenses. The idea of showing him how she could efficiently manage his household improved her spirits and when she went to bed, she could hardly wait for morning to come.

She woke early and felt at ease to implement her plan as she made her way to her father's study. She knew her father worked at the duke's residence and would not be home until dinner, giving her plenty of time to assess his household. She took a seat at his massive mahogany knee-hole desk and ran her hands over the weathered and decades old writing table. A wave of emotion washed over her thinking about how often he sat at this desk, and she wondered whether her own mama had engaged in the same sentimental manner, running her own hands over the mahogany top.

Christina shrugged off her sobering emotions and pulled the stack of household account books from the top of the desk where her father kept them, and then, carefully opened them one by one. Her review of the week's menu, grocery, coal, staff and household expenditures, confirmed her concerns. She reacted by calling in the servants individually and now, because of her impulsive nature, she was dealing with the result of her actions.

Christina knew if she could not calm her rapidly beating heart, she would soon be passed out on the floor with no one to blame but herself. She sat hunched over the desk with her elbows planted on the surface like two pedestals to support her swooning head in her hands. With her eyelids closed, she silently coached herself to inhale deeply through her nose and exhale slowly through her mouth. She repeated the exercise until she felt better, but her dizziness returned when she remembered what caused her to panic in the first place.

Christina continued to focus on her breathing and was trying to free her mind of worry when the echo of hurried footsteps startled her into lifting her eyelids. She looked up and saw a flash of bright blue cross her sight. Aside from herself, Cook was the only person in residence and the woman moved at a snail's pace compared to the burst of color she just saw. Fearful an intruder stalked her home, Christina tentatively pushed off from the desk and stood. She was considering whether to confront the villain or find safety with Cook until she heard her aunt call her name. A profound relief overcame her, resonating like a cool breeze on a hot summer day. It was as though her silent plea for help was answered. She quickly walked around the desk and greeted her aunt.

"My dear girl," exclaimed Priscilla. "I thought I would never find you. Where are all your servants? I had to let myself in and then ordered my footmen to search the house for you."

"I am sorry, Aunt, you were not well-received, but I am afraid there are no servants, aside from Cook who refuses to leave the kitchen and attend to anything that does not pertain to her duties."

"As she should, but Christina, your papa assured me his household was in order. Are you telling me he spoke false?"

"No, of course not. I acted foolishly and now must put everything to right before he returns, but I am not sure how to go about it. I am glad you have come, Aunt."

Lady Dewksbury set her reticule on her brother-in-law's desk, removed her bonnet and then began to slowly remove her kid gloves. "I expect there is a story to be told. You best have Cook brew up a pot of tea to fortify me before you begin."

Knowing Cook would not respond to the bell cord, Christina made her way to the kitchen, hoping the servant had something to break her aunt's fast. She went about preparing a tray with her father's best china while Cook brewed a pot of tea. She added a pitcher of cream, a bowl of lemon curd, and was happy to see there were some leftover biscuits from breakfast she could offer her aunt. Carrying the heavily-laden tray, she carefully made her way back to her father's study, releasing a curse when her arms started to shake. At that moment, she wished she had the foresight to have kept at least one footman to aid in the tasks requiring strength.

She entered the study and saw her aunt perusing the ledger sheets and menus she had spread out earlier on her father's desk. It was Christina's own review of the household accounts that led her to call in the staff, and one by one, dismiss them all, except for the cook.

Christina set the tray down on the desk and began to serve her aunt. She remembered to pour in the steeped tea first, before adding a splash of cream into Priscilla's cup. Only bone china could tolerate the hot brew without cracking and the ladies of the peerage were quick to observe the quality of their hostess's tea service when the lady of the house poured. Her aunt had taught her everything she knew about being a hostess and she could tell through her aunt's smile she was pleased with her serving skills.

"I believe I know what you are going to say, Christina, but you had best explain yourself first. Then, we will see what needs to be done."

"Well, you have seen the accounts. The agency clearly took advantage of my papa. Even if the servants are experienced and sought-after, as they were kind enough to inform me, we have no need for such talent. And we surely have no need for seven course meals. Honestly, Aunt, it is just the two of us."

Lady Dewksbury took a sip of her tea and answered with aplomb, "Your papa wishes to keep you in the style you are accustomed, Christina. He is not ignorant of his finances. He is an astute solicitor and I assure you, he knew what he was about in putting together his household."

Christina forlornly admitted, "I know. As soon as the house quieted, my better senses prevailed upon me. I understand why Papa hired his staff, but Aunt it is not necessary for him to make such an expense. It distresses me how my living with him costs him so dearly."

Christina began to twist and turn the *serviette* she held in her hand. "I must make it right, but I do not know how."

Lady Dewksbury took pity on her niece, "Do not distress yourself, Christina, we can easily replace your staff and after looking through the ledgers, I can see what your papa can afford. Let us discuss how we can reduce expenses while meeting your household needs."

Mindful of costs, Christina argued against the need for a butler, suggesting a maid-of-all work could answer the door and announce guests, but Priscilla quickly disabused her presumption. Her aunt explained how a butler would manage the servants when Christina was out of the house. Besides being the household's gatekeeper in screening visitors, as a senior servant he would ensure discipline among her staff. Priscilla also insisted Stephen would want someone to watch over Christina when she was home alone. Her aunt's argument reminded Christina how on this very day she had feared an intruder stalked her home, so she quickly agreed to the hire.

Priscilla then suggested Christina employ a footman for the heavy tasks. Her aunt's words prompted Christina to look at the heavy tea service she had struggled to carry. Sighing, she conceded to her aunt's wisdom. Further discussion placed on her hiring list a maid-of-all-work for washing clothes and cleaning house, a scullery maid to help Cook, and a lady's maid for Christina's personal use.

They worked for a better part of an hour before Lady Dewksbury's footman entered and announced, "My lady, you wanted to be home before his lordship arrived. Coachman bid me to call upon you."

"Oh, my! I must leave, but do not worry, Christina. I will send you a temporary staff from my household and tomorrow I will help you interview new applicants."

The next day, Lady Dewksbury sat laughing in her niece's parlour while Christina recalled her father's outrage over the dismissal of his staff. In an uncommon temper, he ranted how he had snared a number of the servants from better households, which explained the high wages he paid them. Once he calmed down, Christina convinced him how there was no need to pay for over-priced servants and to her satisfaction, he designated the replacement of his household to Christina's capable hands.

Christina and her aunt now waited to interview the hopeful applicants. Priscilla had sent a message earlier that morning to a servant registry, commanding them to send over their best candidates for inspection. Normally, the housekeeper would see to the business, but Christina did not have one or any need for one, since her household would be small compared to aristocratic standards.

Priscilla instructed Christina to review the applicant's reference, ask questions pertaining to their experience, and then let her conscience guide her in making a decision. Christina nodded her head to express she understood what to do. Her aunt offered a "very good," and told Christina to have her footman inform her butler he could let her first applicant enter. Christina did as she was bid and waited to interview her first applicant.

A young girl of ten entered the parlour and kept looking over her shoulder until she stood before Christina and her aunt. The girl's fright was palpable with brown eyes as big as two silver crown coins. Christina sympathized, knowing what it felt like to stand in front of authority, waiting for your future to be decided and offered a smile to make the girl comfortable.

The girl wore a serviceable brown dress and weathered brown boots. She looked like the typical street urchin until she delivered her curtsy. Someone, a mother perhaps, had taken the time to school this child in how to show respect to her betters.

Christina asked, "What is your name?"

"Molly," the girl answered rising from her curtsy.

Without offering anything further, Christina prodded the stick of a girl to speak. "You have come for employment, Molly? The agency sent you?"

When silence continued, Priscilla intervened, "Why are you here, Molly?"

Her answer exploded from her mouth with little pause to separate her words. "Me mum is sick and cannot work. Word on the street says yor looking for a scullery maid, so I snuck in through the kitchen ter beat the uvvers waitin' outside. Will yor 'ire me?"

Priscilla looked at Christina to see if the girl's rapid speech had astounded her as well. She turned her focus back to the girl and asked, "Do you have any references?"

Before Molly could answer, Christina asked, "Have you worked before?"

Molly's eyes seemed to open even wider, crunching her brows up into her forehead. She opened her mouth to reply, then clamped her lips firmly together. Christina grinned. Clearly, the girl thought better than to offer an impertinent response which proved the girl had sense. Silently, she chastised herself for asking a foolish question. No doubt, Molly was used to hard work.

Molly finally answered, "I 'ave no papers, but I work 'ard at 'ome and can tidy and tote wiv the best o' them."

Concerned her aunt was ready to dismiss the girl, Christina took over the interview and asked Molly about her family and circumstances. Satisfied with her answers, she handed Molly some coin and immediately saw how the girl misunderstood her generosity. Christina quickly told her she was hired and should report to Cook tomorrow, bright and early. Molly's sadness transformed into giddiness, her smile growing even bigger when Christina reminded her how she knew where the kitchen was located.

The meeting with Molly set the tone for the rest of the applicant interviews. Priscilla sighed each time Christina dismissed someone the agency recommended in preference for someone with less experience. Even so, Priscilla thought the motley crew would serve her niece exceptionally, considering how grateful they were for being employed.

"Well, Christina," stated her aunt, "I had no idea where you were heading with your personal questions, but I believe the men and women in your employ will serve you well. They are grateful to you for hiring them, so they are not likely to leave unless they are dismissed. Definitely more favorable than those servants who hop from household to household. Those bounders do nothing but stir up dissension when they enter a new household."

After a thoughtful pause, she added, "You also have a good balance between young and old servants which will only benefit the whole staff. The young can learn from the experienced, and the older ones will be happy to have assistance with the heavy chores. Cook will definitely enjoy having Molly to command. If you treat them fairly, more than likely they will stay and mature into a fine loyal staff. They will look to you to set the tone in what is permitted in their behavior. You must be firm, yet compassionate, or so I have always behaved. Others in our Society will tell you different. You must let your conscious lead you; mine has always served me well."

"Thank you, Aunt. I could not have done this well without you."

"You are sure you will not want Mary as your personal maid? She has done your hair ever since you came out of the nursery. This Susan you have hired is as young as you and without experience. Plus, I do not know why you insist on calling her Susan. It is easier to call her Mary."

"Perhaps, when you have a multitude of servants, it is easier to call the maids Mary, but my personal maid's name is Susan and I am quite capable of remembering and using it. I like her enthusiasm, Aunt, and she will learn quickly. Besides, I could not take Mary away from all the pomp and circumstance of your household. She would be heartily bored here at Bedford Square and would surely feel her transfer a demotion from her current position. No, I will manage quite nicely with Susan."

"Very well, but I will send Mary to do your hair when you have something formal to attend, until this Susan of yours can manage on her own. Which reminds me, I received an invitation from the Countess of Larksborough to attend her daughter's *come-out* ball. She is a friend of yours, is she not? I thought I remembered you mentioning her name at one time."

"Yes. I consider Amanda a very dear friend, Aunt."

“I was surprised the countess did not extend the invitation to you. I take great umbrage they neglected to invite you, Christina. I will send my regrets, of course.”

“Say you have not done so, Aunt! Amanda has promised to honor me and Papa with our own invitation.”

“I am glad to hear it, Christina. It would grieve me terribly to think someone you considered friend affronted you. I shall send my acceptance when I am assured of your own invitation. I see no reason for your uncle to object if I do not stay overlong. My acknowledgement of you can only add to your consequence. Truthfully, I cannot fault Dewksbury for being overprotective for we have waited a long time for this child I am carrying. However, I am finding his strictures, while born out of love, incessantly annoying, especially when it intrudes on what I wish to do!"

After calming herself, Priscilla asked, "Tell me, Christina, what new gown will you wear?”

Christina’s eyes glinted and she smiled at her devious aunt, who knew, without a doubt, Christina owned no new gowns. “I shall wear my blue silk, Aunt.”

“We must get your hearing checked, Christina. I believe I asked, "What new gown you would wear?'”

“You know very well I have made no purchases. My blue silk is more than adequate for Amanda’s ball. Besides, my role is simply supportive. I need not dress to attract suitors.”

“And why not?”

"To what purpose, Aunt? Why should I set myself up for disappointment? Even if I caught the attention of a lord, what do I have to barter with to secure him in matrimony?"

"You are not common, Christina. You are well connected. Your grandfathers were of the aristocracy. Besides you are a beautiful, intelligent girl of a generous nature who would benefit any lord of good breeding."

"Not common, Aunt, but a commoner with nothing of consequence to offer a lord."

"You disappoint me, Christina. You speak of fiduciary concerns. What of your claims to follow in your parents' steps and secure a union through attraction?"

Christina laughed. "I am no fool, Aunt. Should Providence present me with such a gift, I will greedily accept it. I have not yet resigned myself to spinsterhood, only to marrying above my sphere. Tell me, would you shun me if I found love with a shopkeeper?"

Priscilla cringed. "I doubt if you would let me, Christina. You have always done as you please, even with your uncle's stern hand, you have managed to have your way in the end."

Christina smiled, then offered, "Looking back, I should probably thank Uncle for reigning me in. Who knows what kind of trouble I could have gotten into without his sober guidance."

"You are being generous, Christina. I know he was often too unyielding with you, but you must forgive him for he acted in a manner he believed befitted a guardian." Her aunt's eyes misted "He was never a brute, was he?"

Christina patted her aunt's hand. "No never. I think I just simply scared him with my youthful shenanigans. I think we get along quite nicely now I am grown. Do you not?"

"Yes, quite nicely. Now, enough of this melodrama. I shall make an appointment with my *modiste* and get you outfitted for Amanda's ball."

"Aunt, it is not necessary."

"Who spoke of necessity, Child? I simply wish to indulge myself in shopping. Would you refuse me this boon after I helped you hire your household? That would be most ungracious of you."

"You are a master manipulator, Aunt. Do not think I am easily cajoled. However, I will see your *modiste* as it pleases me to please you. I leave it to you to argue with Papa over who covers the expense. You know he will wish to assume the cost."

"Nonsense, he can find his own pleasure as the purchase of this dress is mine. Now, it is time I return home to rest or else your uncle will fret with worry. Why don't you join me in my carriage? You can drop me home and then avail yourself of its use."

"Aunt, that would be wonderful! I could stop and leave my card for Amanda. I promised her I would pay her a visit when I was settled. Then I could go to Hookham's and open up a subscription to use their library. I am anxious to find something to entertain me in the evenings."

"Do not borrow too many books, Christina. I expect your evenings to fill up quickly enough once I introduce you around at Amanda's ball."

Chapter Four

Christina rushed upstairs calling out for her new maid Susan. After employing the girl, she had sent her up to her room to become familiar with her wardrobe and a wide-eyed maid greeted her when she burst through the door. Christina grinned at seeing her maid's astonishment and commanded, "Grab your things, Susan. We are going out."

Susan did as she was bid, grabbing her hat, shawl, and reticule from the chair where she had placed them, but quickly gasp when she forgot her duty to her mistress. She dropped her things back on the chair and hustled to help Christina into her spencer and bonnet. Then, she hurried to collect her own belongings and catch up to her mistress who had already left the room.

Christina heard Susan's quick steps behind her and the sight of her new butler Giles at attention, with shoulders back, proudly holding the front door open for her to exit made her happy with her hiring decisions. Her aunt stood at the entry, cloaked and ready to leave, so Christina followed her out the door and down the front steps with Susan following. The Dewksbury footman lowered the coach footstep and offered his hand to help them enter her aunt's carriage. Christina took the forward facing seat next to Priscilla while Susan sat across from her where she quickly made herself invisible by keeping her eyes cast down. Her presence was completely forgotten when Priscilla began her discourse on how she did not need to host a ball to introduce Christina to the upper echelons of society.

Priscilla talked about the latest fashions in the ballroom, who she hoped was in town for the Season, and which balls Christina would attend as her guest. Christina's lips twitched in amusement when her aunt kept punctuating her name to ensure she paid attention. Amazingly, Priscilla's speech ended, with a warning to boot, at the exact moment they arrived at the Dewksbury town home. "I will not be deterred, Christina. I will send you a note as soon as I have scheduled an appointment with Madame LaReaux and you will make yourself available."

"Yes, Aunt. I will do as you bid," offered Christina with an affectionate smile and thank you.

The coach door opened, the footstep was put down again and Lady Dewksbury with the help of her footman made her exit. She looked to her coachman and commanded, "You are at my niece's disposal, Thomas. I will have no further need of you or my carriage, so do not hasten her use of your service."

"As you wish, milady."

Christina directed Thomas to take her to the Larksborough town home and sat back on the soft leather squab of her seat to await her arrival and breathed in her aunt's lingering floral scent. She felt the gentle rumble of the coach's wheels as the carriage made its way down the street and thought about how Amanda most likely was out with her mama visiting those families newly arrived to Town. The three months, primarily April through June, when Parliament was in session was the most exciting time to be in London. The Season was full of balls, routs, and musicals hosted by the *haute ton* who wished to showcase their sons and daughters, especially daughters, where hopes of enhancing their social standing and wealth lay through a contracted marriage. Daughters reaching their majority were introduced into fashionable society by first making their curtsy to their sovereign and then by making their debut at their *come-out* ball. Lady Larksborough, like every other lady with a daughter of marriageable age, would be using house calls to inspect her daughter's competition and investigate, in terms of wealth and connections, the eligible bachelors in Town for the Season. She and Amanda would only remain home on those days set aside to receive company.

The coach stopped and Christina wrote her address on the back of her calling card with a short message before instructing her aunt's footman to deliver it to Amanda's butler. If Amanda was literally "not at home" Christina would have to wait until Amanda called on her. Her message informed her friend she was at home most days and would always be home for her. It was common practice for the aristocracy to inform their butler to tell those visitors they did not wish to see, that they were "not at home," which was usually the case for any untitled person.

Christina watched her aunt's footman rush up the steps and rap the lion's head door knocker. Amanda's butler opened the door, accepted and looked at the card, before saying something to the footman. Christina waited and learned from her aunt's footman that Amanda was not home, but according to the Larksborough butler, he had standing orders to receive Christina at all times, even when Lady Amanda was out. Christina grinned at her friend's kindness. She informed the footman to tell the butler how she would not stay, but wait upon Lady Amanda's leisure to call upon her. Once the footman returned and took his perch on the outside of the carriage, she instructed Thomas to take her to Bond Street.

Christina looked at her newly hired lady's maid, or *abigail,* as the aristocracy referred to them and noticed the girl's hands were clasped on her lap, her head bowed in deference. The girl sat adjacent to her and had remained quiet through their ride, reminding Christina how servants were trained to be invisible. It was a common practice in many households for lower servants to turn their backs to their master, to vanish into the walls when they came into contact with him. Even upper servants were known for their stoic expressions in the presence of nobility. However, Christina had little companionship growing up, so whenever a servant offered a kind word or hand she had embraced it with enthusiasm.

As a child she was often called to account and chastised by her uncle for her impetuous behaviors. Her strict upbringing drew sympathy from those who served her and before long, Christina found friendship among the serving class. Her aunt and uncle would have disapproved and reprimanded the servants soundly had they known the help conversed with Christina as an equal.

Christina grew up being told by many children of the titled how her father's position made her too common for them to associate, and as much as her aunt championed her, it was not until she met Amanda did she finally gain a true friend.

Uncomfortable with the silence and how quiet and still Susan sat, Christina offered, “Susan, when we are alone, I am more than agreeable to engage in a conversation with you.”

Christina watched Susan's head lift in wide-eyed surprise and felt compelled to explain to relieve her maid's obvious shock. “I assure you I do not wish us to become fodder for the *gossipmongers*. I understand what should dictate our behavior to one another, but if you do your job to the best of your ability, swear loyalty to me and respect my authority over you, then in return I will respect and care for you. Perhaps, our mutual respect will foster into a friendship and I am sorely in need of friends."

"You, miss? With your aunt a titled lady and you, living in such finery, is in need of friends?"

"Cannot everyone always use another friend, Susan?"

"Indeed, miss. But I never heard of no ladies mixing with my kind."

"I am not a lady, but a commoner like yourself, though my means and situation place me above your class. I am sorry I suggested we be friends."

"Oh! No, miss, it's just that you took me unawares. You know I am new to being a lady's maid and my mouth got the better of me. Please, miss, I swear loyalty to you and would be honored to be your friend."

Christina feared her impetuous behavior would be the ruin of her. If Susan spoke to another servant regarding how she asked Susan to be her friend, the remark would sweep through every parlour discussion as the latest *on dit* and like a wild fire that kills everything in its wake, so would the gossip remove any chance she might have had of a life among respectable society. She could hear the *ton's* vicious speculation wondering which footman or stable boy could also call her friend. She paled knowing the shame she would bring to both her aunt and father. *"Oh,"* she thought, *"Why do I never think before I act?"* Her hands began to shake and before she could contemplate how to retrieve herself from the threat she created, Susan spoke.

"Oh, miss, please do not worry yourself for I would never speak of our friendship to anyone. Is that not what loyalty means? To be obedient to your wishes. I swear to keep silent unless you tell me different. I would very much like to be your friend."

Christina looked at Susan, saw her sincerity, felt her body calm and smiled. "You have already proven yourself a worthy friend, Susan. Thank you."

At that moment, the carriage stopped again and within seconds, the livered footman opened the door, dropped the footstep, and offered his arm to help Christina exit. She looked out, saw how the streets and sidewalks were crushed with traffic, and told Thomas to leave her and return in one hour to pick her up. Thomas tipped his head to convey he understood. The footman helped her and Susan to debark and when Christina saw he meant to accompany them, she kindly refused his service, insisting she could manage alone with Susan. Once Christina was safely on the sidewalk, she saw Thomas move the carriage away.

Bond Street was a fashionable shopping center and like Hyde Park's Rotten Row was an effective means for announcing one's return to Town. The *haute ton* promenaded along the store fronts as much to see as to be seen. Almost anything, if you had the currency, could be found among the many stores and exchanges, even boxing lessons for gentlemen.

The air was heavy with overwhelming smells. The scent of people bathed in flowery cologne and the stench of horse dung fouling the street assaulted her nose, as did the contrary sweet aroma of freshly baked bread from a nearby vendor. Susan's stomach grumbled and brought Christina to an abrupt stop to ask, "Have you not eaten, Susan?"

"No, miss."

"Well, I cannot have your stomach making vulgar noises. I will give you coin to buy yourself a currant bun. Then, you will meet me at Hookham's. It is three doors down and I do not think my lack of servant will cause any remark on my character in the time it takes for you to return to me." Christina pulled two coins from her reticule and looked towards the direction she expected Susan to follow. She gasped and an alarmed Susan asked, "What is it, miss?"

"I am glad we have reconciled to be friends, Susan, or else I would have replied nothing is wrong and left my answer at that, but the truth is I just spied someone I have not seen since my youth."

An amazingly handsome and fit naval officer with blond hair exited the lending library holding two brown parcels tied with string. He was distinguished in his navy blue dress coat and his striking figure drew attention from the nearby ladies. Shiny gold buttons adorned the lapels and gold braid trimmed the coat's lapels, tails, pockets, and pocket flaps. He wore white breeches, white stockings and black buckled shoes.

He stopped on the sidewalk and his bicorne pivoted like a weathervane when he looked to the left then the right as if unsure which direction to take. He decided to turn towards them and Christina's breath hitched again. She stood transfixed and never even noticed when Susan took the coins she still held between her fingers, nor was she aware when Susan pushed her towards Jason.

Susan waved the tuppence at a young boy standing across the street. The urchin made his living by being paid by someone to clear the street of dung where they wanted to cross, so he quickly raced over to her when he saw the tuppence and listened to her proposal. He nodded his head in agreement, grabbed the coins and ran towards the young lady whom Susan wanted shoved into an officer.

Christina cried out in alarm when she began to fall. She feared injury, embarrassment, and visualized herself sprawled on the pavement drawing snickers and condescension. Somehow, two hands caught her and managed to gracefully stand her on her feet. Her legs shook, but she quickly found her composure and nervously smoothed her wrinkled skirt. Blushing, she begged "Jason" to forgive her clumsiness as she straightened her skewed bonnet.

Jason Brentwood instinctively dropped his packages when the body of a young lady came flying at him. He was glad of his quick reflexes and was able to catch her small frame with ease. He set her on her feet and waited until she regained her balance before he released her. He noted she was too flummoxed for her fall to be contrived. He had his share of distressed damsels seeking his attention. Sprained ankles, fainting spells, dropped handkerchiefs were common tricks used by young ladies to catch the attention of an eligible bachelor. Luckily, he did not suffer as often from the juvenile scheming as did his elder brother, the heir to his father's dukedom.

"Are you all right?"

Jason watched the lady do her best to straighten her sprig muslin dress, bunched and twisted from her mishap. She looked up at him and apologized, "I am so sorry, Jason. I cannot imagine who would push me, but I am forever grateful to you for saving me from making a disgraceful display of myself on the pavement. I fear after all these years I am a sorry sight for you to see."

Jason smiled at her frankness and wanted to tip her chin up so he could look under her straw bonnet and see whom this prior acquaintance of his might be. Since his youth, few called him Jason. My lord, Brentwood, Captain, these were the names he answered. "Jason" implied an intimacy he would have remembered having and he did not remember the young lady before him. However, he was not one to dismiss a pretty lady, so he remarked, "You are a delight to my eyes, madam."

The lady looked astonished by his remark and studied him through squinted eyelids as though deciphering the truth of his remark. He knew when her face turned a deep crimson his pretense of knowing her had failed.

Chapter Five

Christina's blush deepened when she realized Jason did not recognize her and she had intimately addressed him by his Christian name. It was *beyond the pale* to speak to a man before a formal introduction, much less address him by his first name and she fretted he would think her of low character. She quickly begged his pardon and stepped back in embarrassment, crying out from the overwhelming explosion of pain from her ankle. She would have fallen again had she not been saved by Jason's sturdy arm to keep her upright.

"Lean on me," he commanded. "Have you a conveyance nearby?"

"I fear not, Captain Brentwood. My coachman is not to return for an hour. He just left."

"You are alone?"

"No, Captain, my maid is nearby." And before Christina could search for Susan, she found her loyal servant at her side, exclaiming, "Oh, miss! Please, tell me nothing is broken."

"Nothing is broken, Susan," replied Christina. "Just sprained, I think." Christina tried to use her injured foot to balance herself and when another shot of pain pulsed from her ankle, she whined, "We must find a hack, Susan. I cannot manage any weight on my ankle and it pains me greatly."

Before Susan could hail a hackney, Captain Brentwood shouted at one of the many lads loitering about, hoping to be of service to a gentleman who needed his horse watched. He ordered the urchin to run and tell his *tiger* to bring him his curricle parked at the end of the block. Jason told the boy he would receive a coin for his trouble if he moved with haste. The boy raced off.

Christina's soft moan caused Jason to return his attention to her and bear more of her weight against him. In a soothing voice, he told her not to worry for he would convey her home. Christina sighed in disbelief of her circumstances. She had not seen Jason since she was eight years old, but she never forgot how much fun she had trying to launch his model ship which had turned into a water battle. He had gifted her the Apollo, even knowing he was to receive a harsh punishment from the duke for including her in his play. She thought him quite gallant to be more concerned for her welfare at the time than his own. Even now, the compassion he showed her was admirable. Over the years, her esteem grew as she followed his war record through newspapers and information shared by her father. She knew he had distinguished himself at Trafalgar. His many successes leading raids to seize cargo on enemy ships had earned him a captaincy, much like Nelson, who had entered the navy at the young age of twelve and became a captain by the time he was twenty. She felt her heart race at the idea of being conveyed home by him.

"That is most generous of you, Captain," she replied in a breathless voice. Christina bit her bottom lip to keep from whining her next questions, "but what of Thomas? Is there some way to send a message, so he does not return to find me missing?"

"I expect you will be home before he even returns to collect you," he remarked.

"I am sorry I misled you, Captain. The coach belongs to my aunt. She is most generous to me and placed the use of her coachman at my service."

"You do not live with your aunt, my lady?"

"I see you do not remember me, Captain."

Christina knew her response was ill-mannered, so it surprised her to see Jason's eyes alight at her bold affront rather than squint in anger. He looked like he wanted to chuckle, but instead he apologized, "No, forgive me, though how I could forget such a lovely face as yours, I do not know."

His roguish manner and glib speech broke through the embarrassment that had caused her to lose her temper. Feeling assuaged, she replied in kind to his apology. "Do not be severe on yourself. I was only eight when we met ten years ago, and I should not harbor any ill will for you not remembering."

"But, you do," laughed Jason.

"Aye," grinned Christina. "But nothing more than an iota."

"Well, I apologize most heartily and hope you will honor me with your name once again."

"Propriety dictates a common acquaintance introduce us."

"But you forget we were introduced ten years ago."

"You will think me a *hoyden* when your memory of me returns, Captain, for even then we were not formally introduced."

"Never, your name, please."

"I am Miss Christina Rothsborn, Captain Brentwood, daughter to your papa's solicitor."

For a moment, Christina's embarrassment grew again, thinking he still did not remember her at all, but then she saw recognition in his eyes and a smile stretch his face. "Your aunt is Viscountess Dewksbury?"

"Yes." Before anything further could be discussed, Captain Brentwood's *tiger* waved to his master. Jason surprised Christina by lifting her into his arms and carrying her to his two-seated curricle where he gently placed her. Susan followed and he managed to squeeze her beside her mistress. Then, he gave the hovering urchin his promised coin. The boy pocketed his earnings and ran over to offer his services to a gentleman dismounting his horse.

Jason turned his attention to his *tiger* and commanded him to wait for the Dewksbury carriage, ordering him to tell the Dewksbury coachman of Christina's accident and how she was being conveyed home. Then, he gave his groom enough coin to hire a hackney to return home.

"You must give me your direction, Miss Rothsborn."

"Captain, I think I prefer you take me to my aunt's address in Grovesner Square. She is *enceinte* and I know word of my mishap will alarm her. I think it best she sees I am fine."

"As you wish, Miss Rothsborn."

Across the street, Lady Lucinda Marsh, was captivated by the gallant scene she just witnessed. At twenty years, she found it terribly unfair her father insisted she marry this year. It wasn't as though she lacked offers. It was just she did not find anyone she wished to wed. However, her father, Lord Harry Marsh, the Earl of Montrose, was determined to see his daughter married by the end of the Season, if not by her choice, then by his. He was tired of squiring her about to all the balls and fetes and was more than ready to relinquish his responsibility of her to a husband. He informed her to either bring a suitor up to scratch or he would arrange a proper match for her, emphasizing three failed Seasons proved Lucinda was incapable of making a choice. It did not matter she made her debut at the tender age of seven and ten. She was the one, not him, who insisted on making her *come-out* at such an early age and after three Seasons, he was done.

"Did you see that officer save the woman from injury?" asked Lucinda.

"No, milady," responded her *abigail*. "I am doing my best keeping your packages in my hands and did not see anything."

"Don't be impertinent, Mary. I insist on knowing who is that man. Papa says I must marry this year and I believe I found the perfect candidate."

Mary, struggling with her mistress's purchases, failed to give Lady Lucinda her full attention and gained her anger.

"Oh, Mary," exclaimed Lucinda pointing to her attending footman, "Give those packages over to him!"

Lucinda did not know the name of her footman for she cared little for her servants, but Mary knew she was pointing to Joseph, who per the earl's instructions, acted as her ladyship's protector when she went out on her excursions. Once Mary was free of packages, Lucinda commanded her to learn the man's identity before returning home. "Do not bother to return if you fail, Mary. I have no use for inefficient help!"

Chapter Six

As much as Jason wished to push his cattle to get Christina to her aunt's care as quickly as possible, he kept them at a sedate pace so as not to cause her further discomfort. He took the most direct route traveling down Bond Street until they reached Grosvenor Street. Even if he wished to put his horses to a canter, the heavy traffic kept him moving at a sluggish pace, so he was relieved when he finally brought his curricle to a stop in front of the affluent Dewksbury town home.

Without his *tiger* to assist, he quickly dropped the leather ribbons, jumped down and ran to take hold of his horses' bridles before a disturbance could make them bolt. He ordered Susan to get a footman from the Dewksbury household to take his place and watched as the maid practically flew from her perch to run up the front steps and bang on the lion's head brass door knocker. Jason saw the door open and the Dewksbury's butler gape, looking astounded that a maid should presume to order him about as if he answered to her. Timmons looked like he was about to deliver a scathing set down, so Jason intervened, his voice booming forth, "Blast it Man! Hurry up and get me some help with my cattle! Your lady's niece is hurt and needs care!"

Duly chastised, Timmons immediately responded like a sailor under Jason's command and ordered the nearby footman to take hold of the horses' bridles. He then yelled afar for someone to alert the viscountess her niece was injured, before rushing down the steps and forcefully moving Susan aside to get to Christina.

Jason released his team's care to the obedient footman, then pressed through the hovering butler and maid, ordering them to stand clear. He surprised Christina by gathering her up again in his arms and racing up the front steps into her aunt's home, holding her close to his chest. He looked about and when he did not find the answer he sought, he turned and asked the butler shadowing him where he should place Miss Rothsborn. Before Timmons could answer, Lady Dewksbury cried out in alarm and rushed to her niece's side. She asked, "What has happened? Where are you hurt?"

Jason saw Christina's brows furrow and knew the one thing she wanted to prevent, her aunt's worry, had happened. His admiration of her grew when he saw how even in pain, she put her aunt's welfare above her own by soothing, "I have only sprained my ankle, Aunt. Please do not fret." Looking at Jason, she said, "I think you should put me down in the drawing room, Captain Brentwood."

"Yes, Captain Brentwood," marveled her aunt. Jason knew by the gleam in her eyes Lady Dewksbury knew him to be the Duke of Aubry's son. He almost blushed from her obvious approval and felt as though he had just been hooked like a fish. He quickly broke her inspection of him by following the butler to carry Christina into the parlour. Gently, he placed her on a giltwood tapestry sofa, before returning his attention to the viscountess.

Quite pleased with Jason's care of her niece, Priscilla extolled, "Thank you, Captain, for your help."

Christina quickly apologized, "Forgive me, Aunt, for not making Captain Brentwood known to you. Captain Brentwood, My aunt, Viscountess Dewksbury. Aunt, Captain Jason Brentwood. His father, the Duke of Aubry resides near your own home in Yorkshire."

"Of course. Well, thank you again, Captain."

"The honor to be of assistance to your niece was mine, Lady Dewksbury." To Christina, he made his bow and said before he left, "I will leave you to the good care of your aunt, Miss Rothsborn."

Christina's dismal sigh at seeing Jason leave had her aunt turning to her in concern. "Are you in much pain?"

"A trifle," she grimaced, glad her aunt attributed her sigh to her discomfort and not to her mooning over Jason. She pressed her hands on the sofa to push herself back to a reclining position, but had to stop when another sharp pain exploded from her ankle. She would have cried out if she had not the wherewithal to bite her bottom lip.

Christina knew her discomfort did not go unnoticed when her aunt ran to pull the bell cord to summon Timmons. She watched as her aunt rushed about the room, picking up and squeezing one pillow after another. It wasn't until Priscilla brought the pillow to place under her ankle that Christina understood her aunt was looking for the perfect cushion to comfort her. Unfortunately, the pain of having her ankle lifted was too much for Christina to bear and this time she was not able to subdue her cry. Her agonizing scream scared Priscilla into throwing the offending pillow onto the floor.

Doing her best to work through her throbbing pain, Christina had little breath to correct her aunt's misapprehension, nor could she keep Priscilla from searching for another pillow. Christina doubted there was anything to make her feel better and she would have shared her dismal news, except the sight of her grinning aunt holding the biggest of the parlour's satin pillows between her hands stopped her. She would have laughed except she knew the movement would only cause her more pain. As it was, she had to suffer having the perfect pillow, which according to her aunt achieved the proper height for healing, placed under her ankle.

Timmons, with his remarkable timing, entered and informed his mistress he had sent for the physician. Then, he presented the bowl of crushed ice and linen he had brought. Priscilla applauded his ability to foresee her needs and took the items from him. She made up a cooling pad by placing the ice in the center of the linen and bringing the corners together to knot them closed. She ignored the gasp Christina expelled when she placed the pad on her ankle and ordered Timmons to place a chair near the sofa so she could sit and watch over her niece until the doctor came.

The man arrived within the half hour and complimented her ladyship's ministrations. He explained there was no bruising or indication of a break and assured his patient the ankle was sprained, not broken. He wrapped Christina's ankle with a strip of linen and told his patient she would feel better the next day if she could refrain from standing and putting pressure on her ankle. He then gave her a dose of laudanum for the pain before he took his leave.

The moment the doctor left, Christina tried to rise to assess the extent of her ability to walk, but her aunt's alarm startled her back onto the sofa. She was in no position to argue for the laudanum made her unsteady. She laid back, carefully placing her ankle again on the perfect pillow and soon fell into slumber. While she slept, her aunt dispatched a note to her father to inform him of her injury, with a post script recommending Christina remain in her aunt's care until her ankle was healed. When Christina woke and learned her aunt suggested she stay a week to convalesce, she adamantly, but politely refused.

Lady Lucinda Marsh clutched her father's arm as they entered the Massey town home. She was anxious to meet the duke's second son. According to her abigail Mary, the gallant navy man she spied was none other than the Duke of Aubry's second son, Captain Jason Brentwood. Lucinda discovered he was quite eligible and more importantly highly esteemed. She liked how he was popular and respected among his peers. She felt an alliance with him would elevate her own standing in society which appealed to her. She had no need for more wealth for she was an heiress in her own right, but being connected to the Duke of Aubry's family was something she found desirable, and so she determined Jason Brentwood was the man she would marry.

Her father had already warned her to pick a man to marry, or he would do it for her and even though she had not met the captain, his handsome face, athletic physique, and family lineage more than recommended him to her. Plus, she found his air of confidence and strength attractive. He was no dandy, a man who worried about the latest fashion, nor was he a man affected with ennui. He was robust and was unlike any other suitor who had courted her. For that reason alone, she was determined to have him.

"Tell me again, Lucinda," asked the earl. "Why did you insist we attend this crush of a ball?"

"If I must, Papa. I wish to meet my future husband and since you are acquainted with the Duke of Aubry, it is only fitting you provide the introduction."

"I cannot fathom why the captain is your choice, Lucinda. I cannot see you take to the sea. Do you understand the type of life marriage to a navy man encompasses."

"Don't be ridiculous, Papa. I have no interest in becoming a naval mistress. He either will resign his commission or we will live apart. It is not unheard of, you know, a *marriage of a convenience*."

"Well, I cannot imagine the duke's son resigning. It is said he has desired a life at sea since his youth, though I do not know why the duke allowed it. Everyone knows the sea is for the gentry. Nobility always purchase their commissions in the army."

"Well, not always, Papa."

"You do know, Daughter, he is but a second son. There is no inheritance."

"Have you forgotten I am a heiress, Papa?"

"No, Lucinda, but I do not think even your dowry of thirty thousand pounds is enough to tempt the captain. He is quite independent."

"As am I, Papa, and for that reason I believe we will suit, content to live our lives as we see fit. Since you demand me settled by the end of the Season, I am quite happy to have a husband away more often than not. Now, I expect your help, Papa, not your opinion, if you please."

"You are impertinent, Lucinda. I have coddled you too much and am suffering the consequences. You are much too obstinate and arrogant, and you need a firmer hand than mine to oversee your bold ways. I have been too soft with my coffers and my hand, but I doubt your future husband will let you get away with your shenanigans where you feel you may do as you please. All I know is I am tired of being responsible for you, so cast your lines. You could not have asked for a bigger fish to hook, but remember, if the captain is not caught by your lure, then I will announce your betrothal to the Earl of Blackthorn.

"You cannot be serious, Papa. You would not wed me to a hermit. Why no one has seen that man in Society in ten years, so I have heard, not since his wife died."

"He is in need of an heir and has no interest in entering the *marriage mart*. He is perfectly eligible and a man of character. He quite impressed me on the rare occasion he spoke in the House of Lords. He has agreed to marry you should you fail in your own endeavor to find a suitable match and since you are only interested in a *marriage of convenience*, I cannot see why you have reason to grumble, one man of nobility should do as well as any."

"The choice is still mine, Papa, and I have set my sights on the captain. I expect nothing less than a grand wedding at St. George's Church in Hanover Square."

"We shall see. Come, I see the duke and your quarry. Let your games begin, Lucinda."

Jason watched the Earl of Montrose approach with a beautiful dark-haired lady dressed in a fashionable primrose satin dress on his arm. The delicate lace trim around her bodice and sleeves brought attention to her attractive figure. *"No doubt his daughter,"* he thought.

He watched as the lady slapped her fan open to cover her nose and mouth with it, drawing his attention to her mischievous blue eyes. He smiled at her and she responded by opening her eyes wide in innocence as if she was a timid debutante. He wished he could laugh at her theatrics for she was obviously an accomplished flirt. He waited for the earl to make his introductions and then he swept her a magnificent bow. He took pleasure in seeing the lady's eyes brighten as though she had read his thoughts. He was used to having debutantes presented to him, but usually their attentions diminished once they realized he was not the heir. That magnanimous post fell to his elder brother Marcus, but since his brother was absent and not available for the *marriage mart mamas*, he surmised he was being flirted with as a way to get close to him.

Her confidence made the hairs on the back of his neck prickle in warning and he wondered what the *chit* was plotting. He watched her glance at her dance card and sighed. Jason decided to take the bait and queried, "I hope we have not detained you from your partner, my lady. Perhaps, I could locate him for you if you give me his name."

"It is not necessary, Captain. Unfortunately, my card is lacking. I fear I am quite available."

"Then, you must allow me the honor of this dance."

"You are too kind, Captain. The honor is truly mine."

Both Lucinda and Jason turned to look at her father when they heard him guffaw. Lord Montrose looked quite embarrassed and swiped his hand across his mouth while clearing his throat. The ruse that he had coughed and not laughed was not convincing. Jason wished he could have contributed his own chuckle to Lucinda's coy performance, but gentlemanly manners prohibited him. Instead, he offered his arm to Lucinda and walked her onto the dance floor.

"Well, Lucinda," declared the earl later that evening when Jason took his leave of their company. "One dance does not a betrothal make. I believe your big fish escaped your hook."

"Not true, Papa. Captain Brentwood seemed quite taken with my charms. He gave no other debutante any particular attention. I am sure he would have requested another dance had he not been called away with a note that demanded his attention."

"Of course," agreed the earl smiling.

"I do not understand the humor you find, Papa. Are you not wishing me success?"

"I am sorry to laugh at your expense. It is just I have never seen you work so hard to gain a gentleman's attention. I do believe the captain has taught you a lesson in humility, something I failed at monstrously."

"You speak nonsense, Papa. You wait and see. Captain Brentwood will be all that is desirable in a suitor."

Chapter Seven

Christina reclined on the same sofa Jason had deposited her upon yesterday. She wore a dreary muslin day dress that looked out of place amongst the splendor of her aunt's Louis XV furniture acquired by a Dewksbury ancestor before the French monarch was overthrown. The delicate pieces, upholstered in the renowned Gobelin tapestry, had roses and laurel wreaths carved into their giltwood curved frames. They were smaller, lighter, and with their slender cabriole legs, looked more graceful than the harsh right angles and bulk of previous furniture styles. The large room was dotted with the gilded pieces and they glowed from the morning light streaming through the tall arched windows adorned with golden brocaded curtains.

She was nestled against the woven threads of the sofa's pastoral design reading one of her uncle's botany books. She gently placed her embroidered cloth marker in the crease of the book to mark her spot and raised her head when Timmons entered and cleared his voice to gain her attention.

"Miss Christina, I would normally approach her ladyship, but as it is your direction his lordship requests, I thought it best to inquire to your wishes."

"I am sorry, Timmons. Who wishes to know where I live?"

"Lord Brentwood."

"The duke's heir?"

"Forgive me, miss. I mean, Captain Brentwood."

Christina felt her heart skip a beat at hearing Jason had come to call. A wash of joy and excitement fell over her and though she wished to bounce up to greet him, she knew better than to act unseemly. Instead, she replied in a contrived calm voice, "I will receive him, Timmons. Please show him in, then alert my aunt of her company and order a tray of tea and cakes."

Christina had been resting since yesterday and now having to greet a visitor, she was feeling rather indolent and rumpled. She quickly sat up from her reclined position, being mindful not to prod her ankle and moved her legs off the sofa, pressing them from knees to ankles together. She placed her book down on the sofa, then smoothed and straightened her skirt to ensure her limbs were covered. Pulling her shoulders back to straighten her spine, she clasped her hands and placed them on her lap to sit as a lady should.

Nervous, she raised her hands to straighten and tuck her lace fischu into the neck of her bodice. She patted her coiffure into place, pushed in the loose pins she felt here and there, and then reluctantly, she pinched her cheeks to give her face some color. She felt she did all she could do to make herself presentable and quickly clasped her hands and placed them back on her lap again.

Her aunt had sent Susan home yesterday to retrieve a clean set of clothes for her and now she regretted choosing comfort over style when she asked Susan to bring an older gown versus a more fashionable dress. She might have despaired about her looks if the sight of the captain had not thrust all thoughts from her mind. In lieu of his naval uniform, he sported a tailored superfine brown tailcoat, a golden brocaded waistcoat with silk blue threads running through it over a crisp white shirt and a simple tied white cravat. A pair of Hessian boots over fitted cream pantaloons finished his attire. Christina felt her heart flutter and the corners of her eyes crinkled when she smiled at the sight of him.

She was not an expert at masking her feelings, so anyone interested could easily see how pleased she was to see the captain. She saw Jason smile back at her and was glad he also preferred the sincerity of true feelings to the artificial ennui most of Society postured.

“Miss Rothsborn, I am happy to see you are up and about, though I admit I am astonished to see you making social calls so quickly after your injury. How does your ankle fare?”

"I am well, Captain. I am here because my aunt insisted I stay overnight. I confess I am most anxious to be home where my every move will not be remarked upon."

"Are you well enough to leave?"

"Yes, my ankle is tender, but I am able to apply weight on it as long as I keep it bandaged. I am in no danger of further injury as long as I am chary."

"Then, I hope you will allow me to see you home."

Lady Dewksbury entered and directed the footman following her to set the silver tray carrying the Sevres pink floral tea service on the small round table near the sofa. Jason turned and greeted her when she entered. "Lady Dewksbury, your servant."

"Captain Brentwood," she returned before allowing her frustration at Christina to be vented. "What is this I hear of the captain conveying you home and why is your ankle not propped up. The swelling will not reduce if you do not rest sufficiently, Christina!"

Lady Dewksbury took the chair near Christina and asked Jason to bring another chair so that he could sit near them. She then turned and frowned at her niece. Christina's patience at her aunt's coddling was wearing thin and she had to clench her lips tight to keep from saying something brusque. She did not want to hurt her aunt's feelings, but she knew if she wanted to go home she needed to assert herself. "Aunt, I am quite improved and ready to return home." When her aunt looked like she would argue with her, Christina blurted out her frustrations. "You know I cannot abide to be idle and we know the sooner I depart, the better both our moods will improve. Your concerns are making Uncle and myself anxious. I cannot move an inch without you worrying. You have the staff coming and going, searching for yet another perfect pillow to plop under my ankle. In addition, you are feeding me enough food to send me into hibernation. I do not know how much more I can bear!"

Jason, to his regret chuckled, drawing a surprised look from the viscountess for his outburst and an icy glare from Christina. Priscilla saw her niece's ill manner and quickly admonished her, "Your manners, Christina!"

"I am sorry, Aunt. I did not mean to be impolite, especially to you. I am most grateful for your care, no matter my churlish behavior."

"Very well." replied Priscilla accepting her niece's rant as evidence of her improved health. Priscilla much preferred seeing her niece confrontational, than suffering. "If you are well-enough to be argumentative, then I suppose you are able to return home." Priscilla's eyebrows rose when she remembered the *modiste* appointment she made for Christina. She quickly added, "and to meet with Madame LaReaux. I will not cancel your appointment, Christina. I shall pick you up tomorrow at eleven."

Lady Dewksbury looked to Jason, "You will see her home, Captain?"

"With the greatest care."

"Then," replied Priscilla. "I will send Susan with your things and see you tomorrow, Christina." She left, pushing the parlour doors fully open on her way out as protocol demanded for an unmarried lady receiving a male visitor.

Embarrassed from her heated outburst, Christina began her duties as hostess as if she had never made an unseemly diatribe. She picked up the teapot to pour Jason and herself a cup of tea.

“Cream?"

Grinning, he answered, “Yes, thank you.”

Christina filled his cup with steaming black tea, splashed in some cream before she stirred the brew and placed the cup before him. She performed the same service for herself and then returned the teapot to its tray. She unfolded her *serviette* and spread it on her lap, taking time to regain her composure before she picked up her delicate porcelain cup to sip. Having recovered from her embarrassment, she finally glanced at Jason. “It is kind of you to convey me home, Captain. Did you bring your curricle?”

“Yes, I had hopes of learning of your direction and then calling upon you to bring you an appropriate token.” With a gleam in his eyes he added, “It is customary, you know.”

“Perhaps, if you had singled me out at a ball with a dance and wished to further your acquaintance, but I hardly think being a good Samaritan requires any such protocol as a day after visit.”

“I am glad you understand it is not good manners that brings me calling, Miss Rothsborn."

Christina practically dropped her cup. She regained enough composure to nervously place it on her saucer before gawking at Jason and asking, "I beg your pardon?"

"You need never beg, Miss Rothsborn. I expect I would gladly comply with almost anything you wish."

Jason was surprised how he felt comfortable teasing Christina. Usually, he would have to be careful with what he said to an unmarried lady. Any particular attention or intimate comment could be construed as an offer and he usually left bold remarks for those older ladies who understood the art of flirting. Christina was far from a flirt, but she was not shy either.

"Excuse me, Captain Brentwood, but it is most ungentlemanly of you to tease me. I hate to think the young boy I admired turned into a rogue. I had hoped our youthful history laid a foundation for friendship."

"You judge me harshly, Miss Rothsborn. It is our previous history as children that encourages me to speak openly. Looking back, I expect you knew very well the trouble we would be in for engaging in water sport. Your dress and shoes were not fit for play, yet you took a risk to engage in an adventure. I liked you then for your intrepidness and wit, and I must tell you I am impressed how your injury has not inconvenienced you. I see no simpering debutante seeking attention, but a strong beautiful woman who will not let her discomfort stop her from doing what she wants. I believe I am smitten, so you see, my remarks were far from teasing."

Jason's jaw dropped at the same time as Christina's own mouth gaped at hearing his precipitous declaration. He had not meant to confess an admiration for her, but upon reflection he knew it to be true. He admired her determination to not let a sprain keep her from doing what she wanted to do. Her resolve reminded him of the little girl who chose to follow him in adventure, rather than mind her father's order to wait for his return. She was different from the young ladies in Society. Those demure darlings would have used an injury to draw a suitor's sympathetic attention. They would never have been bold enough to go off on an adventure and Jason needed someone who would relish being a captain's wife. He found it providential how Christina had been literally thrown into his path right when he needed her.

He had not understood until he met Lady Lucinda Marsh the reason behind his father insisting he attend a number of balls and fetes with him. He assumed the duke only wished for his company while he was on leave and thought nothing of the multiple debutantes introduced to him. After all, the purpose of the Season was for the peerage to find eligible gentlemen for their daughters and so the onslaught of young ladies making their curtsies to him was not alarming. He played the gallant as expected, charming them with appropriate compliments. Being a second son, he never felt the pressure as did his brother Marcus to contract a marriage that would bring prestige to the family with both wealth and property, especially since he had chosen a career in the navy. He had no reason to believe his father would interfere in his life until the duke's interest in Lucinda's substantial dowry was brought to his attention. Now, he worried by attending these events he gave the duke the impression he would be obedient to his will and allow the duke to contract a marriage for him.

Jason had always followed his own conscious and he knew he would do so in marriage. His father's rant about him securing the line, in case his elder brother failed in his duty to produce an heir, reminded him how important his marriage was to the duke. Lucinda's beauty, wealth, and lineage recommended her enough for the duke to covet her for his second son. Unfortunately, those were not the traits Jason desired in a wife. He had no wish to attach himself to a woman for money or prestige. If he needed to marry, then a *love-match* he would make.

He knew his father could be devious to see his will done, so Jason decided in order to preempt the duke from interfering in his life, he needed to marry quickly. He had only meant to see to Christina's welfare on this visit, but their teasing banter revealed an attraction he wished to pursue. Now, having professed he was smitten, he waited for her to speak.

"I am sorry, Captain, but what did you say?"

"Since clarity is in need I will make my intentions known. I would like to court you."

Christina said what they both already knew. “I am quite beneath your station, Captain. I doubt his grace would approve.”

“I am glad you do not disapprove, Miss Rothsborn. As for the duke, he is irrelevant.”

Christina laughed.

“You do not believe I am independent of my father? No matter. I find myself anxious to spend time with you, Miss Rothsborn. I cannot deny something sparked between us and I think it would be a shame not to further our acquaintance and explore our attraction."

Christina blushed and admonished, “You are quite bold, Captain Brentwood.”

“Too bold for you, Miss Rothsborn?”

"Nay," she replied. Jason could tell by her smile she liked bantering with him. He returned her smile until he realized he forgot to ask Mr. Rothsborn for his permission to court his daughter.

“You are frowning, Captain. Have you come to your senses?”

“I am of sound mind, Miss Rothsborn. However, I should have spoken of my intentions to your father before addressing you. You will forgive my lack of etiquette?”

Christina grinned at him and Jason knew he was forgiven. They both turned their sights to the door when Susan entered and said, “I have everything packed, miss.”

Jason watched as Susan helped Christina put on her spencer and poke bonnet tying the ribbons under Christina's chin so the bow rested near her ear. Christina blushed from Jason's attention and before she could stand, Jason rose and gathered her up, bringing one arm under her knees and the other arm to cradle her back to nestle her against his chest. He lowered his head, bringing his mouth down to her ear and softly whispered, “In response to your query, Miss Rothsborn, I am very sensible. My intentions are to sweep you off your feet and as you can see, I have quite succeeded.”

"Are you mad?" gasped Christina. "Put me down before my aunt sees you."

"And how, may I ask, will I bring you to my curricle? I can beg your aunt's permission, if you like. She did not seemed alarmed by my gallantry yesterday when I carried you. In fact, I remember her thanking me for my consideration."

Christina rolled her eyes.

Jason looked at a grinning Susan and said, "We leave now, Susan. Please hail my *tiger* and have him bring me my curricle. You will find him walking my cattle up and down the street awaiting my orders.”

Chapter Eight

"Really, Captain. I am quite capable of walking."

Jason ignored Christina's protest and strode out of the drawing room, through the front door, down the steps to his waiting curricle. He carefully placed a blushing Christina onto the bench seat and handed her the band box Susan held. Then, he helped her maid climb up to sit next to her mistress, before making his way to take his own seat. They were all squeezed together, cozy and tight, on the red leather squab designed for two passengers. Christina sat erect, keeping her arms tight to her side while Jason took his reins in hand. Jason also kept his elbows tucked, so as not to poke Christina or bring attention to how closely they sat. The idea was ridiculous since he felt the side of her body pressed against his own the moment he sat down. The phrase *snug as a bug in a rug* came to mind and he had to clench his lips together so as not to utter the teasing phrase, or some other inane remark he was sure Christina would not appreciate. He could tell she was anxious by the rapid heartbeat he felt pulsing from her body and he had no wish to make her more uneasy.

His *tiger* released his horses' bridles at his nod and then his groom raced to jump on the platform at the back of his curricle where he would stand until he was needed to take charge of his horses again. Jason jostled the leather ribbons and his high-stepping cattle started. His thoughts made him grin and when it looked like Christina was about to ask him what he was smiling about, he slapped his reins again to bring his horses into a canter. The carriage jolted forward and any question Christina might have made was forgotten. She would not have been amused to discover he was puzzling over whether she, with her thirst for adventure, would have been the one to stand on the platform with his groom if the three of them had not fit on the seat.

His fanciful thoughts made him cheerful and it was all due to the lady sitting next to him. In that moment, he decided he was not ready to part with her company, so he asked, "Well, Miss Rothsborn, am I to take you directly home or are you rested enough for an adventure?"

Sighing, she replied, "I am not dressed for public display, Captain."

Her dejected response, reminded Jason of the Grimm Brothers folk tale of Cinderella, the scene where she receives an invitation to a ball and has nothing to wear. Shaking his head at the ridiculous comparison and to refute her own harsh appraisal, he quickly countered, "I happen to think you look wonderful, Miss Rothsborn."

Jason saw her eyes alight at his compliment, but quickly dimmed as if she had come to her senses. "I think it best you return me to Bedford Square, Captain."

"I had not thought you a coward, Miss Rothsborn. Is it truly your dress that concerns you or my company? What if I promise we never leave my curricle? Will you consent then?"

"And where Captain will this adventure take us?"

"You decide."

Jason knew the minute he saw Christina's reticence evaporate that his quirky smile had convinced her to agree faster than any argument he could have offered.

"Very well, Captain. I will admit I am enjoying the brisk air and would like to prolong the ride, so I will agree to a jaunt through Hyde Park. It is too early for the park to be populated, so there should be no one to remark on my attire; but truly, I am not dressed to be seen by the *ton*, nor is my ankle strong enough to meander about." Her escalating voice punctuated her concern. "I expect you to keep your word and we will not debark!"

Jason liked her emotional response. It showed strength and determination, traits he particularly admired. He assured her, "My word is my bond, Miss Rothsborn. We will not debark."

At that moment, a young girl at the corner of South Audley Street caught Christina's attention. They were making their way towards the Grosvenor Gate of

Hyde Park and the girl's obvious stare had Christina asking her maid, "Susan, do you know her?"

Susan grinned. "Aye, it is my younger sister, miss, no doubt on errand for the household where she works in the kitchen."

Jason pulled on the reins to halt his cattle and looked at the young girl being discussed. The look on her face suggested she feared a reprimand if not for herself, then for her sister Susan. "What do you say about letting your maid join her sister, Miss Rothsborn. It will be an hour at least before I bring you home and our open carriage satisfies all rules of propriety for driving without a chaperone."

"But how will she return, Captain. The walk to Bloomsbury is too long to ask it of her."

Jason dipped into his pocket and retrieved some coins. He proffered the currency in his outstretched hand to Susan. "Hail a hackney to return to your mistress, Susan, but do not take longer than an hour. I will not have her without your services."

Christina chided, "Really, Captain, Do you not think it is I who should direct my servant."

"Do you object to my orders?"

Before an argument could ensue, Susan grabbed the coins out of Jason's hands and jumped from her seat onto the street. She yelled her thanks and hustled to her sister's side. Both Jason and Christina watched the two of them walk away, heads together, talking with alacrity, causing Jason and Christina to bellow a guffaw at Susan's fearless departure.

"She is a bold one," remarked Jason.

"Aye," agreed Christina, "but she is loyal and trustworthy. I find no offense in her manner, Captain. Tell me, do you feel terribly abused?"

"More amused than anything else."

With Susan gone, Christina scooted herself away from Jason's side and he felt the loss of her body heat immediately. "You should stay close to me, Miss Rothsborn. I would hate to see you bounce out of the carriage should the wheels hit a rut. Besides, I am suffering a chill from your leave."

"I am quite capable of keeping my seat, Captain, and I am sure the sea winds are harsher than anything Mayfair has to offer. Why don't you start up your cattle and tell me something of yourself. I have tried to keep abreast of your career, but I would love a firsthand account."

Christina almost bit her bottom lip hard enough to draw blood. She could not believe she revealed her admiration of him so carelessly. She felt his smug confidence and knew his ego swelled exorbitantly at her confession. She tried to detract from the evidence of her obvious infatuation by remarking, "It is only natural I know something of your career. Oftentimes, the duke read excerpts from your letters to my papa, who then shared the news of your exploits with me. Papa, you know, admires you."

"Of course. I can only hope you share in his esteem, Miss Rothsborn, for nothing would please me more."

Christina blushed. It was humiliating for him to know she liked him and she wanted to tell him she did not admire him, but she knew by his growing smile he would not believe her. A heated reply would only prove her infatuation further. The idea embarrassed her so much she could not form a sensible string of words. Luckily, the shout of the captain's name brought her and Jason's attention to the mounted officer riding up to greet them.

She was surprised they were already on Rotten Row the bridle path where the *ton* converged in the late afternoon hours to show off their finery in both carriage and dress. The serene Serpentine, a long curving body of water that originated at one time from eleven pools being merged together, caught her view. It was easy to understand with ducks and toy boats gliding across its glistening surface, and children playing on its lush green banks, how it was a favorite subject for artists to capture.

Christina returned her attention to the man being introduced to her, Lieutenant Oliver Bradshaw, and ignored her fluttering stomach. She had not considered how she might be introduced to an acquaintance of Jason's, for if she had, she would not have agreed to go on a ride with him dressed so poorly. After being cooped up for a day, she had just wanted to enjoy his company while taking in the sights and sounds of nature. Instead, she managed the one thing she did not desire, public scrutiny.

Lieutenant Bradshaw's warm smile helped put Christina at ease and after engaging in a light discourse with him, she returned his salutation of being pleased to meet him. He no sooner left, than two ladies in an open carriage moved into the spot he vacated. Christina thought Jason looked like he had no idea who the ladies were in their wide brim bonnets, but surprisingly he introduced the Honorable Claudia Dash and her mother to her. Lady Dash was thrilled to meet Miss Rothsborn, cousin to the Earl of Marksby, of whom she and her family were acquainted. It never surprised Christina how she did not become relevant to the aristocracy until a connection could be found for her. She very much doubted Lady Dash knew her cousin the earl, since he rarely came to Town.

Jason clucked his cattle into service, but before he could move his curricle past the Dash's carriage, he was hailed by the indomitable Lady Jersey. Christina watched him skillfully hold his restless bays steady so they would not canter off, before bringing his curricle over to the countess's barouche. Christina was impressed.

The Almack Patroness sat in her open carriage looking quite proud and perturbed. She was a stickler for adhering to rules that governed the upper echelons of society. She wanted to know with whom the captain was keeping company and why she did not know her. Jason presented Christina and before he could finish the introduction, Lady Jersey interrupted him by saying she had heard the girl's name mentioned at one of her teas, yet had not seen her before. The countess recalled how Miss Rothsborn was the niece of Viscountess Dewksbury, but before the lady could comment further, Christina informed her ladyship how she just arrived to town and was setting up her father's household. Lady Jersey nodded as though approving of her industry.

Christina could not believe the attention she and Jason were drawing among the small crowd taking a turn in the park. No doubt their pairing was causing a stir and she worried their excursion would make their way to the *gossipmongers*. Two hours passed before she finally reached her home and she was exhausted from being on display. She watched Jason descend from his seat and hand the reins to his *tiger* who had already made his way to his side. She was so tired she did not realize she was slouching in her seat or that Jason's grin had turned her mind back to that day when as children they had engaged in a silly water fight. Submerged in the past, she relived every detail of the day they met.

Chapter Nine

Ten years earlier, May 1800
The Duke of Aubry's Estate, Yorkshire, England

Christina wrapped her arms around her middle, giving herself a hug to settle her uneasiness while she waited for her father to collect her. She sat on an embroidered mahogany carved settee in the Duke of Aubry's enormous entryway with her eight-year-old slippered feet not quite reaching the floor. She had never been in a duke's mansion, but waiting among its grandeur and overwhelming tang of wood polish reminded her of the times she accompanied her aunt on her social calls. She had learned before her fifth birthday the peerage did not associate with the common. Her mama was born a lady, but when she married Stephen Rothsborn, a man with neither fortune nor title, she condemned her daughter to the common class, or so Christina was told by children of the peerage.

Her father was the duke's respected solicitor and like anyone who worked for the peerage, was often called to serve without thought to the inconvenience it might cause them. Unfortunately, the day the duke required her father's services they had begun their long-awaited holiday together. They were not long on the road to London when their hired coach was intercepted by one of the duke's grooms with orders to bring her father to the duke. With no other recourse, she was brought along to await him and put into the care of a very severe and staunch butler. The servant led her to her current location and like a piece of baggage, was placed without thought until its owner retrieved it.

With nothing else to occupy herself, she began to inspect the quality of the duke's household, comparing its tidiness to Dewksbury Hall where she lived with her aunt and uncle. Her Aunt Priscilla maintained a well-disciplined staff and apparently so did the duke for the floors shined and the wood paneling glowed. Even the beeswax candles in the ornate brass wall sconces were freshly trimmed. Christina knew to look at them for her aunt did not tolerate fluttering or smoking candles. Apparently, neither did the duke.

The walls, like her uncle's home, were decorated with beautifully painted landscapes. Some bespoke the hunts she knew the aristocracy participated in and others portrayed the natural wonders of the countryside. Console tables lined the walls with a multitude of gilt and ivory trinkets and vases filled with sweet-smelling purple lilacs were displayed upon them.

Christina looked for something else to occupy herself when she finished her inspection and settled on swinging her dangling legs. She grasped the silky threaded seat with both of her hands to keep from teetering off and then hunched herself over to try to count the black and white tile squares making up the expansive floor. She soon tired of the activity and thought she would have to suffer greatly from her boredom until she let her imagination design a scenario where the curio boxes on the console tables were filled with jewels.

She looked about expecting her father to appear and scold her for not staying put the moment she rose from her seat. She was prepared to explain how her legs needed stretching should she be caught. The ready excuse was more for the frowning butler who had brought her to her current location than for her father. Christina knew her papa would do nothing worse than shake his head at her for being less than honest with him.

Confident no one was present to observe her bad manners in touching property that did not belong to her, she placed her hand on the delicate floral curio. She was about to take off the lid when she heard the murmurings of an interloper and quickly pulled her hand back. She squeezed her transgressing hand with her other one as though soothing a burn caused by touching a candle's flame. Guiltily, she turned to face the reprimand due her.

Christina expected to be scolded by the duke's butler, so she was surprised to see a boy a few years older than herself smiling at her. She wasn't sure if his amused face was because of the toy boat he held or because he had caught her touching the duke's treasure. He wore nankeen breeches with a fine linen shirt, cravat, and a serviceable waistcoat. His golden hair and sky blue eyes made him remarkably comely and she almost returned his smile until she remembered how often friendly faces turned haughty when they learned she was not a lady. Unsure of herself, she stammered, "I-I am Christina Rothsborn." when he asked her name.

"Not anymore," he mischievously replied. "You are hereby a sailor pressed into His Majesty's Service."

"I-I b-beg your pardon?" Christina knew it was impossible for her to be forced to serve His Majesty's Navy since she was both a female and a child, yet there were ghastly stories about men who were coerced into service. Common men were literally being pulled from the pubs situated near the docks, or so she overheard last week in her uncle's library while hiding in her favorite spot, a sort of alcove overlooked by visitors.

She liked to spend time there because it afforded her a private retreat where she could hide whenever she felt overwhelmed by all the rules she was expected to abide. As yet, no one had discovered her refuge where she liked to ponder her musings, not even on the occasion where her uncle and his guest spoke of press gangs. Christina's recollection made her wonder what the boy meant by his statement. Puzzled, she took his measure and watched how under her scrutiny he began to frown. His blond eyebrows scrunched together and his lips pressed tight in distemper.

Fearful she was the cause of his anger, she took a step back only to find her retreat stopped when he grabbed her wrist.

Twelve-year-old Jason Brentwood had entered the main hallway in time to see a young girl playing with one of the many gifts presented over the years to his mother, the Duchess of Aubry. He almost laughed at her obvious mortification at being caught. She was lucky it was he who saw her and not their butler who would have admonished her soundly. He shook the idea aside, remembering his task at hand and how fortuitous it was he came upon her.

Jason was used to having his wishes granted without pause or question, so when the young girl just stood and looked at him as though he was a prized bull at the fair, he grabbed her wrist and began to pull her down a side corridor. Unfortunately for him, the girl was stronger than he expected and effectively countered his pull. Frustrated, he stopped to reconsider the reluctant child he held captive. When she yanked from him again, he immediately released her, afraid she would cause him to drop his model ship of the HMS Apollo. Her unwillingness to accompany him continued to surprise him. "Don't you want to help launch her?"

"Do you mean your toy?"

Insulted, Jason raised the model to her eye level and with superiority over her ignorance, explained, "This is a replica of one of the finest frigates in our navy's fleet. Father had her made special for me. I want to see if she floats and I thought you would like to join me."

"Oh, I wish I could, but I must wait for my papa."

"Is that the man who is speaking with my father?"

"Is your father the Duke of Aubry?"

Jason nodded his affirmation and added, "You have time to join me. My father's desk is full of papers your father is reviewing with him. It will be half past the hour at best before they are done." He encouraged, "Come on now. I need a shipmate and you are as good as anyone. Marcus cannot be bothered and my sister still wears nappies and is perfectly useless for my current needs."

"Who is Marcus?"

"A tyrant of a brother and the future Duke of Aubry. I would keep out of his way for he is mighty high in the instep and would no doubt give you the cut direct, unless you have some lofty connections."

Her brows furrowed in anger. "My uncle is Viscount Dewksbury. Is that esteemed enough for you and your brother?"

Her heated retort surprised Jason and he almost laughed at seeing her injured expression. "Oh! Do not look at me so furiously. It is not I who requires good breeding to make an acquaintance." Grinning, he added, "but indeed your connections are more than respectable for me or any of my family to receive you. I believe we are expected to snub anything lower, but I cannot say I am obedient to that rule. I look to settle myself in the navy. It would make for a sorry life if I adhered to socializing with only the most elite, don't you think?"

Jason could tell his words had appeased the girl and commanded, "Come on, let's go."

"You are sure I will return before my papa seeks me?"

"We have plenty of time." He took her by the hand and pulled her down the wide corridor, hearing her rushed steps to keep up with him. She ran into his back when he stopped abruptly and Jason almost fell forward. He had halted in his step to answer her question of what was his name, but her forceful shove had him turning to deliver her a heated scold, that is, until he saw her pretty face. Eager to launch his ship, he hadn't paid attention to her features when they first met, but looking at her now, he realized she was exceptionally pretty. She had intelligent blue eyes framed with curly locks that matched his own blond hair, and wore a stylish dress and kid slippers that were far from serviceable. He began to worry his nautical exploit might damage her dress for which he undoubtedly would be blamed and reconsidered his invitation, until she laughed.

"Do you not know your own name?"

Jason's eyes widened at her impertinence, then relaxed when he understood she had misinterpreted his silence. Grinning, he replied, "Of course I do. My name is Jason Brentwood. I did not answer right away because I was noticing your fine clothes. I do not think you are fashioned for play. Where are you going today dressed so fastidiously?"

"It is nice, isn't it? My aunt had it made especially for me in honor of my turning eight years old. My papa is taking me to London on holiday."

"You don't say. A birthday celebration. What day were you born?"

"I am eight years today. How old are you?"

"That is very bold of you. It is very gauche to ask someone their age."

"You asked me," stated Christina in a vexing voice.

"I did no such thing. I asked you what day you were born. You had already informed me how old you were and besides if you don't want anyone to know your age, then you should not be giving the information away so freely."

He could tell Christina was mulling over his words and waited to see what she would say. She surprised him when she admitted, "Oh. You are right. I did tell you my age, but I don't mind that you know. Do you dislike your age so much you must keep it a secret?"

Jason chuckled. "You are a clever one. No, I do not care who knows how old I am. I was only trying to correct your ill manners so you do not repeat the offense with someone who might care."

Grinning, Christina prompted, "Well then, how old are you?"

"Old enough to join His Majesty's Navy."

"Really?"

"Father is to purchase me a midshipman as soon as I turn thirteen. I wanted to join now, but my mother insisted I wait another year."

"How nice it must be to know what you wish to do with your life."

"I imagine your expectations are good with such a pretty face." Jason saw Christina's cheerfulness diminish. You would have thought he said something terrible the way her mouth turned down and his guilt made him ask, "Why do you look so sad?"

Christina soberly asked, "You think I am pretty?"

"Indeed," and then he laughed when Christina's eyes brightened with glee and her mouth turned up into a grin.

Christina could not think of a time when someone praised her for being pretty. She felt ridiculously pleased to learn she had something to entice a gentleman in the future to marry her. She was old enough to know a pretty face was a valuable commodity and she was glad this boy informed her she owned one.

"Hasn't anyone ever remarked upon what a pretty face you have?"

"Never," she replied honestly.

"Well, one day, I expect you will have a slew of beaus, waiting to call upon you."

"I do not know about that for I am told breeding above all else is important."

"Ah, but your uncle is a viscount."

"Yes, my uncle, not my papa."

Christina saw Jason's immediate frustration when he tired of their banter and was not surprised when he grasped her hand and began to tug her again along the corridor. She practically ran to keep up with him until he pulled her outdoors. Then, the assault of brilliant light caused her to stop and pull her hand free from Jason's grasp to shield her eyes. She had suffered the blinding phenomena before when she moved from a dark area to a bright one and knew she only had to wait a few moments before her vision returned.

She closed her eyelids and immediately smelled the earthy scents of freshly cut grass, evergreen, and flowers. When her eyes adjusted to the light, she marveled at what she saw. Colorful primrose flowers bordered the walkways, expansive rolling lawns carpeted the grounds, and magnificently sculptured hedgerows in both box and animal shapes decorated the estate. There were multiple gardens blooming with a variety of flowers and Christina wished her young host would suggest a tour of them instead of launching his wooden boat. She was about to make the suggestion when she heard him holler, "Come on now. We don't have all day."

Christina found Jason at a distance, his legs spread apart, his arms akimbo with fists on his hips looking like his temper was ready to erupt. She immediately ran to meet him and was glad to see him grinning. Her uncle, Viscount Dewksbury, would scold her soundly if news of her running like a boy reached him and she hoped that would not be the case.

She followed Jason until they reached a small ornamental pond flanked by tall blades of grass, verdant shrubbery, and a gnarled oak tree. A bed of large rounded grey stones lined the graded side of the lake where they stood. Christina waited to see what Jason would do next.

He made his way to the water's edge and explained how his father stocked the small pond with trout and carp for fishing. Christina looked at the water, completely still without ripple or movement, and wondered if there were really any fish in it.

A harsh scream turned Christina's head towards the nearby oak tree in time to see the white rump and black tail of a wary Jaybird disturbed by their presence dash through the branches. The bird's appearance heightened her senses to nature's sounds and she intently listened to hear what else her surroundings offered. Soon, a frog croaked and she searched the water's edge where she found the yellow-brown amphibian nestled in the tall stalks of green grass. Captivated by the wonder of nature she failed to witness the pomp and circumstance involved in launching Jason's frigate. It wasn't until he muttered an oath she realized she missed the important event.

"What's wrong?"

Jason grumbled, "Can't you see?'

"See what?" Christina looked where Jason glared and saw the wooden frigate floating a few feet from shore. She couldn't understand his frustration. "Isn't it suppose to float?"

"Silly girl, of course, it is suppose to float, but with no wind, it seems she is not going anywhere. I had not expected to leave the frigate stranded. I am sure father

would not appreciate me abandoning the ship after owning it for only a day. I expect I shall have to get the servants to fish her out for me."

"Can you not retrieve it yourself? It is not far out."

"Of course, I could fish her out, but that is a servant's job."

Christina ignored his self-importance. "Why don't you just get a stick and move it towards the shore. I am sure I can grab it when it gets near."

"Your shoes will get muddy," he chided. "I won't get into trouble for soiling your shoes. No, it is best I return you to your father and command a servant to do my bidding. They are used to seeing to my needs."

"I can clean my shoes," Christina retorted even though she knew she would likely ruin her fashionable slippers. The thought of rescuing a stranded frigate seemed much more interesting than launching one and Christina was not ready to give up on something sure to offer her amusement. "Maybe you don't need to reach for it, perhaps if we create a wave, the current will take it to the other side of the pond."

Jason's eyes and mouth flashed wide. "Say, that is a capital idea!" With enthusiasm, he crouched near the water's edge, rolled up his shirtsleeves, dunked his hands in the water and began to push the water towards the frigate, causing the wooden boat to bob up and down with each swell. Christina squatted by his side, also pushing the water to make waves until she squeaked when a backsplash hit her face. Jason turned and saw her face drenched, but before he could offer his apology, his own face dripped with water. Without thought, he splashed Christina back and within seconds, a water fight ensued. They were laughing and splashing without thought to the damage they were causing to each other's clothes and would have continued if not for the duke's outburst. They both sobered and rose simultaneously. A deluge of water streamed from their hair and clothes.

Jason's drenched linen sleeves clung to his arms and were completely transparent, his cuffs dripping with water. His serviceable vest kept his chest discreetly covered, while Christina's once pristine silk dress now drooped and was marked with dark spots of both water and dirt. Their hair hung limp, saturated with water that dripped down the sides of their gleaming faces. Whether from embarrassment or nervousness, Christina laughed while Jason ground his teeth, finding no humor in the moment.

Towels were brought forth to dry them and as they made their way back to the mansion, they saw a footman trying to retrieve the wooden frigate. They watched him attempt to corral the ship with a long branch, only to lose his balance and fall into the water. Jason and Christina turned to each other, eyes shining with delight, and quickly smothered their chuckles in the towels engulfing them.

Chapter Ten

May 1810
Bedford Square, London

Christina's childhood reflection quickly ended when she felt herself lifted from the curricle to be secured tightly in Jason's arms. She blushed at the idea her neighbors were witnessing her improper arrival and could only hope her father was not at home. She had no idea what her papa would think of Captain Brentwood's proprietary behavior. Jason carried her into her town home, past her wide-eyed butler who held the door open for them. Then, after asking Christina to direct him to her parlour, he carried her into the room and gently placed her on the dimity couch.

Curious of Jason's particular search of the room, Christina asked, "What is it you seek, Captain?"

"A cushion for your ankle, Miss Rothsborn."

Christina remarked with candor, “It seems silly you continue to call me Miss Rothsborn since I have been in your arms twice today. When we are alone will you call me Christina? I think it is more conducive to fostering a friendship.”

“Only if you will return the favor and call me Jason. By the way, I hope to foster more than a friendship with you.”

“Jason, why do you continue to tease me with your flirting?"

Smiling, he asked, “Do you abhor my attentions, Christina?”

“I do not wish to be confused. I will admit I have liked you from the moment you pressed me into service at the tender age of eight. Even so, you must know your family will never sanction a union between us, so why do you play with my feelings? I did not think you so callous.”

“You mistake me, Christina. Should you ring for your maid? The door is open, still it really is not proper for us to be alone together.”

Christina blushed and started to rise. Jason raised his hand to halt her movement. “Allow me.” He walked over to tug the bell cord to summon the butler. Giles arrived and Christina asked if Susan had returned. Her butler assured her Susan was above stairs and he would summon her immediately if that was her wish. Christina nodded and remembering her manners, informed Giles to have Cook prepare some tea and cakes for her guest.

Jason sat himself down in the chair near Christina, so he could take her hand into his own. He leaned forward to bring his head close to hers and whispered so only she could hear. "Most gentlemen wed because they are in financial difficulty or need to produce an heir. Neither of those reasons apply to me, nor do my circumstances suggest I wish to marry. You see, I am anxious to command my own ship, so my time here in Town is not of long-standing."

Christina's eyes widened at hearing Jason's confession, but before she could ask him why he was telling her his private thoughts, he grinned at her obvious surprise and continued his disclosure.

"However, I find I like you very much, so much the thought of losing you to another man, before I have figured out my own feelings have caused me to pay my addresses precipitately. I can only hope you like me enough to muddle through a courtship to learn if we are indeed suited. You see, I desire a *love match*, not a *marriage of convenience*, so while we get to know one another, you need to think of the particular lifestyle married to me presents, and whether it is something that appeals to you. You need not worry about my family. My prize monies have made me solvent and I am well able to support a wife. Are you interested in seeing where our feelings take us?"

Christina's jaw dropped, astounded that a man of Jason's stature wanted love over wealth, class, and property. She doubted his family's opinion was irrelevant, but the idea of spending time with him, was a dream come true. She could not keep a grin from forming on her lips when she whispered her trademark, “Aye.”

At that moment, her father walked in and balked at the intimate scene. His displeasure revealed itself in a curt tone, “Giles informed me you were entertaining a guest, Christina. Imagine my surprise to learn you were here. I thought I was supposed to convey you home.”

Jason released Christina's hand, rose, pulling his shoulders back as he stood to address Mr. Rothsborn as if he was his commanding officer. With pride, he explained, “Sir, your daughter gave that honor to me.”

Christina saw her father frown and knew he was worried the infatuation she held for Jason would bring her grief. They both knew a duke’s son was far from her touch, so both their eyes widened in surprise when they heard Jason ask, “May I beg an audience with you for tomorrow, Mr. Rothsborn?”

“As you wish,” Stephen replied soberly.

“Will noon be convenient?”

“Yes, Captain," replied Stephen sharply. "However, I think it best you take your leave now and allow my daughter to retire. She looks tired and I am sure her ankle needs tending.”

“Of course, until tomorrow.” Jason surreptitiously winked at Christina and made his bow to her father before taking his leave. He no sooner made his exit than a troubled Mr. Rothsborn spoke, “There is only sorrow there, Christina. I have worked for his grace for over a decade and have never found him tolerant of a marriage without prestige. Definitely, not for one of his own where a great alliance can be made."

"I know, Papa, but I find I cannot refuse him. I have admired him since the first time I met him. He is most confident he is free of the duke's wishes. Is there harm in enjoying his company for the short time he is here? He awaits a new ship. Surely, a few weeks in his company will not hurt me."

"What of your heart, Christina? Will you not suffer?"

"I think I would prefer risking it to own some cherished memories I can tuck away, than to never have experienced what can only be marked as my own personal fairy tale. You know, Papa, perhaps this courtship is the tonic to cure me of an infatuation I have owned since I was a child."

"You wish me to permit him to court you, Christina?"

"Yes. I would very much like to get to know the captain, no matter how short the period."

"Very well. It will be as you wish, provided he knows the choice is yours."

"Thank you, Papa."

Jason was in high spirits thinking of a future with Christina and decided to contemplate that future at White's. He drove his cattle through the main thoroughfares to bring him to the heart of London and to St. James Street where the oldest gentlemen's club in London was located. The traffic grew thick as other members of society ventured out to shop or visit the city's clubs and parks. Frustrated from his lack of progress, he called forth his *tiger* to take the reins when they turned the corner at St. James Street and practically jumped from his seat the moment his groom had his cattle in hand. Jason ordered his groom to retire the curricle to the duke's stables. He would make his own way home by either friend or hack.

He quickly reached White's and fairly pranced up the steps, causing the majordomo to raise an eyebrow at him. The club's gatekeeper let him pass because he knew him to be the Duke of Aubry's son and a member in good standing. Feeling like a man who just inherited a great deal of wealth, Jason winked at the butler as he passed him and chuckled at the servant's wide-eyed response.

His mind was full of courting Christina and how his father would have no say in the matter. He had never allowed anyone's opinion to govern his behavior, aside from the Admiralty, so he had no regrets in marrying as he pleased, instead of being obedient to his father's will. Still, he had hopes of bringing his parents around to accepting Christina as his wife, and only a well thought-out strategy to show how he and Miss Rothsborn suited, *if* they suited, was his only chance.

The Duke of Aubry expected his children to contract marriages worthy of their position, but Jason knew he could never find happiness in a marriage negotiated for alliance versus affection. It would take a special and courageous woman to marry a naval captain, a woman who could abandon the gaieties of Town life, not to mention the comfort of a home, to join her husband at sea. It was rare for women to travel with their naval husbands, but a captain was the law at sea and if he wished his wife or any other wife to sail, there was no one to gainsay him. Usually, ladies of ranking officers made passage to the nearest port closest to where their husband's ship cruised. They were then able to secure a house and see their husband each time his ship docked for refurbishment and supplies. For some, it was easier than remaining in England, separated for years at a time.

Jason looked for an empty table in the coffee room, a large dining room whose walls were papered in red silk and adorned with a number of giltwood framed paintings. Long crimson brocaded drapes flanked the tall windows facing the street, a stark contrast to the white table linen covering the numerous dining tables. He could smell the lingering tobacco from those who preceded him and eagerly slid onto a seat to think more about what he was asking of Christina.

Dinner would not be served for hours and he thought he could contemplate in relative quiet, since the room was fairly vacant when he entered. *Could she really be happy living a life that offered her little in the way of entertainment and comfort?* The memory of an eight-years-old Christina, waterlogged and laughing, and then a vision of her now standing on the deck of his ship, her hair and dress fluttering in the wind made him grin.

His imagination was about to expand on that image when his daydream broke, his mind having registered his father's face who sat at an adjacent table. The duke had nodded at him and not until his father raised his eyebrows did Jason realize he was being summoned, much like when he was a boy in short pants. He cursed himself for not going to one of the newer clubs where the younger set of the peerage frequented. He had come to White's because he found the conservative group of lords, who made up the club's membership, comforting. There was something pleasing, knowing the same people with their same opinions could be found at the inveterate institution. Unfortunately, his father was one of those members.

"Hello, Father, Not going home for dinner?"

"I will make an appearance, Jason, but I prefer the peace at White's to the chatter at Aubry House. What of you?"

"Same, though I have plans to meet up with some friends. In fact, I am running late, so you will need to excuse me."

"Your mother is hosting a party to attend the opera on Saturday. She will expect you to make an appearance. I would not be pleased to see her disappointed."

"Nor would I, Father."

The Duke of Aubry inspected Jason's countenance. "There is something," he paused and waved his hand as though he could conjure up the appropriate word, "cheerful...yes, cheerful is the correct word about you. Is there something you wish to share?"

"Not at this time. If you will excuse me I see my friends are beckoning me."

The Duke of Aubry looked over his shoulder and indeed saw two gentlemen signaling his son over. "Of course, but we will talk later."

Jason nodded and was happy to see Lieutenant William Croft and Lord Anthony Breckman encouraging him to join them at a table shadowed in a corner. It was his good fortune they waved him over right when his father began to interrogate him. It was as if they knew he needed rescuing from a parental scold. He did not want to inform his family of his interest in Christina until he met with Christina's father. Mr. Rothsborn did not seem the type to discount his daughter's wishes, but he was an astute man. He would know better than anyone else what Christina faced married to him, so much so, he might refuse him as a suitor.

Lieutenant William Croft stood and extended his hand to Jason in greeting. Lord Breckman remained seated, swirling the port in his balloon glass snifter. He kicked out a chair for Jason to take a seat, "Sit down, Brentwood, before you make a spectacle of yourself."

Jason laughed. Both gentlemen were friends from his boyhood. Lieutenant Croft, to the dismay of his parents, followed Jason into the navy instead of the army. William was a fourth son with little promise of inheritance or prospects for an advantageous match and had joined the navy, hoping for promotions and prizes to secure his future. He owned a boyish face with light brown hair that always fell forward, an amiable countenance, and a keen wit that drew people to want to call him friend, especially when they discovered he was an equably honorable man.

Lord Anthony Breckman was the heir to a viscountcy, so his behavior was more fribble than not, since he did not have to worry about his future. His father gave him a generous allowance provided Anthony fulfilled a minor duty designed to teach him estate management. Like all gentlemen of the peerage, Anthony spent most days at his club conversing with his peers. If that bored him, he might visit Tattersalls to inspect the new round of horseflesh on auction, seek a lesson to hone his pugilism and fencing skills, or any other number of things a gentleman of means did to keep boredom at bay, even attend a ball or two where ladies of the *ton* described him as a devilishly fit and handsome man with blue eyes. Jason liked Anthony because he did not engage in those licentious behaviors or risky wagering common among the peerage. His friend had a superior intellect and an unfailing integrity that kept him grounded. Jason knew when the time came for him to step into his title he would execute his responsibilities admirably.

Anthony asked, "Who is the pretty filly with whom I heard you kept company in the park today?"

"The young lady is an acquaintance of long-standing, Breckman. Why do you ask?"

"The rumor mill is already full of chatter wondering of her."

Jason looked to William for confirmation and the young man nodded. "You must not concern yourself, Captain. You know anything concerning your family is fodder for discussion."

"What are they saying?" inquired Jason.

"Nothing much, just speculation," responded Tony. "Who is she?"

"An acquaintance from my youth. Her aunt is Viscountess Dewksbury, her cousin, the Earl of Marksby. Perhaps, you know her, Breckman, Miss Christina Rothsborn?"

"Never heard of her, Brentwood, but I am anxious to make her acquaintance. Say, is she a shy debutante or a girl with sense?"

"Why do you ask?"

"My sister has, most cleverly I might add, coerced me into escorting her to see Barrymore's *The Blood Red Knight* at Astley's Amphitheatre. What do you say we make a party of it and you can bring along Miss Rothsborn. My sister is married and more than an adequate chaperone."

"I don't know, Breckman," replied Jason. "The spectacle is receiving rave reviews, but I am not sure if it is a suitable excursion for a maiden."

"Well, if she is a silly debutante, then of course don't bring her, but you must come. I refuse to keep my sister company alone."

"Miss Rothsborn is far from silly. I will let you know tomorrow."

"With or without her, Brentwood. I expect your company."

Chapter Eleven

"Just a few more, miss," remarked Susan to Christina as she fastened the last of the many buttons running down the back of her walking dress. Christina sighed. She was sorely fatigued, thinking how as soon as she returned home she would need to suffer the same ritual of standing in place, this time waiting for Susan to unbutton her dress to change into a simple ensemble. Being fashionable was exhausting. She stood before the full-length cheval glass mirror in Madame LaReux's dressing room and saw how her eyes were heavy and glazed. She had been disrobed and measured after spending hours reviewing fabric swatches and fashion plates. She struggled to keep from yawning and stared at her image until she no longer saw herself. Her weary mind had drifted to recall the last few hours.

She and her aunt had arrived at Madame LaReaux's shop where Priscilla informed Christina how only those with appointments were served. Her *modiste* prided herself in giving the best of attention and service to her patrons and she did so by scheduling one client at a time. Christina followed her aunt through the door which the Dewksbury footman held open for them. The thick cloying smells of its previous customers immediately assaulted her and Christina turned to her aunt with a ready remark, but refrained when Priscilla delivered her particular look that conveyed, "Do not!"

The shop resembled a parlour with a Queen Anne sofa and mahogany tea table set to one side of the room; a long wooden table covered in white linen with chairs tucked under were set against the opposite wall. Between the furniture in the open space lay an oblong medallion carpet where ladies could promenade and showcase their new dresses to whomever awaited them on the sofa. The walls were papered with a floral design and overhead, hung a crystal chandelier that added elegance to the room.

A small middle-aged woman with brown hair arranged in a soft coiffure, wearing a simple, but stylish dress, approached them with a friendly smile and thanked them in her French accent for their business. She was not obsequious, but appreciative and Christina understood why her aunt liked Madame LaReux. She knew right away the *modiste* would not press her into buying anything she did not wish. Madame directed them to the table where a number of fashion plates and swatches of material were organized in piles of style for perusal. She left them to take their seat and make their selections while she hustled through a door opening covered with a swag and tasseled curtain. Located on the other side were the dressing and work rooms, as well as the small kitchen where she went to collect a pot of tea and plate of sandwiches for her clients.

Christina pulled the pile of fashion plates for ball dresses toward her. She looked through them and with her aunt's prodding, narrowed down her selection until she decided on the one she wanted above all. She made her choice of material and being done, she started to rise from her seat, but was stopped when her aunt placed a hand on her shoulder.

Priscilla pointed to the pile of patterns for evening dresses and asked Christina to pull them forward so they could take a look at them. Christina complied and watched as her aunt carefully looked at each plate, asking her opinion, before selecting a number of patterns which Christina agreed she liked as well. Before long, they were looking through each set of fashion plates. It did not go unnoticed to Christina how the runner-up designs for ball dresses from their first review were not returned to their particular pile of fashion plates, but set aside with the other patterns for day dresses, evening dresses, and riding habits Priscilla favored.

Christina had thought her aunt was shopping for herself until Priscilla asked her to pick the material and trim for the dresses. She must have looked astonished for her aunt explained, "Your uncle may have refused my sponsoring your *come-out* ball, Christina, but that does not prevent me from engaging in those activities that make me feel supportive of your entry into Society."

"Uncle does not wish to see you fatigued, Aunt. It has nothing to do with me. Besides, I only agreed to let you buy me one ball dress."

"Of course, Christina. I have no intention of purchasing anything else and to address your uncle's concerns, I am far from weary. If anything, browsing these fashion plates has exhilarated me."

"Well then, I guess if we are just amusing ourselves, I wouldn't mind looking at walking dresses. I very much like the one I'm wearing and wouldn't mind owning another when I have saved enough of my pin money."

Christina was wearing a high-waist white muslin layered gown with two deep double flounces of muslin pointed around the edge with a running pattern. Over her plain bodice she wore a rose-colored long sleeve spencer with a standing collar that supported a frill of lace. The jacket was made of sarsnet and ornamented with frog fastenings to keep the front and cuffs of the sleeves closed. Christina liked to wear the light and frilly ensemble with matching crown bonnet whenever she walked out to be seen in society.

Christina was startled from her thoughts when her maid exclaimed, "Oh! Miss! You will look so fine in your new dresses!”

Christina shook her head and quickly corrected Susan's assumption regarding the number of purchases made for her. She explained, "Only the azure satin gown for Amanda's ball was commissioned, Susan. You do know the other selections were not purchased."

"I do not think so, miss. I heard her ladyship tell Madame LaReux to bill the balance to your father's address when you went to be measured. She also told the *modiste* to order gloves and slippers to match your gowns."

Christina turned so fast her maid almost tore off the top button she was fastening on her dress. "You must have misheard, Susan."

"No, miss. If you will just turn around, I will finish buttoning you up. I am sorry if I spoke in error. Perhaps, the gowns are to be a surprise and I have just ruined it!"

Christina left the dressing room as soon as Susan closed the frog fastenings on the front of her spencer. She grabbed her bonnet and briskly exited the back room, leaving a fretful Susan to follow in her wake. She fairly stomped to the viewing parlour where Priscilla waited and when she saw her aunt's "do not" look, checked her outburst. Obviously, her aunt knew she was bothered and expected Christina to hold her tongue until they could speak in private. Her body bristled while she waited, anxious with worry over the costs her father was about to incur on her behalf.

She followed her aunt out of the shop and into the Dewksbury carriage. She took the seat next to Priscilla while Susan took the seat across from her. Before she opened her mouth, her aunt raised her palm, scolding, "Do not speak, Christina!"

Dumbfounded, Christina kept quiet. Her aunt quickly soothed, "We will speak at home where we can be private."

Christina nodded and realized her aunt would not discuss anything personal in front of Susan no matter how loyal she thought her maid might be, so she sat in rigid silence until the double doors to her parlour were shut. Her total focus was on her own worries, so she did not pay attention to her aunt's movements until Priscilla pulled the bell cord to summon a servant. Christina silently cursed herself for being a negligent hostess.

She felt her aunt's eyes on her when Giles entered the room and quickly took her cue, ordering a light repast for their consumption. Once her butler left, she watched her aunt sit on the dimity couch where she calmly removed her gloves and placed them on her lap, before motioning Christina to sit next to her.

Christina sat, took a deep breath to settle her temper and asked, "Aunt, did you commission more than the ball dress for Amanda's debut?"

"I understand Christina, Captain Brentwood met with your papa this morning and asked permission to court you?"

Blushing, she replied with a touch of exasperation "Yes, but that is no answer to my question, Aunt."

"I believe it is, Christina! Do you think your papa would allow you to enter Society in last Season's fashions?

Do you think he would have you judged on your wardrobe instead of your character? That he would allow the *gossipmongers* to criticize your state of dress?"

Her aunt's outrage, surprised and humbled Christina. She quickly explained, "But, I am only to keep Captain Brentwood's company for a short period of time, Aunt. He knows my circumstances and does not beg my company because of my sense of fashion. I believe he enjoys spending time with me."

"No doubt, but where do you think the two of you will venture to spend time with one another that does not include the company of others."

Christina paused and then informed, "Why, just yesterday we took a ride through Hyde Park."

"And do you think that drab dress you wore is not the latest *on dit* in today's parlours? Already the *ton* is remarking upon the company the duke's son is keeping. Why your character and position in Society are being speculated upon as we speak."

"I never even debarked, Aunt. How could anyone criticize my dress?"

"Oh, Christina, you should know better. Did we not just spend hours discussing this Season's changes in style: the new colors, the lower cut bodices, the change in sleeves and flounces? Any lady in Society can identify whether a dress is in current fashion or not. If you intend to keep company with Captain Brentwood and not generate gossip, then you must remember your dress and actions will always be commented upon."

"Oh, Aunt, I do not like the sound of speculation. I am not of your sphere and have no desire to pretend to be."

"I do not know why you have let others dictate where you belong. You are equal to any lady's manner. I have seen to your education and you have lived in my sphere long enough not to be intimidated by it! As far as fashion goes, after today, the only remarks you will receive will be compliments."

At that moment, Giles opened the door to allow a maid to enter with a tray of tea and sandwiches. As soon as the servant placed the tray on the round mahogany table near the settee, Priscilla commanded her niece, "Please serve, Christina. I need my nourishment and we both need to relax. Do not worry so much. Your papa and I have everything in hand."

Christina watched her aunt finish the last of the tea sandwiches and was pleased to see her color restored to normal. Their earlier confrontation had wearied them both, but after she accepted her aunt's counsel, it seemed their moods both improved. Christina wiped a crumb from her aunt's chin and saw her blush when Giles entered at that exact moment to ask if she was home for Lady Amanda. Christina's exuberant face answered the butler's query before her resounding "yes" reached his ears. He left Christina with a "very good," and went to escort Amanda to her. Meanwhile, Priscilla remarked, "I will leave you to your company, Christina, and see you for dinner tomorrow, unless your Captain Brentwood requests your company."

Christina blushed at her aunt's teasing. She would have made a retort had Amanda not just been announced. She rose to bid her aunt goodbye and welcome her friend.

"Amanda, I am so glad you have come. Aunt, you remember my friend from school, Lady Amanda Larkfrey."

Amanda made her curtsy. "It is good to see you, my lady. I do hope you and the viscount will honor my family by attending my *come-out* ball."

Lady Dewksbury made no reply other than present Amanda with a stern and unyielding face. It took only a moment for Amanda to understand her ladyship's affront. She pulled from her reticule an envelope and proffered it to her best friend. "I have brought your invitation in person, Christina. As you know, it would mean everything to have you attend."

Christina laughed. "You are *too high in the instep,* Aunt. Amanda is all that a friend can be."

"Very well," sighed Priscilla. "I will leave the two of you to your visit. Amanda, you may tell your mama she may count us among her guests."

Amanda curtsied again and held her breath until the viscountess left, making Christina chuckle when she heard her friend's heavy exhalation of relief.

"She is a fierce one!" exclaimed Amanda. "I had no idea. You always make her sound docile and loving."

"She is, Amanda, but she is like a bear protecting her cubs when she thinks I am being abjured."

"Well, I would never shun you, Christina. As you can see, I am here personally presenting you with the promised invitation, so there is no excuse for you not to attend."

Christina looked at the beautifully scripted invitation with gold edging. Bursting with excitement, she giggled, "Yes, I will come. Oh, Amanda! My aunt has commissioned the most beautiful ball dress for me to wear. The sleeves are off the shoulder and the square bodice is cut so low there is no doubt I am a woman grown. If not for my aunt's assurances, I would think the dress indecent."

"It is the current style, Christina. My mama assures me it is quite proper, but enough of fashion. Tell me your news!"

"What news?"

"Why the parlours are wagging about a poor relation keeping company with the Duke of Aubry's son, Captain Brentwood. While the "poor relation" sounds peculiar, the description of the woman reminded me of you. I know Captain Brentwood is the man you admired from your youth because you shared enough news of his life with me. Tell me, was it you?"

"Amanda," sighed Christina. "I told Jason I wasn't dressed for viewing. I knew I should not have agreed to ride with him and now look at the gossip I created."

"It was you!"

"Yes."

Amanda stared at Christina and waited for her to continue her tale. "Well," she prompted.

"Oh, it is nonsense of course. We are only friends. He enjoys my company. That is all. He is waiting for a ship to captain and I have agreed to keep him company during his leave."

"Exclusively?" Amanda asked.

"I dare say, I do not know."

At that moment, Giles entered again bearing a silver salver. He presented the tray to Christina who picked up the card belonging to Captain Brentwood.

Christina asked her butler, "He has called?"

"He is aware you have company, miss, and requests only your response."

Amanda walked to Christina's side, so she could read the card with her. She nudged Christina's arm and told her to turn the calling card over. Written on the back was the question, "Would you like to see *The Blood Red Knight* with me and my friends tonight?"

Christina walked over to a writing table with Amanda following in her wake. She picked up a pen and wrote her answer on the card. "Yes, if a chaperone is invited. What time?"

Amanda asked, "Christina, Do you not need permission from your papa?"

"My papa has granted the captain permission to keep me company whenever I wish."

Amanda gasped, "Granted? Oh, Christina! Do you mean the captain is courting you?"

"Do be quiet, Amanda. The answer is yes, but you know as well as I that an alliance between us could never be realized. His family would never condone it. Please, do not speak of it to anyone. We are simply enjoying each other's company until he receives his orders to sail."

Christina handed the note to Giles to give to Captain Brentwood. "Please tell the captain if his time permits, I would gladly receive him."

As Giles left the room, Christina returned her attention to Amanda and saw her shake her head from side to side.

"What?"

"I wish you could see yourself as I do."

"And how is that?"

"A woman of uncommon character and beauty. A woman worthy of a duke's son."

Jason entered the parlour and saw Christina smile at him. He thought she looked quite fetching in her walking attire and though her gown could not compare in extravagance to her friend's fur-trimmed pelisse, he thought she outshone every lady of his acquaintance. He made his bow and waited for Christina to make the introduction of her friend.

"May I present my friend Lady Amanda Larkfrey to you, Captain Brentwood. Amanda, his lordship, Captain Jason Brentwood."

Amanda curtsied and Jason delivered his bow while greeting, "Your servant, my lady."

Amanda grinned at Christina and then apologized for not being able to stay. She made a speedy exit and Jason saw Christina's face crimson over her friend's blatant maneuver to give them some privacy before Susan joined them. To put her at ease, he remarked, "I am so glad you are available to attend Astley's. My friend Lord Breckman was maneuvered into escorting his elder sister, the Countess of Hartwell, to see *The Blood Red Knight*. It is receiving excellent reviews, but it is a very dramatic piece. I have heard how some women swoon during the theatrical production. I would understand if you prefer not to attend."

"It sounds like a marvelous adventure, Jason. When will you pick me up?"

"First, is the Countess of Hartwell sufficient to act as your chaperone?"

"Yes."

"Then, we will see you at eight o'clock."

Chapter Twelve

Overly excited, Christina practically skipped out of her room the moment Susan finished the final touches on her hair. She had been anxious to be released from her maid's tentative ministrations ever since her butler conveyed Captain Brentwood had arrived and awaited her in the foyer. Her better senses prevailed when she reached the top of the stairs. She knew if she did not slow down, she would embarrass herself to be seen acting like a giddy school girl. She breathed deeply, but forgot to exhale when she saw the man she admired looking up at her from the base of the staircase.

Jason looked simply magnificent wearing a superfine worsted black tailcoat, a crisp white shirt, and black pantaloons. His embroidered white waistcoat shimmered with silver threads running through it and the starched white cravat wrapped around his neck was pristinely tied. The sight of him made her heart pound in her chest, or maybe it was from the pressure of the breath she was now forced to release.

Everything about Jason from his head to his toes was perfect. His trim physique was shown to advantage in his fitted evening clothes and his regal posture was a reminder of how unequal they were in both stature and wealth. Even so, her heart was too enthralled to let reality dampen her spirits.

She heard Jason clear his throat as if it had gone dry and had no idea his discomfort came because she looked like a Grecian goddess to him. Susan had pulled her hair atop her head into a bun, braiding a number of hair strands to wrap around and decorate her coiffure. Using heated tongs, her maid curled strips of her blond hair into coils to hang down the sides of her face. The hairstyle complimented the sky blue empire *Naples de Gros* gown she wore. The silk dress made her look slim and graceful. The skirt had a sheer net overlay, the hem trimmed with lace floated like a cloud when she walked. Her arms were covered in long silk sleeves bounded tightly with a silk cord. The overall effect brought attention to her bosom and the silkiness of her exposed shoulders.

Her reluctance to descend the staircase had Jason racing up the steps to collect her as if he thought she was about to turn tail and run back into her bedroom. The foolish idea made her grin until he took her hands into his own and said, "You look magnificent, Christina."

His praise reminded her of the gossip Amanda told her when she visited earlier that day and apparently, she was still smarting from the blatant slur for she blurted, “Not like a poor relation then?”

He cringed. “Ah, you heard the latest *on dit*. Have you?”

“Yes. My friend was kind enough to share the chatter making its way through the parlours." Christina wondered if the remark had embarrassed him as well, especially after seeing him wince from her disclosure. She prepared herself for disappointment. "I must ask, Captain, in light of the speculation, if you still wish to keep my company?”

Surprised by her question, Jason looked earnestly into her somber blue eyes and proclaimed, “Christina, it is my greatest wish."

His remark pleased Christina, even though she knew nothing could come of their courtship. “You, Captain, are way too glib. I must keep my wits about me or I shall fall prey to your charm.”

Jason chuckled, “Well, nothing would please me more.”

Christina's mouth gaped at his bold response and her cheeks blushed when she saw Jason tap her chin with his knuckles to close her mouth. He took hold of her hand, tugged and commanded, “Come on,” and then proceeded to walk her down the steps. His actions sparked her memory of the day they met and how even then he had led her where he wished to go.

Giles had their cloaks in hand and Jason took hers and placed it on her shoulders, his eyes twinkling as though he hated to cover her loveliness. Christina saw his amusement and was about to inquire what he found funny, but was adeptly deterred when he gently pushed her through the door Giles held open for them.

A black lacquered carriage, with a coat of arms belonging to the Earl of Hartwell blazoned on the door, awaited them at the curbside. The earl's footman stood at attention, holding the door open for them, but Jason waved him off and helped Christina into the carriage onto the forward facing seat himself.

Christina smiled at the well-dressed and welcoming lady sitting next to her, before her attention was drawn back to Jason who bounded into the seat across from her. He quickly greeted and introduced his friends. Lord Breckman insisted they be informal and use their Christian names, but Christina shook her head and refused. She insisted upon protocol, though later she relented to Lord Breckman's sister and called her Claire. The countess was just too friendly and engaging to refuse.

Claire was Anthony's elder sister by only two years, so the discrepancy was not so marked that Christina felt out of sorts in her company. In fact, after a brief conversation, she felt quite at ease with the young, giddy, and emotional countess.

Claire asked Christina, "Have you been to Astley's before?"

"Only once and not the present theatre. I was eight when my papa took me in honor of my birthday celebration. I was quite amazed at the trick riding. I had never seen anyone standing bareback on a horse, or doing headstands on a saddle. I even recall a man playing a pipe while riding astride two horses." Christina almost jumped out of her seat when she exclaimed, "Oh! I also remember there were clowns, ropewalkers, and acrobats. It was more than a child of eight could comprehend."

Claire grinned while Christina excitedly recalled her youthful visit to Astley's, but cautioned, "Tonight, will be quite different of course. It is an epic tale we are to see, surrounding the tale of the villainous Sir Rowland who tried to force himself on his brother's wife, Lady Isabella, while he was away on crusade."

"Really, Claire," reprimanded Lord Breckman. "I do not think you must overdramatize the play. I am sure Miss Rothsborn is capable of picking up the innuendos."

"Oh, forgive me, Christina," apologized Claire. "I forgot you are unmarried and how I should censure my conversation."

"Nonsense, I am well-read and too sensible to become emotional over a play."

Christina raised her brow in question when she saw Lord Breckman nod in approval to Jason.

Jason chuckled when Christina's brow rose and quickly explained, "Breckman warned me not to bring an emotional girl for he feared she might swoon."

"It seems," replied Tony, "That I should have been more concerned with my own sister."

Claire laughed. "Why do you think Frederick would not escort me, Tony?"

"Why that bounder of a husband," he bellowed. "This was all his idea! He gave you the ammunition to provoke me into attending."

"Now, Tony," soothed Claire. "Do not be out of sorts. You are scaring Miss Rothsborn."

"Impossible," he replied after regaining his composure. "She, unlike you, is quite sensible."

His remark broke the tension and by the time they reached the theatre, they were all in good humor. The carriage left them in front where the white portico of the building reached the street. A crowd was already making its way into the theatre and within seconds the gentlemen were taking care to hold their ladies close. Claire gasped when a common man bumped into her. Her eyes widened in anger and before she could berate the lout and demand an apology, Tony forcefully pushed her through the crowd, scolding, "What did you expect? This is not legitimate theatre. It is open to all."

Christina stayed near Jason, her eyes and ears on alert. She saw people from all walks of life and heard plenty of bawdy jokes and exclamations being shouted. As a child she must have been impervious to the coarse side of Astley's for she did not remember anything tarnishing her experience, not even the stench currently assaulting her nose. Bodies reeking of sweat, tobacco, liquor, and cheap perfume overwhelmed her to such a degree she had to breathe through her mouth. She wanted to stop, retrieve her sweet-smelling handkerchief from her reticule, and place it against her nose to mask the odors, but there was no way she was letting go of Jason's hand and risk being lost in the unruly crowd.

Christina held on tight as Jason continued to pull her through the horde of people towards the first tier of box seats. She followed blindly for her eyes were looking at the grand crystal chandelier hanging from the ceiling, until the large stage surrounded on three sides by tiered boxes and galleries caught her attention.

Her abrupt halt jerked Jason back to explain how the stage could be made bigger and stronger to support horses and carriages driven over them by adding platforms. He also told her the circular dirt-packed riding pit in front of the stage, forty-two-feet in diameter, could accommodate as many as thirty-six riders performing simultaneously. Christina marveled over the four-foot painted mural stonework fence enclosing the riding pit and was so enthralled, all she could offer Jason was a head nod to communicate she heard him. She was still gawking when Jason finally guided her into the amphitheatre's first tier.

Jason removed her cloak and helped her to a front row seat where she immediately scooted her chair forward to look over the low balcony railing. She instantly recalled how as a child she had taken a similar view of the equestrian ring and had been surprised to come face to face with a performer standing on his horse. The memory made her anticipation build and she could barely contain her enthusiasm or keep her seat. People were shouting and waving as if they were trying to get her attention and the resounding chatter overexcited her. She knew they were not calling to her, but she automatically looked every time someone gestured or yelled. She was ready to swivel in her seat again at hearing an outburst when she caught Jason grinning at her. The man seemed to think her erratic movement, turning to look this way and that way, entertaining. She was about tell him how ungentlemanly it was of him to laugh at her when the crowd silenced, drawing her attention back to the stage.

She watched as the crimson curtain slowly rose to reveal a pastoral backdrop with two young women and one boy child sitting center stage. The characters' dialogue identified them to be Lady Isabella, her young son Henry, and a young maid named Emma who sat apart from them reading a letter. The loud sounds of horses clopping and revelry blasting surprised her and signalled the actors to rise and bustle about in fright. Isabella sent Emma to investigate. The maid exited stage right and returned, running and waving her arms to tell her ladyship to take her son and hide for the Blood Red Knight, the villainous Sir Rowland, approached. Lady Isabella grabbed young Henry and fled.

Masses of soldiers on horses appeared with a crowd of peasants to fill the stage and pit. The music swelled igniting exclamations and panic in the audience. The Blood Red Knight rode across the boards to take center stage and his fierce persona hushed the crowd. He bellowed, “A thousand marks to those who finds and retrieves Lady Isabella and her son!”

The soldiers and peasants made chase in the direction of Lady Isabella's flight. Claire's nerves got the better of her and she grabbed her brother's arm for comfort. Gasps of fear, cries of warning, and shouts of obscenities were heard from the mixed crowd. Scene after scene, fear and flight were performed on stage assaulting the audience's nerves. Thunderous and smoky battle scenes and bloody displays of violence captivated everyone who watched. When the loyal knight Edgar, introduced as a relief comic was slain, the tragedy overwhelmed the audience and their voices created an uproar of such magnitude the screams of men and cries of women were fused into one enormous bellow.

Claire stood and cried, “No more! I can bear no more! Tony, take me home!”

Anthony stood and enfolded his hysterical sister in his arms. He looked over Claire's shoulders to apologize to Christina and Jason for having to leave. They immediately understood Christina would also have to return home without Claire to chaperone her. They rose from their seats and then another blast of gunfire exploded. The terrifying noise provoked another wave of screams from the frightened with Claire among them.

Claire pushed out of Anthony's arms and flailed backward in distress. Christina tried to move out of Claire's way, but was pushed back by Claire into the low railing, her back bending over the safety bar. Tony quickly pulled Claire off Christina, not realizing his sister was the only thing anchoring Christina's feet to the ground.

Without Claire, Christina's body reached its tipping point and she fell head first over the rail. Jason reached to grab her, but missed. He frantically looked over the railing, his friends at his side, all hoping to find Christina hanging onto something. The vision of her lying on the riding pit floor injured or worst, dead from a broken neck had Jason's heart throbbing so hard he heard the beat in his head. He released a swoosh of air when he finally located Christina being held by a rider exiting off the stage. He had no idea how she managed to end up in the arms of a horseman, but he thanked the Almighty she was alive.

The ten foot drop from their first tiered box seats was reduced by half when Christina fell into the arms of a rider. Somehow, a mounted performer dressed as a soldier had caught her. He managed with amazing dexterity to keep his seat and hold onto his distressed damsel before cantering off with her in his lap to exit stage left. Those who saw the debacle applauded the soldier's heroism and nervous laughter followed. *The Blood Red Knight* drama continued without a hiccup and Jason, Tony, and Claire rushed to find Christina backstage.

It was not hard to locate Christina once they made their way to the wings of the stage because she was surrounded by a mass of actors and horsemen. They were applauding the rider who caught Christina and the lady for what they deemed a magnificent feat. Claire, in what she would later term a gross behavior, ran to Christina and begged for her forgiveness. Both Jason and Tony waited until Christina's band of well-wishers dispersed. Then,

Jason took her hands in his and looked her over for any sign of injury. He realized he was shaking, but managed to ask, “Are you hurt?” He was relieved to see mirth in her eyes, but could not relax until he heard from her own mouth she was unharmed. Again, he asked, "Are you hurt?" When he saw her shake her head side to side, he felt profound relief.

“Oh, Jason! I am not harmed, but thoroughly embarrassed. What will the *gossipmongers* say tomorrow regarding the company you keep?”

Christina placed her fork down when she heard her uncle exhale. She looked over to where he sat at the head of the table and realized, with the forceful release of his breath, just how much her first tier tumble had worried him.

“You know, Uncle,” she added in response to his query for a detailed explanation. “The only rational thought I had as I fell backward over the railing is how my skirts would rise and reveal my unmentionables to the audience. I remember trying to hold my skirt down by grabbing it against my legs. Before I knew it, my hands flew out when I hit something."

She laughed at the memory. “That something was the rider, dressed as a soldier, into whose arms I ungraciously fell. I don't know who was more wide-eyed from the impact, but I am heartily grateful he was there.

He later told me how he heard a scream from above and instinctively put his arms out, keeping his thighs tight against his horse to control him. He said he practices stunts all the time with other performers and is always ready whenever he hears a shout. Apparently, he and his horse are used to the unnatural shifts in weight from catching performers or when he dips down to pick something from the ground. I know when we started to slide from my impact, he made some type of maneuver and kept us seated."

"Well," interjected her aunt, "I am sorry for your peril, Christina, but I am very glad everything turned out well." With a smile, she added, "so much, I will not rebuke you for discussing your undergarments in mixed company."

"I know you have an adventurous spirit, Christina," interjected her father, "but I ask you to please refrain in the future from engaging in such death defying stunts."

"Here! Here!" exclaimed her uncle.

After a pause, her aunt asked, "I am surprised the captain did not seek your company this evening, Christina?"

Christina blushed and replied, "He had a previous commitment, Aunt. He is to make an appearance at his family's box at the Theatre Royal."

"And he did not think it appropriate to invite you?"

"Do not think ill of him, Aunt. He invited me today when we rode together in his curricle through Hyde Park, but I refused, explaining I had a previous engagement."

"You could have sent me your regrets, Christina. Did I not tell you so?"

"Yes, Aunt, but until my new wardrobe arrives, I prefer not to bring undo attention to myself."

"Well, your fiasco at Astley's is not the way to remain anonymous!"

"Oh, Aunt, please tell me the rumor mill is not spreading news of my debacle."

"No, my dear. I did not mean to scare you. The captain's friends must be very discreet for I have heard nothing of it."

"I believe the Countess of Hartwell is fearful of her own conduct," remarked Christina. "Other than her husband, I do not think she will speak of it. Funny, how she worries someone might have seen her running and not how she thrust me over the railing."

Her aunt explained, "Well, a swoon can be excused; however, a lady running is *beyond the pale*. The act would mark her a *hoyden*, she is right to be concerned."

"Speaking of your wardrobe, I have some of it here for you. I was near Piccadilly and decided to stop by Madam LeReux's shop. Do you know she was going to wait for Monday until the entire wardrobe was ready before sending it to you? I scolded her of course; I explained how a lady must always have her ensembles as soon as possible, even if it must be sent in batches. She will be more diligent in the future after my chastisement. Of course, I secured what she had and brought it here."

"Oh, Aunt, is a riding habit among the articles you have?"

"Yes. Why, Christina?"

"I accepted an invitation today to picnic with the captain and some of his friends tomorrow and I would love to wear something fashionable."

"Enough," bellowed her uncle. "This sounds like parlour talk. Stephen and I have had enough, Madam. I suggest you retire, so we can enjoy our port."

"As you wish," smiled Lady Dewksbury. She rose from her seat and Christina followed her lead to exit. She looked to her father and saw him smile.

Chapter Thirteen

Jason wished he had accepted Christina's invitation to dine with her family instead of having to join his mother's party at the Royal Opera House in Convent Garden. He hated being pressed into making these appearances where he was inspected and assessed. He did not understand how his brother Marcus managed his own temper having to engage in all the galas, fetes, and events that made up the *marriage mart*, though in Marcus' case, as a future duke, he was most assuredly the buyer and not the trophy to be purchased. It was moments like this when he was happy he spent the majority of his time at sea, away from his family's demands and the crush of Society.

However, these moments did not compare to the enjoyment he felt when in the company of Christina. He felt his mouth stretch into another grin recalling their morning curricle ride and could not remember the last time he had laughed so heartily or enjoyed the companionship of a lady so much.

Last night, the memory of Christina's perilous fall had kept him from sleeping peacefully. He was convinced when he woke that she suffered from an injury that realized itself in the night. With an urgency he could not explain, he rose and dressed as though he was at sea and had just been woken to learn an enemy ship was sighted on the horizon. He left minutes later, leaving caution behind as he raced his cattle to Christina's home. He fairly brushed the Rothsborn butler aside, not waiting to see if he would be received and paced the foyer until Christina presented herself.

Mr. Rothsborn following in his daughter's wake did not look pleased to have his morning meal interrupted, but Christina's obvious pleasure over Jason's concern for her well-being soothed his temper and removed the frown from his face. Jason offered to take Christina on a morning jaunt through Hyde Park in recompense for disturbing their morning repose and Christina agreed before Stephen could intervene. Stephen rolled his eyes at his daughter, then returned to his breakfast, while Christina retrieved her bonnet, gloves, and reticule.

Jason no sooner boarded Christina in his curricle and started his cattle than he inquired into her health. She assured him she suffered no ill effects from her harrowing fall and then asked him if he thought any of the *ton's* highest sticklers could have done any better than she did at Astley's. The picture of these noble ladies falling head over heels, with bloomers billowing for all of society to see, had him laughing so loud he expected his behavior to be discussed in every *ton* parlour.

It amazed him how easily they conversed, teasing and discussing all facets of their lives, though admittedly, his anger had risen one time when he misunderstood Christina's queries into his life at sea. He thought she wanted to know of battle and had been brusque with her, "You ask of war, Christina? Gallantry?"

"No," she explained, blushing with embarrassment. "I would not ask you to recall those tragic times, though should you ever feel a need to do so, I would gladly lend you my ears. No, I refer to the ship. I once heard you climbed up to the masthead and almost fell to your death."

Jason concentrated, trying to remember the incident she referred and then laughed when the memory surfaced. "Where did you hear about that embarrassing and *jejune* fall?" He raised an eyebrow and prodded, "Confess, Christina. I should hope that story was not shared with the *ton*. My pride would take a direct hit to think the *gossipmongers* enjoyed amusement at my expense."

"His grace might feel my papa betrayed his trust if he knew I learned the story from him. He only told me because I so often asked about you. I have never spoken of your escapade from the time I learned of it to anyone and would not for the world embarrass you. I hope you will not tell the duke how I came to know."

"I am only teasing you, Christina. I was very lucky the fall did not end tragically. Instead, I learned a valuable lesson. You must always secure yourself when aloft."

"What is it like to be so high you can see nothing but ocean for miles around?"

"It is more than sight, Christina. All your senses are peaked. You not only see, but taste, hear, and feel the power of the ocean. The brine is carried in the wind and it settles in your hair, drying your face and lips. When you try to moisten your lips with your tongue, the taste of salt is there. You can hear the roar of the ocean in the cresting waves, and feel the power of the wind in how it whips your body and billows the sails. The experience makes you feel alive and vulnerable all at once. Alive in triumphantly climbing the masthead and vulnerable in knowing the roost can bring you to your death. Only when you are settled and have secured your safety, can the masthead offer a peaceful respite. It is not uncommon for a sailor to fall asleep tied to the masthead."

"You jest, Jason!"

"No, it is true. On a smooth sail, the sounds of the ocean, the rocking ship, the warm breeze can easily lull a sailor to sleep. That is why it is important to secure yourself so you don't fall. There is not much to keep a sailor alert on watch unless there is land or a ship on the horizon. It is easy to understand how drowsiness prevails."

"I have climbed a tree before," confessed Christina.

Jason smiled, knowing Christina's admission to anyone else might mark her a *hoyden*, but he felt honored she trusted him enough to risk sharing her adventure with him. "Perhaps, climbing up the masthead sounds more like an adventure than a chore to you."

"Aye," laughed Christina.

Their attention turned to the two distinguished navy officers mounted on a pair of prime horseflesh riding in the company of two young ladies making their way towards them. Jason brought his curricle next to them.

Lieutenant Croft was first to speak. "Captain! I am glad to see you. May I present Lady Irene Caulfield, daughter of Baron and Baroness Chadwell and Miss Mary Smith. Lady Irene, Miss Smith, I present, Lord Brentwood, my captain and fearless leader. You know Bradshaw, of course."

"Your servant, ladies, Croft, Bradshaw. Allow me to introduce Miss Christina Rothsborn. Her aunt is Viscountess Dewksbury and her uncle is the Earl of Marksby."

Before Jason could finish the introduction, Christina intervened, "And even more important, my papa is Mr. Rothsborn, a respected solicitor. It is my honor to make your acquaintance."

Christina's outburst flummoxed the party. Christina blushed at her impertinence, but she hated how Society overlooked her father. She feared her rash behavior embarrassed Jason and for that she was sorry. She waited to be *cut* for her ill manners, but to her surprise, she saw wide smiles breaking across her newly met acquaintances. Lieutenant Bradshaw was the first to speak.

"I am glad you are not *high in the instep*, Miss Rothsborn. It is gracious of you to make Miss Smith comfortable."

Christina felt guilty the lieutenant misunderstood her reasons for her unladylike outburst, but when she saw Miss Smith's eyes alight with appreciation, she chose not to explain, saying instead, "I would be happy to call you all friend, if you will permit."

"That is a capital idea," remarked Jason. "And to foster the relationship, why don't we all plan a picnic for tomorrow? The weather looks to be fair and I think it would be a fine way to spend the day."

Everyone agreed. Jason promised to invite Lord Breckman and his sister Lady Hartwell to act as chaperone which he did before he left for the opera that evening.

The corridor of the Royal Opera House was empty when he first arrived. He was halfway to his father's ducal box when the first act ended and the doors to the other private boxes along the corridor opened. The hall quickly filled with the peerage looking for respite, refreshments, and gossip. The noise of people competing with one another to remark on who they saw and with whom grew as more observations were made. Jason caught a number of ladies whispering about him, no doubt speculating whose company he kept and why he looked so severe.

His mood was far from congenial and unless he was waylaid by one of his mother's schemes, he hoped to be long gone before the curtain rose for the second act. He was still smarting from the chastisement he received from his father earlier in the afternoon and he doubted he could bear the duke's company. The accusation was false, but he had suffered the charge anyway. Apparently Lady Lucinda had stayed home waiting for him to pay her a call the day after the Massey Ball. The duke was aware of this fact because the Earl of Montrose had called upon him and in elevated tones emphasized the extent of his daughter's disappointment. The duke in turn passed on the earl's displeasure to his son.

Jason had been irked to be commanded to his father's study. He was no longer a boy, but a man capable of managing his own life and he believed a request should have been made, not a order if his father wanted to see him. His anger had rose instantly when he read the terse message, but diminished when he considered something might be wrong. His concern made him rush to his father's study, only to be duly astounded and speechless to learn the reason behind the duke's summons.

He was informed the Earl of Montrose paid a call; and in tones indicative of an angered parent, he was berated for not behaving as should a gentleman. His father's harangue emphasized how his ill manner reflected badly on his family.

Jason waited until his father expelled his last word and then refuted the accusation. His words began to come out faster and louder with every breath. He reminded his father how both he and Marcus were drilled in etiquette as children. At five, he knew how to address his betters and make his bow. At eight, he was a proficient dancer and knew every rule of etiquette demanded of his station and by twelve, he could hold a conversation with an adult, so he very well knew to send a bouquet of flowers the day after to any lady he paid particular attention the night before! Why, he expounded, the duke's own secretary ordered the flowers for him.

Jason was so incensed by the earl's effrontery and his father's rebuke, he told his father he owed no particular consideration to Lady Lucinda and made a point of saying how in the future he would avoid the *chit* to assure she could not misinterpret his intentions. He left feeling the matter was settled.

His reflection did not help his temperament when he entered his father's ducal box and saw the lady who had instigated his earlier quarrel with his father. She was striking a pose with her fan and he had to quickly mask his anger before he made his salutations.

“Oh, Jason!" called the duchess. "Finally you are here. You know our guests, the Earl and Countess of Montrose, and their lovely daughter Lady Lucinda. I understand you paid her particular attention at the Massey Ball.”

Jason pressed his lips together to keep from denying his mother's assertion and made his bow to the ladies. He gave a nod to the earl, but made no effort to acknowledge Lucinda other than the initial bow he made to all the ladies. His neglect to speak to her was profound;

the quiet so embarrassing his mother began to chat about the weather. Her effort to initiate a conversation fell on deaf ears, for everyone's focus was on him.

It was clear to Jason, the Earl of Montrose was waiting for him to grant his daughter a compliment. He did not like to be manipulated and had no wish to bolster the lady's ego, but he knew until he played Society's game, they would all be stuck in this impasse. At present, the only thing he liked about Lucinda was her brightly painted fan. A picnic scene was painted on the thin vellum and reminded Jason of a Gainsborough painting. A young fashionably dressed couple sat on a blanket enjoying a glass of wine while they watched their young sons push a toy boat on the ultramarine water. The composition of a picnic on a clear day amid a lush evergreen lawn by a still lake reminded Jason of his childhood and he wondered if Lucinda had selected the fan herself or if it was purchased for her.

Jason had seen Lucinda dramatically open her fan with a quick flick of her wrist and then cover the lower portion of her face with it when he had entered. She had kept the fan positioned to lure Jason to look at her eyes. Unfortunately, he found her fan more alluring than its owner and marveled at it until Lucinda snapped it shut from his view. Her obvious anger at being ignored placated the resentment he felt toward her and offered him the solution to appease the earl who awaited a compliment for his daughter.

"I find your fan incomparable, Lady Lucinda. Tell me, is it of recent purchase?"

Jason received her icy glare with satisfaction. He knew she was not happy to learn it was her fan and not her beauty he admired. The next few minutes passed tediously with idle chatter from the women about who was seen today, who sat in whose box, and who was expected to attend the Merriweather Ball. Jason cared less about who saw whom and no longer paid attention to what was being said. He simply gave the requisite nod when necessary and would have continued thus if Lady Montrose's voice had not risen to gain his attention. "You will join your parents tomorrow for our luncheon, Captain Brentwood."

Stunned by her presumption, he quickly declined.

"Nonsense," interjected the duchess. "It is my wish you join us, Jason."

"Forgive me, Mother, but I am already engaged."

"I know of no other engagement," she huffed.

"No doubt," he replied. "But, I am occupied."

"Perhaps I may join you, Captain Brentwood," queried Lucinda brazenly. Her request was bold, but Jason doubted if any gentleman had ever refused her. She practically pouted when she said, "If you are to be absent at my parents' luncheon, I fear I will be left without a partner."

He countered, "I can offer you no solution, my lady, for I am already engaged with another for a picnic."

Lucinda crimsoned at the refusal, yet pushed her request with resolve, "I do enjoy a picnic. May I join your party if I can secure someone to accompany me?"

Jason wanted to laugh at the girl's audacity. He retorted, "Perhaps you prefer that someone join your parents' table."

"It would be easier to find a companion to attend a picnic than to sit at my parents' table, as you can attest."

"You are too severe, my lady."

No sooner had Lucinda volleyed a witticism than Jason returned it. The duke had enough of their childish display and intervened to settle the matter. "I am sure my son would enjoy your company tomorrow, Lady Lucinda. He is more than capable of attending to two ladies at one time."

Jason bit his bottom lip to keep from telling his father to mind his own business. He was angry Lucinda would get her way for he would never disrespect his father by contradicting him. "As you wish, father."

He asked Lucinda, "Do you own a mount?"

"Of course."

"Then, my lady, you can expect Miss Rothsborn and myself to pick you up at one o'clock. I hope you do not keep our horses waiting."

Lucinda grinned as though she had won a battle, while the Duchess of Aubry soberly queried, "Who is Miss Rothsborn?"

Jason was angry; especially at his father who ordered him about like a child. He was tired of his parents interference and wanted them to stop trying to match him with someone they thought would bring him money and prestige. He was a grown man capable of securing his own wife. In fact, unknown to them, he was courting the lady he hoped to marry. The idea of telling them he was betrothed to stop their matchmaking schemes seemed ideal, until the words left his mouth. "Miss Rothsborn is my betrothed."

He knew he blundered when his mother faltered and his father had to steady her by cupping his hand to her elbow. The duke did not look pleased, especially when the earl bellowed, "What?!"

Jason quickly took his leave and the possible repercussions of his falsehood flooded his mind. It would not surprise him if his father ordered Mr. Rothsborn to Aubry House the minute he returned home from the theatre. He felt a sense of urgency to warn Christina's father, but first he had to confess the lie he told. He hailed a hackney commanding the driver to make speed to Bedford Square and when he arrived, he was glad to see the parlour window bright, telling him the household was awake.

He rapped the door knocker and presented his card to Giles when the servant opened the door. The butler knew the captain was an approved suitor and welcomed him into the foyer. He said his master and mistress were in the parlour and he would announce him. Jason removed his black cape, top hat, and white gloves, placing them on the hall settee before following Giles. He waited at the parlour threshold until he was announced before entering. He saw Christina and her father wore dressing robes. Christina's hair was down, plaited, and she sat opposite her father at a table playing chess. He balked, not wishing to interrupt them.

Christina rose in concern and made her way to him. "Jason, has something happened?"

Stephen followed, stood next to his daughter and waited for Jason to explain himself.

"Do forgive my intrusion, but I am sorry to say my temper got hold of my better sense and I have acted rashly. I hope you will forgive me for the chaos I am sure to bring to your household."

Christina whispered, "What have you done, Jason?"

"I have announced our betrothal to my parents."

"You what?!?"

Mr. Rothsborn looked at Christina and asked, "You have accepted his offer of marriage?"

Christina saw the hurt in her father's eyes, realizing he thought she superseded him. She quickly corrected his assumption. "He has never asked, Papa. We are not betrothed."

Christina's father roared, "Explain yourself, Captain!"

"Oh! I do beg your pardon, sir. I told you I acted without thought. However, you do know I court Christina in earnest. Tonight, I found my parents attempting to play matchmaker and no matter how hard I tried to deflect their machinations, they would not desist. I did not want the young lady at the center of their plot to be misled. Especially after they forced her company on me for tomorrow's picnic."

He informed Christina, "By the way, we pick up Lady Lucinda tomorrow at one o'clock."

Christina laughed. "Are you telling me, because you did not want this lady to join our party, you announced to your parents we are betrothed?"

"To my parents and Lucinda's," he confessed guiltily.

Christina rolled her eyes and looked to her father for guidance.

Jason warned, "Sir, I expect the duke will ask you to call upon him. I hope you will not let him bedevil you and that my announcement in no way jeopardizes your position."

"I knew it was possible when I allowed the courtship, Captain."

"Papa!" shouted Christina in alarm.

"Let it be of no concern to either of you," he calmly stated." I have had a few successful investments and more than one offer of employment over the years. It is only my loyalty to the duke that kept me constant. If he chooses to release me of my services, I will suffer no hardship."

Jason confessed, "I am glad to hear that, sir, for I cannot relinquish my offer for your daughter.

Christina scolded, "What offer, Jason? Are we not supposed to be enjoying each other's company, deciding if we suit? I think you get ahead of yourself."

"What if I have decided we suit?"

"You cannot speak for me, Captain, and if you think you can than I suggest we do not suit!"

Jason could not help but smile at Christina's fervor. He had to check his laughter, as did Christina's father who also found amusement in her spirit. Jason asked, "Well, what do you suggest, Christina?"

"I suggest, Captain, we continue as we are, getting to know one another. You shall tell your parents our intentions are not to act recklessly, but to adhere to all the rules of courtship."

"What about Lady Lucinda?"

"We will pick her up at one o'clock and be as hospitable as possible. Now is everything settled?"

"I believe so," grinned Jason.

"Sir," he asked. "May Christina have permission to walk me to the door?"

Mr. Rothsborn nodded his approval. Jason took Christina's hand and placed it on his sleeve and escorted her out of the parlour.

She asked, "What are you about?"

"I just wanted to thank you for bringing reason to a situation where I had lost all common sense. I am not an emotional man, but the thought of anyone coming between the two of us made me angry. I will not let you refuse me because of our different stations."

Christina grinned and asked in jest, "Anything else, Captain?"

"Yes," he said and then he lowered his mouth to hers and lightly kissed her before he took his leave. It was a chaste kiss, but he felt its tenderness warm him through to his soul. He was glad he had come, but as he made his way home something still nagged at him. He still had trouble believing how angry he had gotten over his parents' interference. It was not the first time they had tried to thrust a young debutante upon him. He wondered why this particular instance raised his ire and then he realized it was not his parents with whom he was angry, but himself for responding to Lucinda's brazen repartee. The girl had wit and he had to admit he liked sparring with her. The notion made him feel guilty. He already made up his mind Christina was the right woman for him, so he did not think it boded well how he found anything about Lucinda likeable. He did not look forward to tomorrow.

Chapter Fourteen

Jason had no one to blame but himself for last night's debacle at the opera. He should never have announced he was betrothed to Christina in retaliation for his parents pushing Lucinda on him. All it did was anger his father, overwhelm his mother, and alarm Christina who was already apprehensive about the duke learning of their courtship. He was not surprised when after rising from bed he received the duke's summons to attend him again in his study. He no sooner bid "good morning" than he had to suffer through another lecture, this time on what befitted a man of his station. The duke quickly turned his sermon into a scold, berating how a solicitor's daughter, his solicitor's daughter, was far from eligible for a daughter-in-law. Jason tried to expound on Miss Rothsborn's noble lineage and esteemed connections, but his haughty and unyielding father discredited them. Unable to check his own anger, much less assuage his father's, Jason ended the argument by informing his father the choice of a bride was his own to make and he would do as he pleased with or without his blessing. He did not wait to be excused, but turned, left in a temper and stomped his way to the duke's mews.

He could not imagine his day getting any worse until he remembered Lady Lucinda joined his picnic party. He had spent the night thinking of everything Lucinda could contrive to lure him away from Christina and how he could combat her plans. Debutantes were known to create situations to ensnare a nobleman. A sprained ankle, a fainting spell, a lurking villain from which they needed protection were only a few he had experienced. Lucinda was too clever to resort to such obvious tactics. Her strategy would be subtle. She would divide and conquer by concocting a reason for him to have to take her home, thereby abandoning Christina to his friends. He almost chuckled when he thought how surprised Lucinda would be when it was his groom, Johnny, and not him escorting her home.

He reminded Johnny to saddle the spirited thoroughbred Delilah to bring for Christina to ride. The memory of how dissatisfied she was with the docile mare he first brought for her made him chuckle. She had opined she could walk faster than the ancient nag and then apologized profusely for revealing her thoughts out loud.

For their next morning ride he presented her with one of his father's best hunters. He noticed how Christina kept her horse slightly ahead of his own as they made their way to Hyde Park and quickly tested his observation by signaling his stallion to move ahead of Christina's mare. Unable to check his mischievousness, he continued to urge his horse to take the lead whenever Christina heeled her mount to move ahead of his horse. They kept up the unspoken competition until they turned off *Rotten Row's* beaten path. It was then Christina heeled her horse into a gallop.

Jason kept a firm grip on his horse's reins to keep him from following. He had known the minute Christina turned her head and smiled at him, that she was going to take off and challenge him to race. He waited until she had a winning start, before letting his horse sprint after her. Any doubts he had regarding her horsemanship were immediately put to rest. She was more than capable to maneuver around the trees and other barriers she came upon, and barely slowed until she came to an abrupt stop. The wind carried her trilling laughter back to him and he had to fight to keep his own chuckles at bay. He realized how their race brought to the attention of polite society would mark her a *hoyden*, but anyone witnessing her galloping would be hard-pressed to call her anything but graceful, unless they heard her shout, "I won!"

Keeping a straight face until he came upon her, he teased, "I do not remember agreeing to a competitive jaunt, Miss Rothsborn. I do not even recall a start and finish line."

"All that is true, Captain," replied Christina playfully, "but our mounts were in earnest, regardless of our intent, and mine clearly outran yours."

"Only because I checked my reins," he confessed.

Christina's eyes grew wide in indignation. "You let me win?"

"No, Miss Rothsborn," explained Jason mirthfully. "I let you precede me as any gentleman aught, unless the situation provides a danger."

Christina laughed. "I think you have concocted a story to save your pride, Captain, but I will not quibble, for regardless, the victory is still mine."

Their races continued every morning thereafter. The expansive and verdant Hyde Park became their destination for their afternoon curricle rides as well, where sitting intimately next to each other, they were able to speak honestly and become better acquainted.

Jason shook off his recollections when the Rothsborn town home came into view. Johnny had followed him, leading the thoroughbred he brought for Christina by the reins. She stood on her front steps and Jason grinned for she looked very attractive in her fashionable hunter-green riding habit. He unconsciously heeled his horse to reach her more quickly and his obvious impatience to greet her made Christina chuckle. He did not presume to be the reason behind her animation, for most likely, it was the sight of Delilah and not him, that had her clasping her hands under her bosom and rising up and down on her heels.

Christina's joy was testament to how she was not afraid to reveal her feelings and he liked that about her. He couldn't help but compare Christina who was like champagne, a bubbly spirit that made you feel light and merry, to Lucinda who was more like a sobering cup of coffee. Lucinda might be clever, but she had too much pretense and guile for him to ever want her for wife.

"Oh, Captain Brentwood!" exclaimed Christina. "What a beauty you have brought me. Please tell me her name."

Jason quickly dismounted his steed to help Christina mount the horse he brought. Unfortunately her trusty butler had preempted him and placed her in the sidesaddle with the use of a curbside block. Jason had to settle for handing her the reins. Her obvious delight in the mare, reminded him to answer her question. "She is called Delilah."

Christina raised her brows in surprise. "I hope she is not weak in spirit as her biblical name infers."

He laughed. "No, Miss Rothsborn, she is far from weak. She is much like you, owning beauty, grace, and a desire for adventure. My father recently purchased her and I thought you would enjoy putting her through her paces. I hope you do not mind I brought you an unfamiliar mount."

Jason's compliment made Christina blush, but then his absurd remark of whether she minded to ride the beautiful chestnut thoroughbred made her laugh. *Who wouldn't want to ride the sleek and athletic horse bred for speed?* She could hardly wait to see what Delilah could do once she gave the mare free rein. She waited for Jason to remount his horse before heeling Delilah into service.

Once they were on their way, the weight of last night's debacle weighed heavy on their minds and an awkward silence emerged. Neither of them wished to discuss the fiasco, choosing instead to engage in trivialities as they rode side by side. Before long, they fell into easy conversation, laughing and teasing their way to Mayfair.

They approached the Earl of Montrose town home and Jason could see someone peering from a second floor window. He was sure it was Lucinda, no doubt encouraged by the duke to give his alleged betrothal no heed. His father would argue an announcement was not placed in the newspapers, nor was there any knowledge of a marriage being contracted for anyone to believe his son was serious about Miss Rothsborn. The duke most likely convinced Lucinda his son's temper made him speak rashly and if she could be patient, then Jason would realize she would make the better wife.

Jason did not expect Lucinda to come down even though she knew he was here. She was probably schooled from childhood to keep a man waiting and to demand what was due her consequence. Heaven forbid Lucinda should look excited to see any man or anticipate their company. No, he expected to cool his heels waiting for her, just like those men who sought her company. Well, he did not desire her good opinion. It irked him how she had forced her company on him and though it was unmannerly of him, he chose not to dismount and present himself. Instead, he commanded his groom to deliver his card to the butler and to ask Lady Lucinda if her absence was a declaration of regrets. He was pleased when minutes later, a frantic Lucinda exited her door, no doubt, fearing he had departed.

It was obvious to Jason when he arrived and saw the rutted markings of where a mounting block had been situated, that the step, most likely by Lucinda's orders, was removed as a stratagem to get him to lift her onto her sidesaddle. Based on her bold manner to invite herself to his picnic, he could easily imagine the lady making any assistance he gave intimate, so he had commanded his groom Johnny to be made ready to help the lady should she require assistance. He disliked being manipulated, but he hated even more the idea of Christina being hurt by such a display.

Johnny quickly dismounted and offered his help when Lucinda approached her horse. Unfortunately he was not strong enough for the task and struggled. Jason wanted to laugh. The gangly youth had yet to build any muscle and trying to lift the lady with her massive riding skirt was turning into a comedic scene. Jason had to admit Lucinda rallied beautifully and used her foot to push off Johnny's shoulder to pull herself up and onto her seat. However, his good humor quickly diminished when he saw how Lucinda inspected Christina and smirked. Her disdain clearly expressed her opinion of Miss Rothsborn and her unkind judgment enraged Jason.

He knew Lucinda could not find fault with Christina's dress for she looked very pretty in this Season's riding habit styled after the French Hussars uniform. Her ensemble featured decorative braided frog fastenings on the front of her jacket and fringed epaulettes on her shoulders. Her form fitting suit accentuated her figure; the jacket pinched in at her waist and the full riding skirt flared out at her hips. She wore a smart hat adorned with a single ostrich feather at an angle atop her head which drew attention to her pretty face.

Jason took Lucinda's measure and reluctantly admitted to himself the lady owned a more elegant riding habit than Christina. It was made of crimson wool, with the collar, cuffs, and hat all trimmed in mink. Lucinda's ensemble exuded wealth and her deportment clearly marked her a lady of stature, but in his eyes, she could not compare in beauty to Christina. His thoughts made him grin. He returned his attention back to Christina and knew immediately when her shoulders slumped how she must have misread his grin and believed he was admiring Lucinda when in reality he was thinking of her.

To make Christina feel better over his momentary lapse and to bring Lucinda down from her smug pedestal, he ignored decorum and introduced Lucinda to Christina. Protocol demanded those of inferior social class be presented to higher ranking aristocrats; but he could tell Lucinda did not feel the sting of his insult. Instead, she looked amused and ready to engage in a battle of wits with him, at least until he expounded on Miss Rothsborn's connection to the Earl of Marksby.

Jason knew right away by Lucinda's rapidly reddening face she was angry he had the audacity to present Christina as *bon ton* and therefore her equal. She looked ready to insult Christina and he was about to intervene when Christina laughed. "Forgive me, my lady, but I doubt you require my family lineage to make my acquaintance."

"Indeed," smirked Lucinda. "We all know our consequence and should not feel the need to explain it."

Jason opened his mouth to say something back to her in kind, but Christina superseded him. "It is a pleasure to meet you, my lady. I hope we may be friends and that you will call me Christina."

"As you wish," answered Lucinda with no permission to grant Christina the same courtesy. Jason was angry at Lucinda's slight, but any recourse would make Christina uncomfortable, so he heeled his horse forward. The ladies followed his lead and soon flanked his sides. Their silence gave him time to settle his anger.

They walked their horses three abreast and Jason saw how Christina fell back to ride with the groom in order to give way to Lucinda when the traffic thickened with carts and other conveyances. It was protocol to let those of higher consequence go first and for the first time the rule governing society bothered him, especially when he saw Lucinda's smug grin. He was determined Christina not give Lucinda any form of deference. He would drop back himself and let the ladies ride together if there was not enough room for all of them. Unfortunately, Christina had no knowledge of his plan, so when their path narrowed again, Christina dropped back surprisingly in tandem with Jason, which forced Johnny to ride behind them. Lucinda ended up leading the small party. She was not pleased. Jason and Christina looked at each other and grinned, but their amusement diminished when Lucinda pulled on her reins to halt her horse. The action forced Christina's mare to fall back to where she rode once again next to Johnny.

Astounded at Lucinda's rudeness, Jason turned to see how Christina managed. Her crimson blush and downcast eyes revealed her embarrassment and he knew she would not attempt to join them again. Lucinda had put Christina in her place by removing her from their company and Jason feared Christina viewed the act as a vision into their future. When they reached the picnic area, it looked as though Jason's groom and Lucinda's maid had accompanied them.

Jason knew Tony was aware of whose company he wished to keep, so he felt a modicum of relief when his friend came to help Christina to dismount. He was obliged to assist Lucinda since the lady had beckoned him for his aid. It would have been ungentlemanly of him to ignore her, but he quickly regretted his scruples when Lucinda would not let go of his arm the moment her feet touched the ground. He had no option but to let his friend escort Christina to the table prepared for their picnic.

Once the duke had learned about the picnic, he commissioned his servants to put together an ostentatious affair rivaling any gala held in the Aubry gardens. Tables and chairs were carted to one of Hyde Park's secluded lawns. Sheltered among a number of oak and plane trees, their picnic site afforded an area free from gawking passerbys. Fine white linen covered the table set with delicate china plates, sparkling crystal goblets, and glistening silverware. Under silver dome covers were silver platters of roasted meats of pheasant, turkey, and duck. Chesire, Cotswald, and Stilton cheeses were placed among the fruits, breads, and other delicacies making up the meal. Off to the side, were the ducal staff ready to serve and clean up the picnic when all the guests were gone.

Jason watched Tony help Christina to her chair and then take the seat next to her. He wanted to sit on her other side before someone else took ownership and anxiously stepped forward, but Lucinda's strong grip kept him by her side. He found she was rooted like a stubborn mule when he tried to disengage himself. He was not going anywhere unless she wished it, and aside from brute force, Jason realized there was little as a gentleman he could do. It was not until Lord Breckman's sister Claire took the seat he coveted that Lucinda willingly moved to join the rest of the party now seated.

Jason ended up at the head of the table with Lucinda on his right. Since he could not sit next to Christina, he was at least happy he had a clear view of her. He watched his friend Tony and his sister Claire engage Christina in conversation as if they had known each other forever, rallying to raise her spirits whenever her expression faltered.

"I have seen you at Almack's," queried Lucinda to the lady who sat next to Lieutenant Croft. "I believe you made your *come-out* last year."

"Yes," admitted Lady Irene.

It was an insult to bring attention to the number of Seasons a debutante entered the *marriage mart*. It suggested the lady did not take. Of course, it would never occur to Lucinda she slurred herself in the process.

Lucinda added, "I suppose, I will see you all Wednesday."

Jason noted the rising tempers among the gentlemen. It was clear to them and perhaps Christina, how Lucinda was remarking on the different class of stations among her company. The Almack Patronesses were in charge of granting the vouchers needed to attend the Wednesday night assemblies and they only gave them to the crème of society.

Unfortunately, Lieutenant Bradshaw's young lady Mary Smith played into Lucinda's scheme to insult her. "I doubt you will see me, my lady. I have not received my vouchers, but my mama expects them before long."

"Of course," replied Lucinda smirking at the idea Miss Smith could receive vouchers. She turned her attention to Christina to await her excuse.

Ignoring Lucinda, Christina asked the lieutenant, "How long is your leave, sir?"

Oliver Croft beamed, "I await my captain's orders." He grabbed his goblet of wine and raised it in toast to Captain Brentwood.

"I did not know you sailed together," remarked Christina. "Have you always been on the same ship?"

"Since Trafalgar," answered the lieutenant sadly.

Lucinda prompted, "You must tell us of your war exploits, Captain."

Claire gasped. She had enough of blood and glory after the Astley performance and was relieved when Jason rebuked, "I will not speak of such things in mixed company, my lady."

"But what of Trafalgar? I heard you behaved gallantly."

"As did all of his majesty's marines. I am no hero. The man to exalt is Nelson." Jason raised his glass to toast the admiral and Christina watched as all the men at the table raised their glasses, chanting the historic message Nelson sent to his fleet before the battle of Trafalgar. With glasses raised, in unison they chimed, "England expects that every man will do his duty."

The men sipped their burgundy wine and cheered, "Here! Here!"

The moment was lost on Lucinda who like a dog refused to release his bone. "Surely, there is one tale suitable for our ears, Captain?"

"I will not speak of war," he reiterated, "but I will speak of food. Let us eat. This feast is unlike anything a warship can offer after being at sea for days."

Lucinda took a biscuit off the serving platter proffered by a servant. She was about to break a piece off to butter when Jason mischievously said, "You best tap that biscuit to release the weevils inside."

Lucinda screamed. She dropped the ghastly bread onto her plate and pushed back her chair to escape the grotesque black beetle that might crawl from her biscuit at anytime. However, the soft cushiony grass did not yield to her push and Lucinda ungraciously tumbled over her chair. She was so embarrassed she ran off.

Christina scolded, "That was not well done of you, Captain."

"I suppose I must make my apologies," Jason admitted regretfully. He rose from his chair and excused himself.

Jason found Lucinda near a thick oak tree preening. He thought perhaps she was crying, but as he neared her he could see it was her anger she was trying to control. She turned and before he could address her, the rage in her eyes greeted him. Jason held out his hand with his palm up to halt her anger. "I have come to apologize. I thought only to describe how foul the food can become after days at sea. I did not mean to frighten you."

"You meant to humiliate me for no other reason than meanness," accused Lucinda.

"No, only to humble you, perhaps. You are *too high in the instep* for one so young."

Lucinda raised her hand to slap Jason for his impertinence, but his reflexes were quick and he grabbed her wrist before she could connect with his face. He yelled, "You minx! You are to slap me after I apologized?"

Christina feared Jason's temper would get the better of him and he might make matters worse without a mediator, so she asked Lord Breckman to escort her to search out the absentee couple. He agreed and they made their way in the direction they had seen them venture. They did not travel far before they witnessed an intimate scene. It looked as though Jason had Lucinda in his grip and wouldn't let her go. Christina was about to rush to their aid when she caught Lucinda's eyes and saw the girl smile at her. She watched Lucinda move closer to Jason in a sensuous manner and noticed how the man who professed to want to marry her, did nothing to extricate himself.

Christina stumbled and Lord Breckman took note of her pallor. "Come, you need not see this."

"I believe I have the headache, Lord Breckman. Do you mind extending my excuses to the rest of the party? I mean to go home."

"You cannot ride unescorted, nor must you let what you witnessed disturb you. Captain Brentwood is not fool enough to fall for her machinations."

"It was not her behavior that bothered me, my lord, but his. Please will you escort me to my horse?"

"Of course." Lord Breckman helped her to mount her mare only after being assured Johnny would see her safely home. Christina was gone by the time Lucinda and Jason returned.

Chapter Fifteen

Lord Breckman could not stop worrying over Miss Rothsborn. He liked her and hated to see her hurt by Jason's peccadillo. It was really none of his business, but Christina's sorrow after finding Jason and Lucinda in a heated moment played havoc on his mind, so he called on her the day after the picnic. Her butler Giles informed him she was not at home and Tony believed Miss Rothsborn was indeed "out" and not just shunning visitors, since Giles remarked when Christina would return. He would have liked his sister to have made the call for him, but unfortunately Claire was indisposed, refusing to leave her home or receive company until the blemish on her forehead disappeared.

As the days passed, Christina's well-being haunted Tony and he found himself thinking of her to distraction. No matter what his activity, Christina's distress weighed heavy on his mind. His inattentiveness and his inability to hold a decent conversation had his peers asking what was the matter with him. His concern eventually manifested into a nightmare of an inconsolable sobbing Christina. He decided he would never have any peace of mind or night's rest until he saw for himself how Christina fared and decided to seek an audience with her the next day. Satisfied with his course of action, he fell into a peaceful slumber and woke in good spirits, until he realized he had overslept.

He had no wish to suffer through another nightmare, so he jumped from his bed, called for his valet to dress him with all efficiency, and sent a servant to saddle and retrieve his horse from the mews. He was anxious to see Miss Rothsborn and hoped he would find her at home when he came to call.

With haste, he hurried into the courtyard to wait for his horse to be brought to him. He lived in one of the units in the original part of the Albany, a three-story, multi-windowed apartment building, once a mansion belonging to the Duke of York and Lord Melbourne before him. The duke sold York House in 1802 and the new owner reconstructed the mansion that once boasted a great staircase and magnificent reception rooms into twelve bachelor apartments, much to the pleasure of the gentlemen living there. Tony stood in the quad, flanked by the two wings of buildings later added and felt the sun bathe him in its warmth.

Any other time, the uncommonly warm weather would have lifted his spirits, but he was too anxious to be on his way to let nature cheer him. Lord Melbourne had designed his house to sit a hundred feet from Picadilly, so Tony could hear the sounds of carriage and cart wheels rumbling down the busy commerce street and hawkers selling their wares. He was too restless and curious to see what transpired on Picadilly to remain where he stood, so he made his way to the courtyard's entrance where an angry shout and other noises drew his attention.

A cart driver swore at an urchin who had run in front of his team of horses. A laborer slammed a crate onto a cart and a hawker yelled two pence for a currant bun. Tony thought the disharmonious sounds of the busy merchant street sounded like a ragtag band with bits and pieces of people talking, hawkers selling, packages rustling, dogs barking, and horses whinnying.

One of the reasons Tony liked living at The Albany was because he enjoyed watching the hustle and bustle of society. He was a people watcher and often found amusement in silently mocking the fops and popinjays who perambulated in front of the store windows. Since Picadilly was a long avenue that either ended or began at the corner of Hyde Park and Regent Street, depending on which way you were heading, there was always someone or something to observe.

Fortnum and Mason, the upper class grocery store where the *ton* liked to purchase baskets of food for their picnics, or have their midday luncheon in the store's elegant restaurant was located across the street. Next door to it was Hatchard's bookstore and to his surprise was the lady he sought walking with her aunt, Lady Dewksbury.

He quickly made his way to them, maneuvering his way through the conveyances congesting the street, and being mindful not to step in the still warm and odiferous dung left behind by horses. He tipped his hat and greeted with alacrity. “My Lady Dewksbury, Miss Rothsborn, this is most convenient. I was on my way to Bedford Square to call on you and to inquire as to your health.”

Priscilla scolded, “What is this Christina? You were ill?”

”No, Aunt, only the headache and as you can see, I am fully recovered.”

“Well, I am glad, for had I known I would not have burdened you with today’s excursion.” She looked to his lordship. “Forgive my outburst, my lord, but I was unaware my niece suffered. You are kind to inquire after her health. Perhaps, you will join us. We are to luncheon at Fortnum and Mason.”

“It would be my honor, my lady, only let me send word to my servant to return my horse to his stall. I will meet you inside.”

Priscilla watched him with a discerning eye return across the street. He was a handsome man who would turn any lady's eye and meet any mama's approval. “He is a nice man with sound expectations, Christina. Your uncle is a friend with his papa whom speaks highly of him. It would not harm you to keep an open mind to any attention he offers."

Christina said nothing as they entered the store and climbed the stairs to the restaurant. The maître d' nodded his head in obedience when Priscilla informed him she needed a table for three. He excused himself to prepare the table and while he was gone, Priscilla having noticed Christina's reluctance to speak since Lord Breckman came upon them, inquired, "I have not heard you speak of the captain, Christina. Since you have looked as though I withheld your pudding, should I surmise the man has fallen in your esteem?"

"No, Aunt, but it pains me to say we did not suit."

Priscilla patted Christina's hand and comforted, "Oh, my dear girl, well, now is not the time for disclosure. We will speak later. For now, I hope my good news will lift your spirits."

"What news, Aunt?"

"I have secured your vouchers for Almack's. Lady Jersey was most accommodating, especially after your auspicious meeting in Hyde Park. You have a fan there I think. She was all complimentary of you and since your wardrobe is complete there is nothing to keep you from attending."

Christina looked at her aunt wearily, but Priscilla only pushed her wishes further. "It would please me, Christina, to see you attend."

"Then, I shall go and make you happy. Will Uncle allow you to chaperone me?"

"This may surprise you, Christina, but your uncle insists on being your escort. He told me quite vehemently he would not trust any of those gentlemen attending Almack's. He said quite rudely they are wolves preying on corralled sheep. Why dear, I think he fears for your virtue." Her aunt beamed and added, "Isn't that nice?"

"I do not think I like being compared to an insipid lamb," replied Christina. "But it warms my heart to see my uncle show such unknown feeling for me."

It was at that moment Lord Breckman rejoined them and remarked upon the tender scene, "I do not wish to intrude."

"Nonsense," replied Christina. "You have perfect timing, my lord. We are about to be seated."

They were escorted to a table resplendent in white linen where three place settings of silver and china plate were arranged. Tony saw a number of ladies turn their heads to take note of them before leaning into one another to whisper. He knew their rumblings regarding his interest in Miss Rothsborn would make their way into tomorrow's tea parlours. He helped to seat Lady Dewksbury and Christina before taking the seat opposite them. Soon, a tray of cucumber and pâté sandwiches, biscuits with lemon curd, and a pot of tea were served. They enjoyed the repast and Tony listened to Lady Dewksbury share the latest *on dits* which on more than one occasion he was able to confirm. "Yes, His Royal Highness was bitten by Lady Graham's parrot," and "No, he laughed, "the bird was not sent to be hanged."

They engaged in a lively discourse for a full hour without knowledge of the time passing before Priscilla offered a hearty thank you to him and his sister for their discretion regarding the Astley incident. Tony apologized for Claire's outburst, but Priscilla waved him off.

"We are at war with a monster, my lord. Everyone's senses are peaked. Our country may be invaded and ravaged. We women know the peril even though our men try to keep the threats and tales of battle from our ears. Your sister's strong reaction to what she witnessed on stage is understandable."

Priscilla changed the tone of the conversation by announcing Christina's upcoming debut at Almack's. While his lordship did not usually attend the assembly hall, he quickly asked for Christina's first dance. He saw Lady Dewksbury approve of his offer and then expanded on the topic, mentioning some of the people Christina could expect to see there. Christina remembered Lady Lucinda would be there as an eligible debutante and it bothered her how the lady would feel smug over her conquest of Captain Brentwood. She knew Lucinda would make every effort to gloat at her and decided she would not give the viper the satisfaction. Instead, Christina vowed to show Lucinda and the captain, if he attended, how she cared not one whit for either of them. She decided her best revenge was to enjoy herself. Her first dance was secured, but she had no idea how to appear like she was having fun. *What if no one else asked to partner her in a dance? What if her only companion for the whole evening was her uncle? Would she look pathetic without a bevy of suitors?*

Christina worried what she would do until she remembered how Amanda would be at Almack's. She may be pitiful pining for a man that preferred another, but at least with her friend's help she would not look it.

Jason could not understand how his plans for a future with Christina had disintegrated in a matter of minutes. Their courtship was proceeding wonderfully and he had hoped Christina would be at his side when he received his orders to report for duty. He was confident her adventurous spirit would not balk at joining him at sea, or at least creating a home for them at his nearest port. As captain, his job would have him patrolling the waters for Britain's safety. If he was lucky, he would collect some nice prize money for confiscating enemy ships and their cargo. Now the bright future he envisioned was gone.

He cringed remembering the glaring looks thrown at him when he returned with Lucinda. He knew he was gone longer than proper, but Lucinda had been volatile and not interested in returning to his party. It took him quite awhile to soothe her temper and to convince her his friends would not mention her embarrassing fall. Tired of her theatrics and anxious to return to Christina, he had been more than ready to carry Lucinda if he could not convince her to return on her own.

His party had removed from the table and were walking about at leisure when he and Lucinda finally appeared. He guessed their tardiness was what prompted their glares. He immediately searched for Christina and when he could not find her, Lord Breckman informed him, "Your groom escorted her home. I am afraid Miss Rothsborn suffered a headache. She sent her regrets to you and Lady Lucinda."

Jason bit his bottom lip in frustration and guilt. He wanted to go after Christina, but owned the burden of seeing Lucinda home since his groom was now absent. He knew Tony would have offered his own escort of her, but the lady's grip told him and his friend she would not be amenable to the offer.

He had made his way to Bedford Square the moment he saw Lucinda home and was told by the butler his mistress was not receiving. The next day, Giles informed him Miss Rothsborn was out with her aunt and not expected until late. The following day, he was allowed into the foyer. His card was set on the silver salver and sent with a maid upstairs to announce to her mistress she had a caller. Jason waited anxiously until the maid returned and whispered a message to Giles. The butler had the decency to blush as he informed the captain Miss Rothsborn was not "at home." It was the way things were done when guests were not welcomed, but Jason had never been subjected to the slight and it took him a moment to understand that Christina would not see him. His pride was the only thing keeping him from making a scene and demanding an audience with the mistress of the house. He knew very well Christina was home or else Giles would have told him the moment he handed him his card.

With hat in hand, Jason stomped out of the house and decided he would give Christina one more day to receive him before he escalated the matter to her father. Christina was not at home the next day, nor did he find any help from Mr. Rothsborn when he sought out an audience with him. Stephen was completely unaware of his daughter's change of heart in keeping Jason's company and insisted Christina would not have acted rashly. The fault was surely of Jason's own making and Stephen insisted Jason must look to himself to make it right.

Tired of the whole fiasco, Jason thought to ease his frustration by visiting The Albany to share a bottle of spirits with his friend Tony Breckman. His annoyance peaked when he saw Tony dressed and ready to go out, in black breeches of all things. "Where are you off to dressed like a dandy?"

"I have a dance with a sweet girl I would not miss, so you must excuse me, Brentwood, for once I will not be tardy."

Jason looked at Tony again and his attire. He realized it was Wednesday and his friend meant to make his way to Almack's. "Breckman, I thought you swore never to attend that *marriage mart*."

"I go as a gallant. A young miss is about to enter a den of *marriage mart mothers* who can turn quite nasty at some pretty competition, especially a girl with no friend I know of to help her. I thought you would be pleased I have come to her aid."

"And why would I care about a debutante? You know my attentions lay elsewhere."

"Do they?"

"What riddle do you speak, Breckman?"

"Well, you will have to attend if the answer plagues you, Brentwood. I am off and if you wish to come you best make your way back to Aubry House and change into proper attire. The patronesses will not allow you in trousers or to enter if you arrive later than eleven o'clock."

"Well, it is obvious you are determined, Breckman, so I will see you tomorrow. I hope your lady is worth your time."

Tony took his black cape from his butler and just before he made his exit, he replied, "Oh! Miss Rothsborn, is very much worth my time."

"What?!" exclaimed Jason.

Chapter Sixteen

Almack's Assembly Hall was located on King Street, not far from the prestigious Mayfair addresses of those members of the *ton* who attended the galas every Wednesday night during the Season. It was common for gentlemen who were visiting their private clubs on St. James Street, or who lived nearby in their bachelor apartments, to walk to the white columned building in order to bypass the long queue of carriages waiting to debark their passengers. Women did not have the luxury of walking. They had to arrive by coach and bear the time it took to reach the entrance.

Christina sat in the forward facing seat of her uncle's carriage trying not to fidget. She was anxious for the evening to both begin and end. A part of her ached to see Captain Brentwood, while another part dreaded the encounter. Her uncle looked quite handsome in the required dress of black tailcoat and breeches. She was glad he was her escort and not her aunt and papa. They would have noticed her restless manner and interrogated her until they learned the root of her distress. Nothing good could come from confessing what she spied at the picnic between Lucinda and Jason. A full disclosure would only anger her family and make her a subject for pity.

Her uncle, distracted with his own thoughts, seemed quite unaware of her angst. He had already lectured her on duplicitous men: those vanguards who falsely smile with charm. She wanted to laugh during his stern disclosure of the nefarious side of all gentlemen, but managed to control herself. His manner and words displayed an affection for her she never credited him owning and for the first time, his severe and disciplining voice was not as harsh as her memory served.

The viscount's black lacquered coach arrived in front of the assembly hall and Christina watched her uncle debark before her, so as to help her step down to the sidewalk. He escorted her up the steps to the Palladian style building where upon entering, he removed her powder blue velveteen cloak. He handed her luxuriant cover with his own black silk-lined cape, beaver hat, and Malacca walking stick to the waiting attendant.

Christina remembered how her uncle's mouth had turned up in a grin when he first saw her. She had chosen a round evening dress with a low-cut heart-shaped bodice and cap sleeves. The empire-cut dress was made of an embroidered net that lay over a soft sky blue satin skirt. The lower part of her skirt was trimmed in flounces of

Urling's lace, festooned and adorned at its high points with bouquets of bluebells and pink roses.

Hushed whispers scrutinizing her person and dress resounded the moment her cloak was removed. The *ton's* blatant assessment unnerved her and she unconsciously gave each of her long white kid gloves a tug to keep her trembling hands from notice. She was about to pull on her gloves again when she realized how nervous it would make her appear, so instead, she sought comfort by touching the single strand pearl necklace her aunt had given her earlier that day to mark her entry into Society. Even if she was shaking from her core, she was determined that no one need know.

Her aunt had told her to remember she was equal to any lady's manner, and should she falter, to let her upbringing guide her. Still, Christina worried someone would ask her to leave because her papa was a solicitor. Through the years, more than one member of the *ton* had remarked upon her inferior class and those memories made her feel unwelcomed. She was ready to feign a headache when her uncle, standing proud, proffered his arm to her and smiled.

Owning a self-assurance that made her think of a medieval knight ready to smite an enemy, she placed herself under his protection and relinquished herself into his care. He looked like he would strike down any person who attempted to cause her injury and the idea made her smile and settled her nerves. She placed her hand on his arm and was escorted into the assembly hall.

The hall was crushed with the upper echelons of society. If not for the towering strength of her uncle, she would have easily been pushed into the sea of bodies swaying forward as a throng of new people arrived. Christina wondered how anyone was suppose to survive the crush, much less, the odiferous perfumes, tobacco, and sweat rising off the overheated bodies.

Her uncle continued to maneuver her until they found a pocket of space in the large ballroom where they could stand and collect themselves. Almack's had three rooms. The smaller rooms were used as a card room and dining room. The largest was the ballroom measuring forty feet wide to nearly a hundred feet long, capable of holding seventeen hundred members of the aristocracy. Christina feared more than capacity filled the room. Her vision was impeded by the numerous people passing in front of her and she saw little of the room, aside from the gilded pilasters, the classic medallion mirrors, the crystal chandeliers, and the band playing aloft in the balcony.

Through the breaks in the crowd, she caught a glimpse of the dance floor filled with swirling pastel colors and splotches of black. The scene reminded Christina of how her uncle compared debutantes to sheep, and she thought it definitely looked as though predators in black were circling, ready to pounce the innocents in pastels.

She shook off the grisly scene in time to hear her uncle say, "Let us make our way over to the confounding patronesses whose edicts determine who attend these balls and make our required greeting."

"Lord Dewksbury," exclaimed Lady Jersey. "Your viscountess said you would be Miss Rothsborn's escort, but I told her I would have to see it to believe it. I do not believe you have entered our assembly hall since you chased after your wife."

Frowning, he argued, "I do not chase, my lady; however, I admit you are correct in the amount of time passed since I last visited here. As you see, my niece is making her debut."

"But has she made her curtsy, my lord? The Earl of Marksby as head of her household is remiss in not having his wife sponsor her to our sovereign."

"She does not need the Countess of Marksby to present her."

"No, I suppose your lady wife could do the deed, but Marksby's lack of support infers he does not recognize Miss Rothsborn as *famille noble*."

"Do you suggest my credentials are lacking, my lady?"

Lady Jersey laughed and tapped the viscount on his shoulder with her fan. "Of course not, Dewksbury. Do not take offense, but you know the *gossipmongers*. They wonder why Marksby is not here by your side. It is said he arrived in Town yesterday."

"I am not privy to his affairs, my lady. I am sure he will do right for his cousin."

"Of course," the countess replied mockingly.

Neither Christina nor her uncle acknowledged Lady Jersey's insinuation of doubt regarding Marksby's recognition of Christina. Dewksbury simply patted Christina's hand when they walked away as though that settled everything. Christina did not give the matter any heed other than to discount the earl entirely. *Why should I worry if the Earl of Marksby acknowledges me? I have no desire to impose on my mama's connection to him. Why I do not even know if he knows of me.*

Christina searched the crowd for Amanda to no avail. It was so crowded she worried Lord Breckman would not find her in time to secure his dance with her and how pitiful she would look should Lucinda come upon her.

"Uncle, do you think we could walk the perimeter, so I might locate Amanda? She promised to attend and I would feel more at ease to engage in some sort of activity."

"Let us dance, Christina. Would that suit you for an activity?"

Christina knew she was to save her first dance for Lord Breckman, but the strings of the orchestra were alerting the crowd the next set was about to begin and she could not refuse her uncle. There was a night of dances and she was sure his lordship would be satisfied with any one of them. "It would suit me fine, Uncle, but I must admit I did not expect it of you. Aside from my aunt, have you partnered with anyone else?"

Grinning, he said, "Not since I laid eyes on her, Christina."

Christina had rarely seen him smile at her and she thought his smile made him look youthful. They danced a reel and each time they closed in partnership, Christina spied the man with whom her aunt fell helplessly in love. He was a superb dancer, performing the steps with grace and confidence. When they came together, he shared a glib remark that made her smile and relax to the extent she found herself having fun. Her uncle continued his antics of making her smile and on more than one occasion, Christina released a chuckle that resounded louder than she wished. She scowled at her uncle and warned him the patronesses would revoke her vouchers if they found her gauche, but he did not heed her rebuke.

He continued to tease her and Christina could tell he was pleased with himself for improving her spirit and making her laugh. Her eyes were bright like a shining beacon and her cheeks were rosy. She presented quite a pretty picture to a watching crowd. No sooner did the set end, than a plethora of admirers presented themselves to ask her to dance. Christina continued to look for Lord Breckman after each set, but when Tony did not appear, she accepted another gentleman's offer to dance. She was growing weary of dancing by the time Lord Breckman came upon her.

"Miss Rothsborn, I have not been remiss to collect my dance, but you have not been available. A bevy of gentlemen have surrounded you since the moment I spied you. Are you enjoying yourself?"

"Yes, thank you, my lord. Do not think me fickle. I have looked for you and only partnered with another when you did not come to claim your dance."

"You were having so much fun, I did not wish to intrude. Are you ready to dance again or do you prefer to sit this one out?"

"May we sit?"

"Of course."

They made their way over to a niche where a bench was recently vacated.

Lord Breckman inquired, "Your uncle will not object?"

"We are within his view. If he objects, I am sure he will come fetch me. Are you acquainted with my uncle?"

"Yes, but not socially. I have heard him speak in Parliament. He is quite the orator and well-respected by his peers."

Christina was amazed how a man she knew only as a strict disciplinarian had so many sterling qualities. She regretted how her impetuous behavior never gave him the chance to be anything else but a martinet with her. She asked, "Did you come alone, Lord Breckman?"

His lordship grinned. "Did you hope I brought Captain Brentwood with me?"

Christina blushed.

"I do not mean to tease you," he remarked after seeing how he embarrassed her. "I came alone, but it would not surprise me to see the captain if he has the wherewithal to get here before the doors close."

"He is coming?"

"Well, he normally would not attend Almack's, but he found out rather late you would be here, so it is likely he will show."

"More than likely, he will come to see Lady Lucinda. She is here you know."

"It is not Lady Lucinda for whom he has made an effort to see. I understand you have not been home to receive him."

Christina felt her face warm. At this rate, she would look like a ripe strawberry if she could not control her embarrassment. She opened her mouth to explain, but when no words ventured forth, she closed it. Her emotions were escalating and she felt like crying. Tony squeezed her trembling hands, but quickly released them when her uncle came walking towards them. She almost laughed at the idea her uncle would throttle Tony just for touching her, but when Tony let go of her hands, her uncle stopped his approach.

She looked to see if anyone else witnessed the impropriety and found Jason frowning at her. Apparently the captain arrived in time to see Tony hold her hand and misread his conciliatory gesture for something more intimate. She watched Jason turn and be stopped by Lucinda's hand on his arm.

The captain's arrival and turnabout did not go unnoticed by Tony. He turned to Christina and cautioned, "I do beg your pardon, Miss Rothsborn. I meant no disrespect, but I see the captain has misunderstood my attentions. I suggest I escort you over to him and help smooth his ego."

"He chose to engage himself with Lady Lucinda. I will not interrupt what clearly is an private moment."

"As you wish, but if you will accept my counsel, I will tell you the lady will gladly accept your leavings, even if the captain wanted you all along."

Christina jumped to her feet, surprising Tony and without thought pulled him along. As she neared the offending couple, she heard Lucinda say, "I am without a dancing partner, Captain Brentwood, perhaps you would accommodate me."

Before he could answer, Christina intervened, "The captain has promised this dance to me, Lady Lucinda, but I am sure Lord Breckman would partner with you."

Christina thought Jason would call her a liar. She saw Lord Breckman checking his laughter as much as Lucinda was holding her temper. The lady looked at Jason, "Is this true, Captain? Are you already engaged?"

Jason's face relaxed from his earlier scowl. Without taking his eyes off Christina, he answered, "Yes, my lady. I am." He proffered his arm to Christina and walked her toward the dance floor.

Lucinda softly cursed, "blast," which made Tony chuckle, but then he spoke in a serious voice and advised, "There is nothing but disappointment for you there, my lady. I recommend you set your sights elsewhere." He proffered his arm to Lucinda who seethed, "No, thank you, my lord. I am not inclined to dance."

Tony grinned at Lucinda's prideful departure.

Christina was still smiling when she slid beneath her bedcovers. How silly she had acted. All her plans to show the captain and Lucinda she did not care a whit about them evaporated when Lord Breckman offered his sound advice. While she feared to let Jason know how much his attentions or lack of them affected her, she could not in good conscious act falsely. She had taken a risk when she told Lucinda the captain promised her the dance and was overwhelmingly relieved when he did not call out her *faradiddle*. Her lie had been worth it for much was settled with Jason through their conversation.

"I was surprised you preferred to dance with me rather than Breckman," Jason remarked as they began to dance.

Christina explained, "I did indeed promise his lordship a set, but when he came to collect, I chose to keep his company rather than dance."

Raising an eyebrow, he curtly asked, "Is he such an ill dancer?"

"I am told he is very proficient, but I have been dancing with a number of gentlemen this evening and found the respite refreshing."

Jason was in no mood to banter and said, "I will not play these coquettish games with you, Christina. I thought you boldly sought me out because you wished to explain why you left the picnic and did not receive me these past days. I have been concerned for you and out of my wits, until I learned of your attendance here tonight. If you have changed your mind regarding our courtship, then please give me the courtesy of telling me directly."

"Why? Your behavior towards Lady Lucinda spoke volumes as to how you changed your mind regarding our courtship. I do not believe you gave me the courtesy you request."

"What behavior?"

"I saw you, Jason, at the park. You were embracing her. She even smiled at me."

"I was not embracing her," he argued. "I was keeping her from slapping my face because I failed to submit to her charms. I am sorry she used the incident to suggest otherwise. I do not esteem the lady, if anything I dislike her for behaving so calculatedly. The only feelings I own are for you alone."

A sense of calm settled over him as though his outburst had swept away the perplexing feelings that had discombobulated him since he met the conniving Lucinda. At one time, he might have worried his heated dislike of her masked an unwanted attraction, but that concern vanished when she almost slapped him at the park. The moment she cozened up to him, he realized what a gentleman's code of honor would have required him to do should any stickler of society seen them together without benefit of chaperone. Lucinda was more than capable of crying foul to force his hand in matrimony. He had to forcefully disengage himself from her, and as quickly as he could return her to the picnic where he was disappointed to find Christina absent. The following days had been torture for him and now he found it difficult to describe how he felt.

"I cannot explain what I feel." he confessed. "It seems too fanciful to admit my heart beats faster when you are near and my eyes see nothing but you, but if it placates you I will confess it. You must trust in me, in us, if we are to triumph in our relationship. Women will always flirt with me. Not me, actually, but the duke's son who has entrée to the upper echelons of society. I do my best to deter them and frankly, I would appreciate your help rather than your temper. In the future, could you come to my rescue, instead of running away and leaving me to fend for myself? Your earlier intrusion delighted me, extremely. In fact, it rallied my ego of which lately has taken a beating."

"I doubt very much your ego has suffered with Lucinda desiring your attention. You only need to take in the number of eyes glancing your way this very moment to affirm your attractiveness."

"They are not looking at me, but you, Christina. You are beautiful, especially when you are smiling, and it pleases me to see you smiling at me. I trust you will forgive me and receive me in the future when I come to call."

"Perhaps I misunderstood the situation in the park and should most likely apologize to you; however, I am astute enough to know Lady Lucinda is a temptress."

"Christina, if I was foolish where Lady Lucinda is concerned, forgive me. I think she got under my skin because she thought she could get the better of me and my pride would not stand for it. I do not care about her. I only care for you and your good opinion. Do you believe me?"

"Aye, and I will receive you should you call upon me tomorrow, Captain."

A grin bloomed on Jason, crinkling his eyes at their corner.

Chapter Seventeen

Jason whistled the melody of a seaman's ditty as he cantered his horses down Oxford Street and chuckled at the song's lyrics, for he knew exactly what he would do with a drunken sailor under his watch. He was in high spirits, even after being woken early in the morning by the night watchman calling out "all's well." He had dressed quickly, picked up the luncheon he had ordered to be made ready for him and made his way to Christina's town home.

Bedford Square, like Russell Square, sat on property belonging to the Duke of Bedford and was located on the west side of the British Museum in Bloomsbury. The duke had demolished his home to develop his land into townhomes for lease. Many of his peers were following suit, especially after the duke exclaimed how it was easier to collect rents than try to find tenants to farm his land.

Jason pulled his curricle into the square surrounded by three-story brick townhomes and admired the pretty leafy park at its center. He brought his cattle to a stop in front of Christina's home and leapt from his seat the moment his *tiger* secured his cattle's bridles. His excitement to see Christina had him rushing up the steps and banging the brass lion head door knocker. His spirits were so high, he thought nothing could sour his day, until he saw the butler's unfriendly face. Giles looked as though he was about to deny him entrance and Jason wondered, *"Has the butler no idea I am back in Christina's good graces?"*

Having no wish to find out, he crossed the threshold to assert his right of entry. He thrust his hat and gloves to the butler, while expounding, "Miss Rothsborn is expecting me."

"Indeed," answered Giles, pulling the captain's greatcoat from his shoulders.

"She received my note, then?"

"My mistress requests you wait in the parlour for her, Captain. She is changing into an appropriate dress as we speak and has ordered me to assure you she will not keep your cattle waiting longer than necessary."

It was then Jason saw the butler grin at him and realized how he had been the object of the servant's amusement. He would have removed that grin with a sound lashing had the impudent man been under his command. Instead, he was forced to swallow his embarrassment for he knew any rebuke from him would find disfavor with Christina. He checked his temper and followed Giles to the parlour.

The Rothsborn parlour was a small but adequate room, typical of the moderate townhomes located outside the Mayfair District. The walls were painted in ochre. A Queen Anne bottle green velveteen upholstered sofa faced the parlour doors and was the centerpiece of the room with two matching chairs at each corner. A couple of fringed pillows lay haphazardly on the sofa, a corner of a magazine poked out from beneath one of them. On the floor next to one of the chairs sat an embroidery or sewing basket slightly askew and like a plate, the furniture was served up on a hand-tuft flora rug.

Floor-length matching green curtains, topped with a matching triple gold fringe swag framed the window facing the street. Across from the window was a marble-fronted fireplace where an embroidered fire screen stood at its hearth. Near the fireplace was a worn dark-brown leather wingback chair and beside it a circular walnut end table where an opened book and hurricane lamp lay. The walls were adorned with the requisite sconces for light and paintings of amateurish skill. Pushed against the side wall was a square lacquered wooden chess table with its pieces ready to be played. The sight of the chess board recalled Jason's visit when he interrupted Christina and her father playing the game. It also reminded him of his first chaste kiss with Christina. The memory diminished any lingering grudge he had for the butler.

Once again in high spirits, he took a seat on the couch to await Christina and found a golden length of braided silk cord on the cushion. He picked it up and out of habit began to twist and turn the rope into a sailor knot. The exercise reminded him how he learned his trade as a young midshipman. He was still working the silk rope when Christina entered and greeted him. Her curiosity brought her to him. "What are you doing?"

Jason raised the knotted cord for her inspection. “I found this length of rope on the sofa and have been amusing myself with it while I waited for you.”

Christina searched the room for a missing cord. She walked over to where one panel of a velveteen curtain hung loose. “You have one of the curtain tie backs. My father must have picked it up and left it for me to fix.”

Jason began to undo the knot to show Christina he caused it no harm when she exclaimed, "Oh, no!" He looked up and saw her cheeks crimson.

She explained in a softer voice, “I wished to see what you did. I would very much like to learn how to tie a sailor knot. Will you teach me?”

“It would be my pleasure, Christina. However, my horses are probably chomping at their bits, so we will leave the lesson for later. Are you ready to depart?”

“Yes. Susan is in the foyer awaiting us.”

He smiled when Christina bade him to bring the rope along for her lesson and placed the cord in his pocket. He escorted her to the front door with her hand on his arm where Giles waited to help him with his greatcoat, hat, and gloves. Susan helped Christina with her bonnet and then they were out the door Giles held open for them.

Jason stopped at the top of the stairs, took in a deep satisfying breath of having Christina on his arm, and surveyed the scene before him. He offered an approving nod to his groom when he saw him soothe his cattle with sweet words. Then, with a swiftness that spoke of being happy, he descended the steps and quickly settled Christina and Susan onto his curricle. He had just taken his seat and control of the reins when a cheerful Christina asked, “Where are we going, Jason?”

“I am taking you on a picnic of my own making," he answered with a grin. "Our last outdoor luncheon was of my father’s design. I prefer a simple affair which I hope will please you. I had Fortnum and Mason prepare a luncheon for us. We could return to the secluded area we picnicked at Hyde Park, but I think we might draw speculation from the high sticklers. I suggest the open spaces of Green Park."

“Green Park is lovely, Jason. What type of picnic did you order?”

“There are an assortment of sandwiches, a pâté of some sort, fresh fruit, nuts and lots of desserts. I fear there may be more desserts than sandwiches, but they all looked so good and I had trouble making a selection.”

“It sounds wonderful. Should we stop and purchase something to drink?”

"No. I have champagne and lemonade. I was not sure which you would prefer."

They engaged in idle chatter, taking pleasure in pointing out the ridiculous. Jason remarked upon a lady's mammoth hat; while Christina brought attention to a man chasing a mutt with a shoe in his mouth that had them both chuckling.

They were still finding amusement in what they saw when Jason maneuvered his curricle into one of the many dirt lanes crisscrossing Green Park and they heard a jaybird cried out. The single call announced their arrival and before long, a cacophony of squawks, trills, and coos resounded until the birds settled, content their intruders were of no threat to them. Jason kept his team to a sedate walk and turned into another path situated away from Constitution Hill, the main thoroughfare used by those making their way from the Strand to Hyde Park's Rotten Row.

The triangular-shaped fifty-three acre park was located between Hyde Park and St. James Park. It was known for its simplistic beauty with no lake or formal gardens and offered a peaceful environment, unless the kingdom decided to host a war victory celebration, or a balloonist decided to land on the lawn. Then, ceremonial displays, crowds of people, vendors selling their wares, pickpockets, and all kind of riff-raff created all kind of chaos and excitement.

He saw Christina lean forward and swivel her head from side to side to look for a place to hold their luncheon.

He could tell she was enjoying herself and was sure the music of the birds' calls, the smell of the sweet lawn, and the greenery were as pleasing to her as they were to him. He grinned when Christina enthusiastically pointed out the perfect picnic spot and per her recommendation, he drove his curricle within sight of the verdant grass dappled with sunlight. His *tiger* jumped off from his perch to take control of the reins when Jason pulled his cattle to a stop and once Jason was assured his cattle were firm in hand, he helped Christina and her maid from his curricle.

Susan made her way to speak with the groom whose company she would keep while her mistress enjoyed her picnic and Jason gathered the grey worsted blanket and picnic basket he had stored under his seat. He offered his free arm to Christina, who in her excitement to begin their picnic, pulled him enthusiastically to their picnic spot.

He had trouble playing the gallant as Christina insisted on helping him spread out the blanket and organize their luncheon. He took his own seat next to her when she finally settled herself on the blanket and took great pleasure watching her set out their assorted dishes. Her movements were graceful and Jason was amused when she prepared a rather full plate for a lady of her stature. He expected her to suggest they share the plate, so it surprised him when she called out to her maid to come and take the plate of food for her and the groom to eat.

Christina no sooner handed off the plate to Susan when she looked at Jason and said, "Before I forget, my aunt invites you to dine with us this evening."

Jason's silence prompted Christina to pointedly ask, "Do you wish to come?"

Jason was so deep in thought he had no idea his forehead was scrunching with deep lines or how his mouth had turned down in a frown. The sight concerned Christina and she asked, "What's wrong, Jason?"

"It just occurred to me, unlike you, I never even considered my groom's hunger."

"Why should you?" she laughed.

"Well, you thought of your maid!"

"Only because I knew she had not eaten. Your *tiger* was well aware of your plans and he would have seen to his own needs. He probably has his own grub packed somewhere on his riding platform."

"Well, I feel lacking in consideration."

"Do you keep the sailors you command fed?"

"Of course. I monitor everything. As captain, it is my duty. If foul weather keeps us from port, then I make the decisions on what is rationed to ensure we don't starve before we can gain provisions."

"Then, how can you feel lacking when duty guides you to behave honorably? I am sure if your *tiger* appeared hungry, you would have noticed and taken care of him accordingly."

"You are a good woman to placate me."

Christina handed Jason a sandwich and said, “Eat, and then tell me if you wish to dine at my aunt's home this evening.”

Jason took the sandwich. “Christina, it is always my heart's desire to spend time with you, so yes, I will come. Which reminds me, it is time you met my parents. I do not know when I will be called to duty and I would very much like to pay my addresses to you.”

“Jason,” she sighed. “What if we do not suit?”

“Do you truly have doubts?”

“Yes.”

“How can I overcome them?”

“Tell me about yourself and the life you hope to lead?”

“Well, you know I yearned to join the navy since I was a young lad. I enjoyed the sea and have prospered, but I confess it can be lonely, so I would like you with me on ship, at least until we begin a family.”

“What kind of life would I lead aboard a ship?”

“I admit it is not a life for a woman faint of heart. Life is far from what you are accustomed and with little room to wander you may feel quite trapped, unless you are a woman with an adventurous spirit. A woman who can take joy from what the sea and our travels have to offer, and be happy in the company of a man who would only have eyes for you."

"Only because I would be the only woman onboard."

"Maybe not. Many captains are known to allow other wives of seamen to serve the ship as a seamstress, laundress, or cook, so they may accompany their husbands. Your role, should you sail with me, would be to serve only me, not the ship. You would mostly care for my goods. I confess the advantage is all mine, for I will have your care and your company. All I can offer in return is a life of adventure."

"What of the danger?"

"Since Trafalgar, the navy's role is primarily patrolling the waters. Sometimes, we offer protection to merchant ships who carry England's license, other times we confiscate the goods of those ships that do not. Only privateers challenge us and I have never lost a battle to one as yet; however, I would never put you at risk. I would put you off at a port and take chase before I ever engaged in a battle with you onboard."

"What if they engaged?"

Jason felt his eyebrows scrunch in concern, but answered with the conviction of his captaincy. "Then I would ask you to stay below until the danger passed. I am sorry, Christina. I did not think this through. I must admit, those officer's wives who accompany their husbands are not as genteel as you."

"Then, you do not wish to marry me because I am too refined for your needs?"

"No," laughed Jason. "I do wish to marry you. I want you, Christina, but perhaps you would prefer to live apart from me on shore, waiting for when I take leave."

"That does not sound like a good marriage."

"No. In truth, I can be gone for years."

"Is that what my life will be like when we have children?"

"I expect. I don't know, Christina. I had hoped we could somehow make it work, but I must admit it will take effort on both our parts. Many marriages unless they are a *marriage of convenience* fail. You are privy to the gossip of our highest commanders and their peccadilloes."

"Is that what I should expect?"

"Struth! I cannot believe we are having this conversation."

"That is no answer, Jason, and this conversation is relevant if I am to seriously consider your offer of marriage."

"I would not marry you if I could not vow fidelity. What of you? It is common for wives separated from their husband's to acquire *cisceboes*?"

"Not I. You can trust me to stay faithful to you."

"How can you know?"

"Because I have thought of no one else but you in ten years."

"Really," he grinned. "Did I make such an impression at our first meeting?"

"Aye," blushed Christina. "Unfortunately, you cannot say the same for me. You did not even remember me when we reunited."

"I was too taken by your beauty to have reason enough to remember you as the child you were."

"Very charming, but not convincing," she chided.

"We have moved off course, you know. I believe I was asking you to meet my parents."

"Tell me about one of the officer's wives."

"It would be ungentlemanly to speak of them in a telltale fashion. I can only attest they are remarkable women."

Christina frowned.

"Oh, do not look so disappointed. I can tell you of a renowned gunner's wife on the H.M.S. Orion who fought in a battle with a French ship off Cape St. Vincent. Her job was to make and mend the captain's clothes. The tale is while she was sewing one of the captain's flannel shirts, the ship came under fire. It is said she put down her sewing and went to carry gunpowder for the gunners and then helped the surgeon with the injured."

"Truly?"

"Truly," answered Jason.

Christina asked, "Teach me how to tie one of your sailor knots. You still have the cord?"

Jason pulled the silken rope from his pocket. "Yes."

"What will you teach me?"

Jason laughed at her excitement. "The Figure-Eight is simple. It is a stopper knot, prevents a line from sliding out of sight up inside the mast. It was one of the first knots I learned as a midshipman."

Jason slowly demonstrated how to cross over the rope to form a loop and then to pinch and twist the top of the loop before passing the tail of the cord through it. “Now you try.”

The knot resembled the number eight. Christina examined it closely as she unwound the knot and then listening to Jason’s instructions, she worked to make the knot again. They were both so absorbed in their exercise they did not hear the two riders who were making their way over to them until the intruders made their greeting.

“Well, Captain Brentwood,” greeted Lady Lucinda. “I see you are indulging in an outdoor feast again.”

Jason stood, helping Christina to rise. He did not like how Lucinda and her companion remained on their mounts while speaking down to him. He felt at a disadvantage and instinctively stepped in front of Christina to protect her. He moved aside to present her when he was assured no threat existed, “You remember, Miss Rothsborn, of course.”

Lucinda nodded towards Christina. “I see she has no chaperone, Captain. It is not well done of you to put Miss Rothsborn's reputation in question.”

Jason saw Christina stiffen in embarrassment and rebutted, “Then it is good Society accepts a maid and a groom as appropriate chaperonage, Lady Lucinda, or else your own virtue would be bantered about in the parlours. Would you do me the honor of introducing your escort?”

Lucinda blushed at Jason’s rebuke and turned around to search for her own groom. The servant lagged so far behind that Jason felt his remark had hit soundly; especially when he saw Lucinda's ill attempt to mask her vexed expression. She introduced, "Lord Matthews, May I present Captain Brentwood and his companion Miss Rothsborn."

"Your servant," answered his lordship.

"Matthews," offered Jason. "You are welcome to join us if you wish."

Lord Matthews was too good-natured to intrude on the captain's cozy affair and replied, "No, thank you, Captain. I promised not to keep Lady Lucinda long for she has another engagement."

Jason doubted he spoke truthfully, but he was glad he would not have to bear their company.

Lucinda haughtily remarked, "Yes. I am most frightfully engaged, but I do look forward to seeing you tomorrow night, Captain. Your mama invited me and my parents to dine at Aubry House. She assures us of your company."

Jason felt his body tense, but before he could make a retort, Christina announced, "I shall look forward to seeing you tomorrow as well, Lady Lucinda."

Surprised, Lucinda asked, "You are invited?"

"I am."

Jason laughed and verified, "Indeed, she is."

Chapter Eighteen

Jason searched the Dewksbury drawing room for the hostility he felt and was surprised to find a number of eyes, focused on him as if he was the one who meant to do harm. Being a duke's son, he had never been in a position where he was concerned if he was liked. Aside from royalty, most people hoped for his good opinion, not the other way around, but the unspoken message was clear. Christina's family would not brook her getting injured.

He nodded, feeling the necessity to respond even though no words were said, and grinned at Christina when she rose to walk over to greet him. He returned her warm salutation, then presented his arm to escort her back to where her watching family waited. With manners drilled into him from birth, he spoke a number of platitudes, before bowing to Lady Dewksbury, and nodding to the gentlemen, all the while, taking note of the moisture beading the palm of his hands. The sensation surprised him. Even in battle he was never aware of his nervousness, being too engaged in his duty to notice or care, so he was glad when Lady Dewksbury with her astuteness, put him at ease with a discussion of England's inclement weather.

The topic removed him from scrutiny until inquiries into his sea life were made. Before he could answer, Christina stole everyone's attention by announcing she knew a story about an H.M.S. Orion gunner's wife. Having hooked her audience with her admission, she narrated her story. Her voice rose and fell at key points that would have made any theatrical director proud. She added her own insight regarding how the wife might have felt under peril during battle and before Jason knew it, Christina's tale of the wife's feats took on a larger than life heroism. He quickly took himself away to meander about the room when he could no longer withhold the laughter threatening to erupt.

Christina had captivated his attention from the moment she fell into his arms, so he did not remember the drawing room he now inspected. His first thought as he took inventory of his surroundings was how his father would approve the viscount's show of wealth. The walls were paneled in white pine with gilded relief carvings; the ceiling was molded in the Neo-Classical style. Heavy floor-length golden brocaded satin drapes, crowned with matching swag tiers framed the tall arched windows facing Grosvenor Square. A number of Louis XV gilded wood-carved furniture upholstered in Gobelin silk tapestry were prominently placed around the room. Gobelin's was famous, then as now, for the beautiful designed pastoral scenes they wove for royalty. The number of pieces Dewksbury owned, as well as the Gainsborough and Reynolds paintings on the wall, and the Aubusson medallion carpet beneath his feet, spoke volumes about Dewksbury's coffer.

Jason spotted a number of miniature framed family portraits on the tables and fireplace mantel. Unlike the duke's drawing room which also displayed portraits of his family, these frames were slightly askew as if they had been picked up to be admired and then replaced without precision. Another cursory search found an opened book on an end table ready to be read from where the reader left off. Nearby on the floor sat a work basket with a mishap of colored silk threads hanging over its edge. A piece of embroidered linen with the same yellow, green, and rose threads also poked from the basket as though the lady working on the piece was interrupted and in her hurry, thrust the material hastily away. Music sheets were left spread out on the piano forte, a sign the piano was used too often for someone to bother to put them away.

The room's essence spoke of cheerful and comfortable gatherings, not the formal and perfected socials his father hosted. As a child, he remembered the servants always followed after him and his siblings (unless they found a way to elude them) to straighten up after them. It was the untidiness of the viscount's drawing room, (if it could be called such), which marked its coziness, a characteristic much like Christina's small parlour where he had seen a similar work basket placed on her parlour floor. He was about to look for other examples of relaxation and contentment when the butler arrived and announced dinner was ready.

Jason entered the dining room behind his host and immediately noticed how the dining table had been shortened to foster communication for their numbered few. He also saw how the livered footmen did not hover behind each guest's chair, waiting to do their bidding as his father would demand. Only one butler stood ready at the door to call into service those footmen needed to fulfill the viscount's wishes. Jason guessed the butler was highly trusted. Usually, Jason would be chary of what he said, to make sure his comments were not repeated and spread from household to household through the servant grapevine. Upper servants, butlers, valets, abigails would often hear information from servants in other households for which their masters would reward them handsomely to repeat. Nothing profited a servant more than reporting on some type of disgrace to be bantered about in the clubs and parlours of the *ton*.

The table was set with crisp white linen, fine china, polished silver, and sparkling crystal all placed precisely. In place of the requisite silver epergne centerpiece which members of the *ton* used to impress guests was a large elegant crystal bowl filled with water and floating candles. Fresh flowers were situated around the bowl's base and unlike the epergne, which discouraged guests from talking across the table, the low adornment allowed conversation to flow easily. It seemed the Dewksburys did not conform to speaking only to one's neighbor, but encouraged their guests to converse at will. Jason was sure Dewksbury only allowed the informal manner within the privacy of his family, since such behavior would be frowned upon by the high sticklers of Society. The revelation he had been invited to participate in the family affair pleased him.

Priscilla looked at Jason. "It was good of you to join us this evening, Captain Brentwood."

"It is only fair, Aunt," blurted Christina. "If I am to suffer through an evening with Lady Lucinda Marsh, then he should subject himself to a similar experience."

"Miss Rothsborn indulges in the dramatics, my lady," interjected Jason with a smile. "I am far from suffering. Indeed, I consider myself the luckiest of men to enjoy your company."

"Very charming, Captain," replied Priscilla. She looked to her niece pointedly, before saying, "We will overlook your gauche remark and dislike for Lady Lucinda, Christina, for to declare it publicly is unkind. I will even forgive your suggestion our dinner presents a trial for the captain, since I am sure it was not your intent." Having reprimanded her niece appropriately, she turned to ask Jason, "Of what evening does my niece reference?"

"I have invited Miss Rothsborn to dine at Aubry House tomorrow night. I wish to formally introduce her to my parents, my lady. It would honor me if I may inform my mother how all of you could attend." Jason swept a look at Dewksbury and Christina's father.

Mr. Rothsborn replied, "I think it best I decline, Captain Brentwood. I did not wish to make the announcement during dinner, but you must know I gave my letter of resignation to the duke today. I am afraid he did not take it well."

"Oh, Papa!" exclaimed Christina.

Jason asked, "Did he threaten you, sir, with termination?"

"No, Captain, but our working relationship is awkward now that you are courting my daughter, especially since he is used to speaking to me with candor. Lately, he has had to check his comments, knowing the lady he disparages is Christina."

"I have done nothing to provoke him, Papa."

"No, Christina. You have not, but he fears you have ensnared his son."

"Indeed, she has," remarked Jason with a grin. "You must not let his present position concern you. He will come around once he gets to know Christina better."

"Well," remarked Lord Dewksbury. "I can attest Christina is charming enough to change any high stickler."

Christina laughed. "Oh, Uncle, do not tell me you no longer find me troublesome."

"I have never called you troublesome," he corrected, "I have always considered you a *diamond of the first water,* Christina."

Priscilla took her *serviette* and dabbed her wet cheeks, overcome with joy from witnessing the tender scene between Christina and her husband.

"Aunt! You must not become a watering pot, or my most magnanimous uncle will refrain from imparting compliments on me!"

"You will escort Christina, Dewksbury, in my stead?" asked Stephen.

"Papa! I will not go anywhere you are unwelcome. Captain Brentwood will understand my change of heart."

Before Jason could counter, Stephen replied, "I do not consider myself unwelcome, Christina. Did not the captain just invite me? At this time, I decline for my own reasons. Do not question them."

Stephen's reprimand prompted an embarrassed Christina to apologize for her outburst. The silence that followed was awkward until Dewksbury spoke.

"Her ladyship will send the duchess our acceptance, Captain. It is good of you to invite us. Now tell us is there any news on your ship?"

"Nothing formal, my lord. But word is the Apollo is being refitted."

"The Apollo!" exclaimed Christina. "She is the frigate of the model you gave me."

"Yes," replied Jason. "Do you still have her?"

"Yes," answered Christina exuberantly. "She remains pristine."

"Perhaps," commented Lord Dewksbury. "You could let the rest of us in on your conversation."

"I beg your pardon, Dewksbury," apologized Jason. "Before I joined His Majesty's Service as a midshipman at the age of three and ten, my father had a model of the frigate Apollo commissioned for me. As a young boy, I had heard the stories of her many successes and hoped one day to serve on her. Miss Rothsborn visited with her father on her eighth birthday and was gracious to accept the model as a gift."

Stephen chuckled, eluding there was more to the story, but Dewksbury did not demand an accounting. He asked, "I would like to see the model one day, Christina."

"Of course, Uncle."

Priscilla used the pause in conversation to rise, a gesture announcing dinner was over and the ladies were to retire to the parlour while the men enjoyed their port. Christina made her exit with her aunt and once seated in the parlour, felt like she was eight-years-old again under her aunt's glare, the one which had silently checked her words and actions since she was a child.

She opened and closed her mouth a number of times to put together a reasonable explanation for her dinner outburst regarding Lady Lucinda Marsh. *How does one explain to another lady without sounding jealous, that a beautiful woman desires the man you wish to call your own?*

"Really, Christina," remarked her aunt. "You are beginning to look like a fish out of water. Surely, you can put a sensible amount of words together to explain your dislike of Lady Lucinda. I found her manners without fault. She is spoiled of course and arrogant, but what woman with a substantial dowry and consequence is not?"

"You forgot beautiful, Aunt."

"You cannot be jealous, Christina!"

"Annoyed, more than anything, Aunt. While Lady Lucinda likes to put me in my place, it is her trespassing upon Captain Brentwood's gentle manners that riles me. I believe the Duke of Aubry would like to see a match between her and his son."

"The duke obviously disapproves of you if what your papa insinuates is true, but my dear, if it is the captain you want, he seems to be quite agreeable to paying his addresses to you."

"I do not think I would be happy married to him if his family will not accept me. It is hard enough to be ostracized by the high sticklers without giving them ammunition to *cut* me. Can you imagine the parlour talk? The commoner who ensnared the ducal son. I would be cast as a villain."

"You worry for naught, Christina. Once the duke sees you are equal to any titled lady in manners and talent, he will accept you into his family."

"I do not think I can compete with Lucinda. Even I have heard she excels in all she does."

"There is no competition, Christina. You are your own shining star. Be yourself, for that is who the captain admires. Besides, you have your own exceptional talents."

"I am glad you will be there tomorrow evening, Aunt. I fear I am approaching quicksand and every false step will bring me lower into the abyss."

"Your flair for drama was not one of the talents I spoke, Christina. You must stop doubting yourself and embrace the noble blood running in your veins. Your mama never stopped being the lady she was when she married your papa. When you accept you are Lucinda's equal in everything which marks a lady, then you will be just as formidable as was your dear mama. She did not let Society's expectations decide who she should marry and neither should you."

Christina gave her aunt a hug. When Priscilla picked up her embroidery hoop and began to stitch, Christina walked over to the piano forte and took a seat on the bench. She looked at the timepiece on the fireplace mantle and was surprised the gentlemen had not joined them. A quarter of an hour already passed and she wondered what kept them. Distracted, her fingers tickled the ivory keys. She opened the music sheet her aunt must have practiced earlier and began to slowly make her way through the first stanza. A few sharp keys rang through the melody and Christina laughed when she saw her aunt screw her face.

"Really, Christina. If you would only practice, you could be proficient in no time."

Christina continued her play, laughing each time she missed a key. It was during one of her mishaps, the gentlemen arrived. She saw her father and captain grin at her inadequacies, while her uncle frowned saying, "If you must play, at least indulge us with an instrument in which you have a talent."

"Yes, Christina," remarked her aunt. "Will you not play your violin for us?"

"I did not bring it, Aunt."

Jason asked, "You are proficient with the strings, Miss Rothsborn?"

"Some say so."

"You will be adored by my crew. Music onboard ship is one of our few entertainments. I expect your cadre of music would touch the soul of every man in my crew."

"Your words though poetic, Captain, are suspect. I doubt your crewmen would appreciate the classics," remarked Priscilla.

Christina was about to remark she knew one or two lively ditties, but was saved from revealing the news when her aunt asked, "What music is played on your ship, Captain?"

"We sing mostly sea shanties and when we have time to celebrate we gather around a fiddler and my men dance a jig or two."

Jason moved to sit next to Christina. She could smell the redolent tobacco on him as she watched him place his fingers on the keys.

"With your permission, my lady?"

Priscilla gave a nod and Christina laughed as Jason played the piano forte and sang a sea ditty. *"Twas Friday morn when we set sail, and we had not got far from land, when the captain, he spied a lovely mermaid, with a comb and a glass in her hand..."*

Chapter Nineteen

"You look beautiful, Christina," complimented Jason.

Christina thought he was the beautiful one. He was dressed in formal black attire: a black tailcoat, white waistcoat and cravat, black pantaloons and dress slippers all fitting him to perfection. She could easily have spent the evening with nothing more than casting her eyes upon him, until his next words broke the spell she was under.

He placed her hand on his arm and joyfully said, "Come and meet my parents."

Jason's excitement was in complete opposite to Christina's feelings. She had just entered the opulent Aubry formal drawing room when he greeted her and took her arm. Her natural sense of survival told her to turn tail and run, but her aunt's voice steadied her.

"Go, Christina. We are right behind you."

Christina nodded, stiffened her back and walked with Jason over to be introduced to the Duke and Duchess of Aubry. She wore one of her new evening dresses like a knight wears armor, not so much to intimidate, but to impress. The high-waist gown was made of white lace which she wore over a white satin slip. The bottom of her skirt was finished with a deep flounce of more lace and above the flounce, running the width of the dress, were three rows of thin white satin ribbon. A row of white flower wreaths trimmed the top ribbon and multiple pink bows and ribbons adorned her short puffy ruched sleeves. On her golden curled coif sat a wreath of flowers that made her look like a Grecian goddess.

The duke and duchess looked very self-righteous when Jason presented her to them. Even so, Christina managed to ignore their haughtiness and made the appropriate curtsy due them. Considering her frayed nerves, she was quite pleased with her performance and imagined her aunt, who stood behind her, had most likely smiled in approval, until the duke returned Christina's greeting with a nod. Christina knew her aunt would feel the affront as deeply as herself. Manners governed a gentleman to make a bow to a lady when introduced. The duke's slight communicated what he thought of Christina. The insult was made greater when the duchess followed her husband's lead with a tilt of her head which brought attention to her glittering diamond tiara. Had her aunt not adorned herself in a similar fashion, the opulent jewels the duchess wore might have intimidated Christina as they were meant to do, but thankfully, they had an opposite effect. She rallied and offered her best smile, remarking to her hosts the honor of making their acquaintance.

Jason, however, was quick to remark on the offense. "I am presenting the lady I hope to make my wife," he heatedly chastised. "I expect you to give her proper consideration."

"Excuse me," the Duke of Aubry replied with all the self-importance of his rank. "I was unaware a lady was presented to me."

Before Jason could counter, he found himself shoved aside by Christina's uncle. Dewksbury suggested Jason escort Christina and his wife away while he spoke with the duke. The two noblemen looked like challenging King penguins in their black tailcoats and pantaloons. The duchess looked with concern at them and then quickly trailed after her son.

"Aubry," called Dewksbury. "Am I to understand you find my niece lacking?"

"I do not mean to offend, Dewksbury, only to acknowledge a discrepancy in class."

"Well, you do offend and unless you wish to find yourself with my fist in your face, I suggest you remember Miss Rothsborn is my niece. It would be foolish to insult her."

"Are you not being foolish, Dewksbury, for challenging your better in both rank and power?"

"There are all kinds of power, Aubry. Political, fiduciary, financial. Do you really want to test my power or her other protectors?"

"You refer to my terminated solicitor, Mr. Rothsborn?"

"Indeed, but do not discount the Earl of Marksby."

"Marksby," sneered Aubry. "He does not seem to acknowledge the connection?"

"You doubt me, Aubry?"

"If the earl recognizes Miss Rothsborn as family, then I will keep an open mind to her eligibility as a wife for my second son. However, Marksby's decline of tonight's invitation suggests otherwise."

"Perhaps, Aubry, it is your company he avoids."

"Now, who wishes to offend?"

"We shall be civil then, Aubry, and allow Providence to guide us."

"I always knew you were a romantic, Dewksbury. There is no other reason to explain why you spend your evenings at home, instead of at the clubs."

"You should try it and perhaps then, you will not be so prickly. My niece is of stellar character and your son could do no better."

The Duke of Aubry was about to offer a retort, but was checked by Dewksbury raising his hand to stop him. "Do not let your prejudices guide you. Look at your son. He is sanguine in my niece's company. What man could wish for more than to enjoy his wife. Wait until you know Christina better before you judge her. She has her own misgivings and is not the only one being measured this evening. It would not surprise me if she declines the captain's offer because she finds you lacking."

Jason and Christina did their best to engage in trivial conversation with the Duchess of Aubry until the rest of the duke's party arrived. Christina introduced those topics of weather and fashion considered appropriate for a lady. Her apprehension lessened when her aunt offered her own tidbits into the conversation and before long, the duchess was cracking a smile over Jason's absurd comment about the annoying creaks being heard in the clubs from men's corsets. Before long, the butler announced the Earl and Countess of Montrose, and Lady Lucinda. The duke and duchess went immediately to welcome them.

Lucinda looked amazingly beautiful. Her rich dark hair was expertly coiffed with buds of pink roses placed discriminately to match her evening dress. She wore a round robe of rose crepe, with a gathered demi-train worn over a white satin slip that complimented her figure to advantage. Her short puffed sleeves, neckline, and hem were ornamented with puckered white satin and crepe. The exquisite detailing marked her a lady of distinction. Christina saw the duke's approving face and turned to see if Jason admired the lady as well. Her ego was momentarily assuaged when she saw Jason looking at her and not Lucinda.

"My father will come around," he said.

"And if he doesn't?"

"You must trust I know what I want and I want you. Now, as much as I would like to ignore Lucinda and her parents, it would be ungentlemanly of me to do it. Come, let me introduce you to the Earl and Countess of

Montrose. Make me proud, Christina. Show them you are their equal."

"But I am not."

"Who says? Not I and I am all that matters."

Christina laughed at his aristocratic self-importance and allowed him to walk her over to Lucinda's family to be introduced. She saw her uncle collect her smiling aunt and Christina decided in that split moment to yield to Jason's will and her aunt's ever incessant speech about her being equal to any lady of quality. She bolstered her courage and raised her chin. She was determined to show her critics she was more than a lady of gentility. She was a lady of character.

The Earl and Countess of Montrose offered their felicitations to Jason and were quite congenial to her in his presence, but the moment the men took their discussion away from the ladies, she felt Lucinda's and her mother's anger. Their curt manner and condescending tone spoke volumes for what they thought of her as a rival and if not for her very protective and capable aunt she would have easily crumbled under their subtle assaults. The countess had met her match in Viscountess Dewksbury for every time the lady marveled over one of Lucinda's accomplishment's, Priscilla countered with one of Christina's own. It was like playing a game of whist, waiting to see who would trump and win the point. Even when Lady Montrose hit below the belt with a remark regarding class, Christina's aunt recalled a far from desirable Montrose family connection. The battle of wits only ended when the butler finally announced dinner was served.

As protocol dictated, the Duke of Aubry escorted the Countess of Montrose into the dining room as she was the senior ranking female peer under his wife. The earl took the duchess in hand and Viscount Dewksbury escorted his wife. Lucinda smirked, most likely thinking Christina would follow without escort, but her triumph turned into embarrassment when Jason took Christina in hand and made no effort to acquire her company. He was not ungentlemanly enough to leave the lady without an escort, but he made it clear Christina took precedence by waiting for Lucinda to join them before departing for the dining parlour.

Christina was both delighted and mortified when Jason directed the servants to move her place setting so she, like Lucinda, could sit next to him. He was making it clear to everyone he would not tolerate any schemes pushing an alliance between him and Lucinda. Christina almost laughed aloud when the duchess insisted the table looked lopsided with dinner guests sitting mostly to one side. She caught her aunt's eyes and knew she was not the only one who found humor in the incident.

The Duke of Aubry clearly subscribed to the dictates of formal dining where guests spoke only to their neighbors. Artificial discourse broke the silence of the meal as the weather on numerous days were recalled. Christina heard Lucinda remark how the five o'clock hour at Hyde Park was cooler than the four o'clock hour. When she heard Jason chuckle, she was sure the lady was mocking her own mother's conversation to amuse the captain.

Christina waited for Jason to turn his attention to her, but Lucinda would not, as manners dictated, relinquish him. More than fifteen minutes passed. A part of Christina wanted to shove Jason in the shoulder to get his attention, but she had no wish to make a spectacle of herself, even if her pride suffered at being ignored. Before she became too downhearted, she felt Jason fleetly brush his knee against hers. The gesture was so quick it took her a moment to understand what it meant. He was letting her know he had not forgotten her. Knowing his thoughts were on her and not the non-stop chatter Lucinda expounded on him, made her smile so brightly it caught the duke's attention. His discerning stare and frown made her think he knew what caused her to smile and she blushed. She was immensely relieved when the duchess rose, indicating it was time for the ladies to remove themselves to the drawing room.

"You will play for us, Lucinda," remarked the duchess. "Your mama has spoken highly of your ability and it would pleasure the duke, I am sure to hear you."

"I would be honored, Duchess." Lucinda made her way to the piano bench, took her seat and asked, "Do you have a request or should I play Handel?"

Christina was surprised Lucinda did not suggest to play a newer composition, though it did impress her how the lady's repertoire was extensive enough to allow requests. Before she could relax with the knowledge she did not have to play, her aunt announced, "And of course, Christina, you will perform for us. If the duke is a connoisseur of music, then he will be pleased to hear you play as well."

The Countess of Montrose asked with surprise, "She is proficient with the piano forte?"

Christina was happy to interject, "No, I daresay I am not."

The countess smirked.

Before Christina could remind her aunt she did not have her violin with her, she noticed her instrument's case leaning against the wall near the piano forte. She raised an eyebrow in question to her aunt.

"I thought you might have need of it, Christina, so I asked your papa to send it over. I brought it along in the carriage. I believe your uncle had it retrieved while we dined."

"You speak in riddles," remarked the duchess.

The gentlemen arrived in time to hear the comment and the duke queried his wife, "What riddle?"

"It is for Lady Dewksbury to explain, for I am not privy to Miss Rothsborn's musical talent, if indeed, there is one."

The duke raised an eyebrow at Priscilla who simply laughed at his haughty countenance. "There is no mystery, Duke. I brought Christina's violin in hopes she would consent to play for us. Her music always soothes me after a hearty meal."

"Yes! Please!" exclaimed Jason. "I would very much love to hear you play." Jason, with Montrose and Dewksbury present, had just suffered an embarrassing half hour heated discussion with his father where he made it abundantly clear the only lady he wished to marry was Christina. When the gentlemen entered the parlour, only Dewksbury looked pleased and delighted at Jason's steadfast desire for Christina's hand.

Lucinda rose from her seat at the piano forte where she was prepared to play and announced, "By all means, Miss Rothsborn. Please precede me with your particular performance. I am all anticipation to hear your 'soothing' music."

Christina cringed at Lucinda's sarcasm; however, she did not let the retort unnerve her. "As you wish," she replied and proceeded to retrieve her violin from its case.

"Do you not wish to make a request?" Lucinda asked Priscilla.

"Christina could play *God Save the King* and my mood would be improved. Anything she plays is beautiful and heartfelt. I need make no request to ensure satisfaction."

Lucinda blushed at the disparagement to her own talent. She bit her lip for she could not offer a rebuttal to the viscountess without looking foolish. She seemed quite pleased when the duke raised his monocle to his eye and gave Christina a thorough inspection, shaking his head in disapproval and uttering derisively, "I am in anticipation to be among one so gifted."

Lord Dewksbury laughed and broke the tension by adding, "You will find you have spoken truthfully, Aubry. I suggest you enjoy the performance."

Jason had already settled himself in a wing chair separate from the rest of the party, but near enough so he could watch Christina play with no interference from anyone else.

Christina removed her violin and bow from its case and plucked the open strings to ensure her instrument was tuned and thought about what she should play. She needed a score she knew by heart and something to impress her audience. She realized this was her opportunity to show she was equal if not greater in skill to any debutante and decided to play a concerto. The three movement piece would engage the audience for better than half an hour, but would also showcase her talent. More importantly, the Beethoven piece was one she had been practicing and she knew her fingers would recall the music, intuitively.

She liked the popular composer though she felt sympathy for the musician who was said to be going deaf. His innovative music was in high demand with his patrons and publishers, so much so, Beethoven could not keep them from hiring other musicians to arrange his most popular works for other instruments.

Christina liked the excitement his music generated through his change in harmonic ranges and his use of forceful rhythmic patterns. His music was fluid and ultimately, the arrangement told a story. Christina positioned herself for comfort. Grasping the violin's neck with her left thumb and forefinger, she raised her violin to her collarbone, lowering and angling her head until she rested her chin comfortably. She placed the bow on the strings and closed her eyes, taking a moment to gather her thoughts and become one with her instrument. When Christina played, she found herself easily transported to a higher plane where nothing existed but the music. Through her performance, she revealed emotion and passion. The sight of her playing affected her audience so greatly that when she finished, an awe inspiring silence filled the room.

Chapter Twenty

"Aunt," cried Christina. "You must stop. I am beginning to cramp from laughing so much."

"You must not admit to something so vulgar, Christina," chuckled Priscilla.

They were sharing a pot of tea Christina had yet to sip. Every time she brought the delicate Sevres porcelain cup to her mouth, her aunt said something to make her laugh, forcing her to return the cup to its saucer before the warm brew splashed on her morning dress.

Recalling the stunned looks of her audience after her musical exhibition last night had kept them laughing hysterically. They were beyond control, giggling at the most nominal reference to surprise, gape, mesmerized. Christina remembered being pleased she played well and would have taken a cheeky bow, if she had not been met at the end of her performance with silence and gawking from her audience. Even her aunt and uncle were stunned. For the first time, she feared her ears had deceived her and she had played badly. Then, Jason broke the quiet with a resounding applause. Her aunt and uncle followed suit. Christina wanted to laugh when the Duke of Aubry struggled with what to do. He looked ill-prepared to offer his compliments, but of course, he knew to refrain would make him appear churlish, so along with his compliments, he offered Christina a squinty glare as if he realized he had been bested. To which, Christina smiled brilliantly.

"Christina!" Amanda called out as she cheerfully entered the parlour without being announced. "Why am I the last to hear of your success?"

When Amanda saw Christina was not alone, she blushed at her ill-mannered greeting and apologized profusely to her ladyship, silently cursing Giles for not informing her his mistress was not alone. Christina smiled at her friend's uncommon exuberance, rose to greet her, and asked her what she was talking about.

"Lady Montrose and Lucinda came for a morning visit and Mama was quite put out when they never mentioned your musical triumph last night. You see, they spoke of the dinner, how Lucinda herself was a success, and with every word I could see Mama's ire rising. Mama does not like mendacity. She does not mind the white lie, but outright falsehoods are unforgiveable and she knew you had outshone Lucinda at last night's musical performance."

"But, Amanda," retorted Christina. "How did you know I was even at Aubry House last night?"

"The servants pass news around quicker than our *gossipmongers*. Why Mama heard from our butler who heard it straight from the Aubry butler how every servant had their ear plastered to every vent in the duke's home last night. When Lady Montrose called, mama expected to hear an insider's tale, knowing your mastery of the violin is already parlour news. No doubt the reason your salver is spilling over with invitations. You are no longer *sans valeur.*"

"She has never been without worth, Lady Amanda," chided Priscilla.

"Oh, I do beg your pardon, my lady."

Ignoring her aunt's chastise, Christina asked Amanda, "What do you mean my salver is overflowing with invitations?"

"Ring for Giles, Christina," commanded Priscilla. "Let's see who desires your company."

The three of them reviewed a mass of cards and invitations who according to Giles had been dropped off by every footman in Mayfair. Amanda was quick to persuade Christina to accept those invitation she knew she would be attending.

"Oh, please accept the Mattington's Breakfast. Lady Mattington is known for her lovely gardens and soirées, and I would so enjoy your company."

"Are you attending, Aunt?"

"You may join us, Christina, if your aunt is disinclined to go. Mama would be ecstatic to claim you a member of our party."

"You should accept, Christina," encouraged Priscilla. "I doubt your uncle will want me to make the drive and I would not like to be the reason you had to decline the invitation."

"And what invitation is that?"

The women were so engaged in conversation they did not hear Captain Brentwood enter the room. Upset at the flagrant lack of household protocol, Priscilla asked, "Christina, is your butler retired for the day?"

Christina laughed, especially when she saw Jason's affront that perhaps he was unwelcomed. "Aunt, you must not chastise Giles. He knows the captain and Amanda are my particular friends and need no introduction. They are to be received always."

"Well," replied Priscilla. "I suppose all is forgiven. Good day to you, Captain. You will not take offense, of course, to my outburst. We were speaking of the Mattington Breakfast. What are your thoughts on the matter?"

"Well, I believe it is considered *de rigueur*," he replied. "Would you like me to escort you, Miss Rothsborn?"

"Are you invited, Captain?"

"I am a duke's son, so I do not require an invitation. All doors open to me."

Christina laughed. "You are awfully arrogant, Captain."

"But not in error," agreed Amanda. "I cannot imagine anyone of *famille ducale* being refused entry."

Christina informed Jason, "Amanda has graciously asked me to join her and her mama, but it would please me to see you there."

"Oh, Christina!" exclaimed Amanda. "Mama will be so delighted you are joining us. I will leave now and take her the news."

After Amanda left, Christina asked Jason if he would like some tea. "No, thank you. I did not mean to interrupt. I came to see if you wish to take a ride in my curricle through Hyde Park."

"Go, Christina," commanded Priscilla. "I will tell your father where you have gone before I leave. Dewksbury will be beside himself with worry. I left word I would be back within the hour and I have already surpassed it."

Jason maneuvered his curricle down the freshly swept road and agreed with Christina when she exclaimed the day was gorgeous. The weather was cool, but the sky was uncommonly blue without any encroaching grey clouds to suggest an onslaught of England's unpredictable and harsh rain.

"I feel so giddy and restless," she remarked. "I wish you could spring your cattle, so I could feel the cool wind brush against me as your curricle raced along the road. Or better yet, if I was at Dewksbury Hall, I could pick up my skirts and run as fast and hard as I could to expel all the energy bubbling inside me." Christina choked, "Oh, my goodness. I have confirmed I am indeed a *hoyden*."

"No, Christina," laughed Jason. "You are just a lady with an exuberance for life."

"You are too kind, Jason. Any other gentleman in Society would find me mannish at revealing such unladylike behavior."

Jason did not reply because he could not counter her claim. Society's rules for how ladies should behave were explicit and a lady did not run, but how anyone who knew Christina could find anything unladylike about her was beyond belief.

Jason moved his curricle through the Grosvenor Gate at Hyde Park and Christina saw a number of gentlemen tip their hat to her when their carriage passed. One or two even called out to the captain in greeting. She was surprised to see him, completely out of character, ignore them, urging his cattle on rather than stopping to greet them.

"We are drawing a lot of attention, Jason."

"News of your performance has spread widely. I was practically accosted at my club this morning where I went for breakfast. I had to leave without finishing my meal; the intrusions were so great."

"What did they want to know?"

"Everything I know about you."

"What did you tell them?"

"Nothing. I explained a gentlemen tells no tales of a lady."

Jason steered his cattle off into a more secluded lane and Christina asked, "Where are we going?"

"I saw Breckman and his sister riding up ahead. I could not pass them without stopping, so I thought to get away from this overbearing crowd. I would take the road to Richmond and let my cattle have their heads, but without Susan, our jaunt would be remarked upon. The open carriage is sufficient for our rides in the park, but I will not have your virtue questioned because we left the city without benefit of a chaperone."

Jason moved his matched pair of horses onto a grassy patch of lawn marked with plane and oak trees, and then waited for his *tiger* to leave his perch behind their seats to run and grasp his horses' bridles. Once his groom controlled his cattle, he walked around the curricle to assist Christina down from her seat.

Curious, Christina asked Jason what he was about. "I cannot spring my cattle, but I can provide you a spot to run."

"I could not," gasped Christina. "It would be unseemly. Besides, my dress is too confining."

"I shall close my eyes," countered Jason, "and you may show your ankles if you must to run to your heart's delight. No one will witness your indiscretion and the sprint will do you good." Jason laughed. "Your restlessness is beginning to make me feel anxious."

"Well, I admit the idea tempts me. Both you and your *tiger* would need to close your eyes."

"Johnny!" commanded Jason. "Close your eyes until I bid you open them again."

Johnny, who had been listening to the couple's conversation smiled and obediently closed his eyes. Jason raised an eyebrow to Christina, indicating it was her move to make.

"Now, you, Jason, close your eyes."

Christina took in her surroundings when she was convinced Jason's eyes were truly closed and was pleased to see the area was completely isolated. Assured her run would not be witnessed, she bunched her skirt so she would not trip, and ran as fast as she could, laughing when her bonnet flew off her head to dangle by its ribbon from her neck. She felt her heart pumping hard from the exertion and bubbled up with laughter when she finally came to a stop.

The bellow of "Captain!" had Jason quickly opening his eyes and ordering his *tiger* to follow suit. He scanned the landscape to look for Christina and was glad she had the sense to hide when she saw an approaching rider. Jason turned his attention back to the gentleman who had hailed him and recognized Lieutenant William Croft.

William asked the moment he reached Jason, "Is one of your horses lame?"

"No" replied Jason. "Just a rock. I saw him chary of his step and pulled off the road to check his hoof. I was just giving him a moment before I put him to task."

William nodded his head in understanding, then asked, "Is there any news of our ship?"

"Nothing, yet. Where are you off?"

"I am hoping to run across Lady Irene in the park. She usually strolls with her sisters this time of the day."

"Well, don't let me keep you."

"You are sure I can be of no assistance?"

"No, thank you, Lieutenant," replied Jason. "My cattle are fine. Be off with you and enjoy this fine day."

Jason waited for Christina to reveal herself once Lieutenant Croft left. When she did not, he went in search of her and was surprised he could not find her. He stood akimbo, hands on his hips and scanned the area. His senses were alert, so when a small rock bounced off the grass near his foot, he turned and braced himself. He saw no one, but he heard a giggle among the rustling tree leaves and made his way to a sturdy oak from which he thought the sound came.

Just before he reached the tree, Christina darted out from behind its trunk and ran to seek refuge behind another one. He followed in pursuit and their cat and mouse game proceeded, with laughter and shrieks, until Jason caught her by the arm. They were laughing wholeheartedly until they both became aware of their secluded proximity. They stared at each other, never breaking their gaze, not even when Jason took Christina's gloved hand into his own. Her rapid pulse matched his own. Unable to resist the temptation, he raised her fingers to his lips and kissed them. Her sigh, prompted him to candidly remark, "I believe we suit, Miss Rothsborn."

"Dewksbury," hailed the future King of England. His Royal Highness, Prince George, was walking along Bond Street with Lord Alvanley, a particular friend of his known for his wit, when he spied the viscount across the street. Dewksbury went to him, made a proper regal bow and greeted, "Your Highness."

Prince George, known as Prinny to his intimates, waved his hand to hurry him through his deportment and then asked, "Who is this lady being spoken of who rivals Paganini? They say she is your niece and a maestro. Why have you not brought her to Carlton House?"

"When does Dewksbury venture from home?" laughed Alvanely at his own jibe.

Ignoring him, Dewksbury answered, "She has not made her curtsy at St. James."

"For heaven's sake man, why ever not? Who is the head of her family?"

"Marksby," informed Dewksbury.

"What is the girl's name, so I may be on the lookout for her."

"Miss Christina Rothsborn."

"How old is she?"

"Eight and ten."

"Ah, well then it is to be done. Tell Marksby, I look forward to the introduction."

Two hours later, the Earl of Marksby stomped into Dewksbury's study full of rage. "Who are you to summon me, Dewksbury, like a child about to be scold? You are lucky I came."

"You are lucky I share my business ventures with you, Marksby. Did you think I did it from the generosity of my heart? It is time to pay your debt and own your responsibility."

"What nonsense do you speak?"

"Of your cousin and my niece, Miss Rothsborn. It is time to acknowledge your connection."

"The upstart. Aubry told me how she is worming herself into his household."

"You are a fool, Marksby. Do you not realize he insults your own blood? Miss Rothsborn is the granddaughter of your uncle and had he been fortunate to bear a son, then he and not you would own the title."

"Why does it matter I take notice of her now?"

"Besides the fact she has come of age and it is your duty to do so, Prinny commands it."

"I will not burden myself with the costs of a *come-out* Season. If you think so highly of this girl, why don't you present her."

"First, no one is asking you to dip into your coffers, must I remind you, I helped fill. Second, nothing would please my lady wife more than to present her niece, but you know as well as I, the *ton* will wonder why your lady wife did not do the honor. Do not be obtuse, Marksby! You are straining my patience."

"You say the prince commands it?"

"Indeed."

"Aubry will not like it. He has other ideas for his son and the girl's acknowledgement by the queen will not serve him."

"No doubt, but Prinny takes precedence over the duke and you are too savvy to offend His Royal Highness."

"Ho-ho," laughed Marksby. "Aubry will see red!"

Chapter Twenty-One

Christina and Amanda sat across from the forward facing seat where the Countess of Larksborough sat in her luxurious carriage practically purring like a cat. Amanda's mother was grinning, not at them, but at her own private thoughts. Both girls expected she was congratulating herself on having Christina, London's newest sensation, among her party.

Every Season, the Earl and Countess of Mattington host a breakfast for the *haute ton* at their Richmond residence. The Mattington's principle seat was in Cheshire, but when duty called the earl to Parliament, he brought his household to Richmond instead of Mayfair. Early in his marriage he purchased the private estate on the Thames when he saw how much his young countess suffered living in London. The air, she complained to her peers, was too dense for her delicate lungs, but the earl knew better. He knew she missed the country and her gardens, so he purchased the estate in Richmond where she could grow flowers and plants to her delight.

Mattington was an avid horseman and did not mind traveling the ten miles to London, but the distance was too great for his countess to make the daily social rounds required of her station. To keep her happy he allowed her to host any soirée and entertainment she wished. No expense was spared to bring the *ton* to her. Her invitations were eventually coveted when word of her exquisite gardens and delicious fare became the talk of London. Her garden party was the premier event of the Season and anybody who was anybody attended.

Her guests were encouraged to walk the gravel paths where they found breathtaking views of colorful, fragrant, and well-tended plants and flowers. Lady Mattington was known to cultivate new species of roses, many rivaling those found at nearby Kews Royal Botanical Gardens. Only a few knew her rose bushes began with samplings her friend Sir Banks gave her from the foreign lands he had visited. Anyone traveling along the Thames, easily identified the Mattington Estate from the swath of brilliant colors covering their land to the river.

"I am so glad you did not bring your violin, Miss Rothsborn," remarked Amanda's mother Leticia as she returned from her musings. "I hope you will wait until Amanda's Ball to perform again."

"Mama," chastised Amanda. "She is to be my guest. I did not invite her to perform."

"Of course she will be your guest, but surely your friend would perform to ensure your ball is a success."

Christina felt she could do nothing less than to offer her talent if it helped Amanda. "If it would make Amanda happy, then I would be pleased to play one piece at her ball; however, I do not know how it will ensure its success."

"The *ton*," responded Amanda's mother, "is a fickle group, Miss Rothsborn. Right now, you are all the rage. I expect many will try to get you to perform for them by inviting you to their events." Frantic at the idea, she exclaimed, "You must promise not to yield to their requests before Amanda has her ball!"

Alarmed by her raised voice, Christina quickly agreed.

"Now," Leticia announced reverting back to her normal and reprimanding tone, "You both look lovely in your walking dresses and will no doubt draw attention. I want you to remember as debutantes your behavior will be scrutinized, so do nothing that can be remarked upon. The *gossipmongers* are more than happy to spread the smallest scandal. You must stay in my view or chaperonage. Mind you, the gentlemen will try to persuade you to see the gardens."

"But, Mama!" exclaimed Amanda. "Surely, if we stay together, there can be no concern."

Leticia made a puckered face, then added, "You must seek my approval. I will determine if the gentleman's escort is appropriate and then you must promise not to sit on any of the stone benches lining the gravel paths. You must keep moving and not be gone for longer than ten minutes."

"Ten minutes is not very long, Mama," sighed Amanda.

"History among other things have been made in less," she argued. "You will abide me in this, Amanda, or else we will return home."

"As you wish, Mama."

"And I caution you, while Lord Matthews is very eligible, he will not come into his title or fortune until his papa dies. He is young and wild, so do not fall for his charm. He has no plans to marry soon, nor is he required to do so. Do not put your aspirations where only heartache lies."

Amanda and Christina smiled at one another, secretly laughing at the countess's concerns and warnings.

They no sooner arrived and were announced *al fresco* when the Countess of Mattington cheerfully rushed up to greet them. "I have been in anticipation of your arrival. Leticia, please introduce me to this young lady whose musical talent precedes her."

"Really, Sylvia," she criticized. "You did not even acknowledge my Amanda."

Sylvia Matthews, the Countess of Mattington smiled and greeted Amanda and then glared at Lady Larksborough as though the woman had been impertinent. Leticia grinned at her small victory and introduced Christina.

"Sylvia, may I present Miss Christina Rothsborn to you. "Miss Rothsborn, the Countess of Mattington."

"Oh, you are a pretty thing," commented Sylvia. "Tell me, did you bring your violin?"

The countess's question reminded Christina of Lady Larksborough's claim that her invitations were requests for her to perform. Embarrassed, she fairly whispered, "No, my lady."

"Do not be gauche, Sylvia," chided Leticia. "Miss Rothsborn is your guest, not a hired musician."

"Really, I did not mean to be rude. I only wanted to hear her play. You cannot fault me, Leticia."

"Well," she responded. "You can hear her play at Amanda's Ball."

"And you call me tactless. Well, be glad I do not take offense you will not share her, Leticia. At least her presence today will provide enough talk to make my breakfast a success."

Both Amanda and Christina were amazed at how the noble ladies argued with one another as though they did not exist. They were glad when Lady Mattington waved her son over and commanded him to show them her garden. They awaited Lady Larksborough's approval and then happily allowed Lord Matthews to escort them onto the garden path, but not before Amanda's mother reminded them "ten minutes."

Lord Matthews looked pointedly at them and asked, "ten minutes?" Amanda balked, but Christina with her usual aplomb answered, "You have ten minutes, my lord, to show us your mama's garden. We are under strict rules."

"Rules? Are there others?" he asked.

"Well," answered Amanda this time. "We are not allowed to sit, but must keep moving."

"Indeed," replied his lordship. "How odd. Is there anything else I should know? I would hate to engage in a behavior where you think me ungentlemanly."

"I am sure we can count on your decorum to guide your manner, my lord," stated Christina.

"I am honored in your confidence, Miss Rothsborn and may I say it is a pleasure to see you again. As we are under a time constraint, I would like to show you the renowned Lady Banks Rose Arbor. My mother adores it, even though its prodigious growth would overtake the garden if not for our laborers. Mother says its beauty compensates enough for all the work required to keep the climbing rose in check."

His lordship escorted them into the garden and the sweet perfumes and colors of various flowers aroused their senses. Pink carnations, white daisies with their yellow centers, orange marigolds, red peonies, purple lilacs all clustered into geometric patterns and were bordered by low verdant box hedges; oftentimes a bird bath stood at their center. Other flowers and plants grew rampantly in plots, confined by a border of masonry to keep them from spilling onto the gravel path. Numerous potted plants were decoratively placed on the ground, atop pedestals, even hanging from structures made specific for their use.

As they walked along the gravel avenue, nature's sounds abounded, keeping Christina and Amanda curiously searching for the buzzing bees, shushing dragon flies, and fluttering butterflies making themselves heard.

Lord Matthews turned and directed them to where a long arbor, thickly entwined with yellow Lady Bank Roses, stood. The thick blanket of sprawling flowers over the man-made frame kept the sun out and created a shaded tunnel. The long cool passage was lined with stone benches and offered a private respite for either reflection or intimacy for its visitors.

His lordship laughed when they passed the first of several stone benches and assured his mother's guests, "Fear not, Lady Amanda, Miss Rothsborn, I would not think to betray your trust. You will take note my feet are moving diligently along without decreasing speed."

"Your behavior is above reproach, my lord. Amanda and I applaud you prodigiously for refraining from what must be an overwhelming temptation to persuade us to sit."

"You wound me, Miss Rothsborn, though I admit justly," he grinned.

Amanda laughed at their banter and then in an effort to direct their conversation to more appropriate topics remarked, "The flower is named after Sir Joshua Banks' wife I believe."

"You are familiar with our nation's esteemed botanist?" he asked.

"Well, I know his expeditions introduced many plants to our society. The rose specifically came from China."

"Indeed. Sir Banks named variations of this climbing rose, which smells very much like a violet, in honor of his wife. He gave my mother her first cutting and ever since, she has plagued the man for other foreign flowers. If we turn at the next crossing, I will show you the bougainvillea he brought from Brazil when he accompanied Captain Cook on the Endeavour Expedition in 1766. However, to see the glory of his work, you need to visit nearby Kew Gardens where he is Director."

"The garden is very beautiful," remarked Amanda.

Lord Matthews released a dramatic sigh, then said, "I fear our time is at an end. I dare not keep you longer, though there is much to see. Perhaps, we shall approach the garden as a relay race and I shall release you to another gentleman whom your mother finds acceptable."

"You are impertinent, my lord," laughed Amanda. "But I must admit your idea has merit. Shall you return us to my mama, then."

They made their way back to the plush lawn area where guests hovered around tables covered with fine white linen offering a large array of food and drink. Liveried footmen served guests, weaving their way around them to present trays of crystal flutes filled with champagne and delicious appetizers for their indulgence. Lord Matthews delivered the ladies back to Amanda's mother and left them with a proper bow and improper wink.

Christina looked to see if Jason had arrived and though she did not spy him, she was pleased to see Lord Breckman. She rushed forward to greet her new friend and informed him he was needed as an escort to view the gardens. When he agreed, she enthusiastically pulled him over to be introduced to Amanda and her mother. Lady Larksborough approved him as a proper escort for her girls and watched him take them back to the garden from which they had just returned. As they neared the gravel path to the garden, Lord Breckman, in answer to Christina's query, remarked he had seen Captain Brentwood near the French doors exiting to the east lawn. Christina's widening grin did not go unnoticed from her friends and needing no excuse to leave them, she hurried to the doors of the Mattington mansion where she was told Jason was last seen.

She was disappointed not to find him there and ventured through the French doors and deeper down the hallway in search of him. The heavy smell of polished beeswax beckoned her to enter a room she guessed was either a library or study, and was stunned to see the Duke of Aubry sitting at a chess table sans partner. She could make out the pieces from where she stood and saw the duke's bishop was at risk.

Aubry looked up to see who interrupted his concentration and raised an eyebrow when he saw Miss Rothsborn was the culprit. He waited for her to speak, to explain her presence, or to bob her deferential head and leave.

He did not rise as he should to greet her as he would a lady of the realm. He knew his son would not be pleased, but he meant his obvious insult to frighten her away, especially since his stern gaze had proven ineffective. He waited for her to scamper off and was surprised when she walked forward and remarked, "Your bishop is in jeopardy, your grace."

"Another hidden talent, Miss Rothsborn?"

"If you wish, your grace."

He was tired of waiting for Mattington to return and if the chit wished to challenge him, then he was happy to oblige her. "Well, sit down and make yourself useful. Our esteemed host was called away and I do not expect him to return. How well do you play?"

"My papa finds no fault with me."

"How is he? Unemployed?"

"You underestimate him, your grace. He prospers."

"Good. I always liked him. Do not think I did not value him just because I did not wish to call him family."

Christina sat down and immediately took his bishop with her knight. He responded by taking her rook, setting himself up to check her king.

"You must not let emotion cost you your game, Miss Rothsborn."

"Tell me, your grace, aside from class, why do you find me so ineligible for your son?"

"He is second in line to a dukedom. Should something happen to my first born or should Marcus have no sons, then Jason would be the next duke. If you were married to my son, then you would be his duchess for which you are ill-qualified."

"You find fault with my manners or my ability to run a household?"

"Not with your skills, but with your nature. You do not own the disposition to be a helpmeet to my son. I have seen you with your betters and have seen you falter."

"You speak of arrogance, self-importance?"

"The *noblese oblige* must be confident in their decisions and judgments. We are responsible for many and must use our power decisively. It is not a role for the meek. A duchess must be commanding and intrepid. You are neither."

"You think I am afraid?"

"Yes."

"But not of you."

He laughed. "And there lies the conundrum, Miss Rothsborn, and perhaps the reason my son finds you most fascinating."

"It would need to be more than fascination, your grace, for me to become a naval mistress."

"You would accompany him to sea?"

"Yes."

When Christina rose as if to depart, he heatedly exclaimed, "We are not finished, Miss Rothsborn!"

"I fear I am, your grace." Christina looked at the board, smiled and left. She was so intent on making a proud exit, she failed to return the way she came, instead trespassing further into the Mattington mansion. She saw no one as she walked down the wide hallway lined with matching inlaid mahogany console tables, acclaimed wall paintings, and polished brass sconces. A thick Axminster carpet below her feet covered the breadth of the hallway, silencing her steps, but not her thoughts, *"Am I a fool to think Jason and I could find a future together. Do I have the fortitude to be the wife he needs, deserves?"* Before she could answer her own questions, she was startled out of her reflections when someone grabbed and pulled her into a private alcove. She was about to scream until she saw it was Jason who abducted her.

"Where have you been, Christina?" he chastised. She thought it bizarre he should be upset when she was the one nearly scared out of her wits. The more she thought about it, the more her placid face scrunched in anger. She was ready to offer her rebuke when Jason quickly softened his tone to explain, "I have looked everywhere for you. I even waited outside the woman's retiring room for the better part of a quarter of an hour, until one of the ladies offered me her company in compensation for my missing lady."

Unable to mask her tinge of jealousy, she asked, "And how did you respond, Captain?"

Jason grinned at her obvious dislike of the lady's proposition and quickly explained, "I thanked her prodigiously, of course, but then I declined, telling her I belonged to another. I made my bow and moved my feet as fast as possible to remove myself from her person. I was just making my way outdoors when I spied you."

Soberly, she informed, "I have been keeping company with the duke in the library."

Jason's brows drew together in concern. "Did he insult you?"

"Nay," soothed Christina. "He challenged me to a game of chess."

"And the victor?"

"You are looking at her."

He chuckled. "Excellent. It is good to humble the old man on occasion. Is that all that happened?"

"He told me of my inadequacies."

"What do you mean? I asked if he insulted you?" Jason released Christina and she thought he was going to challenge his father, so she held onto him and explained, "I asked him why he found me ineligible. Do not be angry with him for being honest. He finds me too meek to become a member of his family. I am sorry to say I do not bear enough arrogance to become a Brentwood."

Jason laughed. "I must disagree, Christina. I often find you full of yourself."

Christina pushed at his chest in exasperation. It was then she realized how close they stood and her heartbeat quickened.

"Do be serious, Jason," she chided softly.

"I am being serious. I have already seen you acclimate yourself to our mighty *ton* coming to be one in their company. At present, you are being coveted for your musical abilities, but once they get to know you, then you will be sought after more genuinely. I fear marriage to me cannot compare to Town life, especially when it has embraced you earnestly."

"I am a commoner."

"As is Beau Brummel, yet he is an arbiter of fashion and Prince George's esteemed friend."

"Your point is taken, but you know an alliance with me brings you no dowry or advantage of any kind."

"I beg to differ. Will you not bring me your love and fidelity?"

"Yes, but is that enough?"

"More than I could hope. Christina, do you love me?"

"Yes."

"Will you marry me?"

Christina did not even hesitate. She spoke a fervent "yes" from her heart before her mind had a chance to impede her, and within seconds she found herself wrapped up in Jason's arms being kissed. A frisson of excitement and warmth engulfed them, making it remarkably difficult to stop, but Jason remembered where they were, broke their kiss and stepped back.

In a rush, he explained, "I will call upon your father tomorrow. There will be no time for banns. I can be called to duty any day. As soon as I speak with your father, I will secure a special license." His speech left him breathless. Christina saw his shoulders rise when he took another breath and soberly asked, "You are sure?"

"I am sure."

"Even if my father does not accept you. You will have no regrets?"

"Will you?"

Smiling, he replied, "Never."

"Nor will I," grinned Christina.

Jason kissed Christina quickly and then escorted her back to the *al fresco* party. Christina looked forward to spending ten minutes in the garden with Jason and hoped for a repeat performance of his kiss in the Lady Banks' Rose Arbor.

Chapter Twenty-Two

Christina practically yelled, "What do you mean I am to be presented at St. James Palace? I am no debutante."

Christina and her father had just settled themselves in her aunt's drawing room when Dewksbury explained why he summoned them. The idea frightened her out of her seat and had her pacing the floor as though her movement could change what she heard. To and fro she went, her heart racing. She only paused when a member of her family spoke.

Her uncle countered, "That is debatable, Christina, since the act of making your curtsy to our queen marks you one."

"But, Uncle," she asked, "Why now? My position in Society has not changed."

"I beg to differ, Christina," answered Dewksbury. "Prince George himself requests your presentation. In addition, your salver I understand is filled with cards from the highest echelons of society. You will need to be formally introduced to Queen Charlotte to accept many of those invitations where royalty is included."

"Papa," she begged. "Captain Brentwood asked for an audience with you today. You know why. There is no need for me to do this."

"If for no other reason than that, Christina," Stephen replied. "I must admit it pleases me, as it would your dear mama, to see you accepted by her peers."

Priscilla exclaimed, "Christina, she would be so happy for you. Why do you hesitate?"

Stephen prodded, "Are you afraid, Christina?"

Christina remembered the duke's words. *"I have seen you with your betters and have seen you falter."* The memory angered and resolved her. "If I was, Papa, I am no longer. You are right. If I wish to marry Captain Brentwood, then I cannot ignore the sphere into which he was born. I will make my curtsy."

Priscilla informed her niece, "I have had Mary looking through all my old trunks in the attic for my presentation dress, Christina. It is old, but the queen still insists on full court dress. A few alterations and fresh ostrich feathers for your hair and you will be ready to make your curtsy tomorrow."

"Tomorrow? Why so soon?"

"Prince George wishes to hear you play," answered Dewksbury. "I would not want you performing to his particular group of friends at Carlton House, so I suggested he hear you play at Amanda's Ball."

"Lady Larksborough must be thrilled," commented Christina. "The prince in attendance will make Amanda's Ball the most talked about event of the Season."

"Let's retire to my suite, Christina, where I told Mary to bring my court gown. We have a lot to do to prepare you for tomorrow. Besides refitting the dress, you must practice walking in it and making your deep curtsy. You know you must exit walking backwards, never turning away from Queen Charlotte. The three foot train can be a challenge if you do not practice."

"Very well." Christina looked at her father and frantically rattled off, "You will return home to await Captain Brentwood....Oh! I forgot I have my rehearsal with Monsieur Gervas this afternoon. I will not be at home later to receive Captain Brentwood. You must ask him if he wishes to call on me here. No...do not ask him...tell him he should call on me here."

"Do not worry, Christina. I will await his call and convey your message."

Before Christina left the parlour, she said to her uncle, "It is very kind of you to let Aunt sponsor me, Uncle. I am sorry to burden her with something you preferred she not do."

"I have misrepresented myself badly, Christina," he replied. "It would honor me for your aunt to escort you to meet the queen, but I believe to do so, would initiate gossip. I am sorry, you thought otherwise."

"But if Aunt is not sponsoring me, then who?"

"The Countess of Marksby, of course. Your cousin, the earl, is the head of your mother's family and the highest rank of us all. The honor is his to administer."

"I doubt he even knows who I am," she retorted.

"That will be corrected. Marksby and his countess will meet us at St. James Palace tomorrow. He has not been much of a cousin, but he will do his duty to you."

"But why?"

"Because, dear girl," replied her uncle. "You are worthy. Chin up. All will go exceedingly well."

Christina followed her aunt into her bedroom suite in time to see Mary laying a large bundle of material on her aunt's bed. She exclaimed, "Aunt! This could not possibly have been your *come-out* dress. The skirt is mammoth!"

"You forget, Christina, formal court dress requires hoops. The fashion is of our early queen's reign. She insists all debutantes wear the outdated style as a sign of respect."

Christina walked over to her aunt's bed and ran her hand over the crystal and pearl trimmed bodice with lace edging the neckline and sleeves. She noticed how the beading traveled down the overlay skirt in lanes and picked up a swath of the skirt to feel its weight. Shocked, she exclaimed, "Aunt, it is extraordinarily heavy! How on earth did you manage to carry so much weight on your person?"

"Very carefully. Had I known you were to make your curtsy, Christina, I would have had a lighter dress commissioned for you. As pretty as the jewels make the dress sparkle, the weight is an unnecessary burden for any debutante to carry. Especially when the young lady is already worried about falling over when she makes her regal curtsy. However, at the time, proclaiming my family's wealth took precedence over my comfort."

Christina laughed. "Did my mama wear such an ostentatious gown?"

"I dare say she did and carried herself magnificently, as you shall. Now, we don't have much time, so let's get you in your undergarments and hoops. You can practice maneuvering in them, while Mary goes and airs the dress. Then, she can press it before you try it on."

Christina waited with her uncle, and the Earl and Countess of Marksby in the long gallery room at Saint James Palace. As the minutes ticked by, it seemed more debutantes and their sponsors filled the royal room to capacity, which was not hard to do considering the large hooped dresses the young ladies were required to wear.

No one would have guessed Christina wore her aunt's old court dress, for it was fashioned like every other newly-made dress worn by the other debutantes. Her low-cut bodice fit her remarkably well and her skirt fell to a perfect length. Even so, the dress was far from comfortable. Her stomacher pinched her waist, her beaded skirt and train were enormously heavy, and her hoops made it impossible for her to sit down, or to walk around with ease. Everything about her attire was a trial. The delicate lace hanging from her cropped sleeves and protruding from her bodice scratched and irritated her skin to distraction. It was all she could do to keep from rubbing her chest and arms for relief.

The stagnant air smelled of perspiration and conflicting perfumes. Christina feared she would be the first debutante in earnest to swoon before her name was called to meet her queen. Her unforgiving dress prevented her from taking a much needed deep breath. Overheated and exhausted, she felt like one of the limp ostrich feathers pinned into every debutante's coiffure.

Her introduction to the Earl and Countess of Marksby was an astounding disappointment. She could discern no familiarity between the earl and her loving aunt. If he was ever handsome and charming, as her aunt was beautiful and graceful, it did not show. A life of overindulgence in food and leisure marked his features. His girth was wide. Everything about him was pudgy and grim. His conversation was insipid, and like his supercilious wife, he acted as if they were royalty themselves. The diamond parure she wore sparkled their brilliance in the light and were equal if not superior to the other jewels displayed in the room. The smirky smile she made as she nodded to her peers confirmed her satisfaction in knowing she had outshone them. She was far from friendly, too busy with her own consequence to give Christina any notice.

Christina could see nothing to recommend the Earl and Countess of Marksby, and she hoped after today, she never had to engage in their company again. She wished she could pace to dissipate the energy making her nervous, but she could barely turn in her hoops with all the debutantes waiting to make their curtsy. No doubt, they were as nervous as she, though her worries began the day before when Jason failed to meet with her father. He was not negligent, he had sent a note asking to meet today instead, but he had failed to mention the reason behind his absence yesterday. Christina wished she could make her way to Aubry House and ask him directly what was wrong, but protocol kept her from boldly seeking an audience with him. She was so absorbed with possible scenarios for his absence she did not hear her name summoned to the Presence Room.

Her uncle smiled at her and kissed her cheek, assuring how he would be waiting for her return. She gathered her train over her arm and with Lady Marksby made her way to meet her queen. The countess presented her card to the Lord-in-Waiting and together they waited for Christina's name to be announced. In preparation, another Lord-in-Waiting spread out Christina's dress train.

Christina heard her name and bolstered her courage. She pulled her shoulders back, lifted her chin and took a deep cleansing breath before presenting herself to her queen. Queen Charlotte did not recall her family name and Christina saw the queen search her features for something familiar. She thought a glimmer of recognition sparked the queen's eyes, but it must have been a weak one for the queen asked, "Who are your parents, girl?"

The Countess of Marksby intervened, "She is my lord husband's cousin, Your Majesty."

"I do not believe I addressed you, Lady Marksby. Remember not to speak unless I give you leave. I asked who are your parents, Miss Rothsborn?"

"My papa, Your Majesty, is Mr. Stephen Rothsborn. My mama was Lady Elizabeth Marlowe."

"Ah. Now I know why you look familiar. Your aunt is Lady Dewksbury."

"Indeed, Your Majesty."

"I remember when your mama made her curtsy. You look a lot like her. She died young if I remember correctly."

Christina did her best to check her emotions, but having someone say she looked like her mama made her want to cry. Pulling from years of training under her aunt's guidance, she controlled herself enough to reply, "I was but two years old."

Queen Charlotte looked tenderly upon Christina who knew grief at such a young age and who now held herself regally. The queen commanded, "Make your curtsy, Miss Rothsborn."

Christina, with all the eloquence she possessed, made a deep curtsy, practically kneeling on the floor and then took the queen's proffered hand and kissed it. Before she could rise, the queen kissed her forehead, an act reserved for a peer's daughter. She was surprised by her queen's benevolence and almost burst into the tears she worked hard to keep at bay. Before she took her leave, her queen remarked, "Your mama would be very proud of the lady you have grown to be, Miss Rothsborn."

The queen's words made Christina wonder if her dear mama had prompted the queen to speak them, to communicate she was indeed proud of her daughter. The idea warmed her, it was as though she had been hugged. She backed out of the room, taking care of her steps. She was impatient to share the news with her uncle and hurry home to her family, but her success had raced ahead of her. News of the queen acknowledging her as a daughter of the realm spread like wildfire. She found her uncle inordinately pleased and full of congratulations. They were ready to depart when Christina spied the Duke of Aubry exiting the Queen's Presence Chamber and realized he must have witnessed her presentation. As they made their way down the gallery to exit, she saw the duke proffer a small bow at his waist to her. She hoped it meant, like the queen, he also saw a daughter of the realm.

Chapter Twenty-Three

Standing at the threshold of the Larksborough ballroom, Christina's mouth formed an "o." She was amazed at the results Amanda's mother achieved in creating a "heaven-sent" theme for her daughter's *come-out* ball. The walls were covered with glittering white diaphanous material from floor to ceiling. Swaths of the fabric billowed from above like heavenly clouds and had cut-outs of golden stars resting in their hulls. Even the opened French doors were draped with panels of the sheer gossamer and were fluttering from the evening's breeze in a soft and ethereal way.

There was so much material floating about the room Christina worried the candles would set the ballroom ablaze, but then she saw how none of the wall sconces were lit. Only the candles in the grand crystal chandeliers were afire to illuminate and shimmer the room with refracted light. Their flames did not reach the gossamer which eased Christina's concern.

She stepped into the ballroom crafted for an angel and spied a number of subtle details adding to the ambience. Amanda's mother decorated the room with a number of golden cherub statues placed on top of white Corinthian pedestals. The chubby angels looked like sentinels assigned to watch the revelry and Christina had to chuckle when she saw they were robed in Roman togas. Clearly, the countess wanted her cupids covered to censure those young maidens who wanted to look back at them.

There were garlands of ivy and white gladiolas wrapped around the ballroom's structural white columns. Bouquets of various white flowers and greenery filled the tall standing vases embellishing the ballroom. The room smelled fresh, like spring after a rainy day.

Christina had arrived early to ensure the strings of her violin were properly tightened and tuned. She wanted her instrument ready to play when it was time to perform. Lady Larksborough had agreed to the pairing of herself with Monsieur Gervais, a renowned pianist, when Christina reminded the countess how it should be Amanda's name humming in everyone's parlour the next day and not hers. It had not occurred to Leticia how Christina's performance could overshadow Amanda's debut. The suggestion had her quickly agreeing to the duet.

The stage looked like a Roman folly. Six foot Ionic pillars were decorated with ivy and placed in a half circle with shiny gossamer draped between their columns. The white *piano forte* did not surprise Christina and she was glad her pastel azure dress would not contrast starkly with the background, nor bring undue attention to her person. She opened her violin case and assured each string of her bow was tuned before making her way to Amanda's room where she found her friend sitting in front of her toilette table.

"Hello, Amanda," greeted Christina as she entered her friend's room and dropped her overnight bag.

"Finally, you are here!" exclaimed Amanda who looked very relieved to see her friend.

"Are you ready for your big night?"

"Hardly, but I suppose I will manage once my nerves settle down a bit. I am glad you are spending the night and you will be able to console me should I falter at my ball." Amanda opened her first finger on her fisted right hand to illustrate a point. She recited, "Mama has assured me the butterflies and shivers are normal." She raised her second finger. "And that one's own ball is like performing on a stage." Her third finger unfolded. "I must remember everyone's eyes are on me." Finishing her recitation, she sprung her fourth finger and said, "So, I must not trip and fall on my face."

"Amanda," laughed Christina, "you will not fall. You are the most graceful woman I know. Now stand up and show me your beautiful gown."

"I fear I will blend into the scenery. Why Mama insisted decorating everything in white when every debutant will be wearing it or a pastel color I do not know.

I hope I am not trampled. No doubt, I will become invisible in the ballroom."

Christina laughed again at her friend's barbs, then quickly sobered remembering her own anxiousness. She said, "You know, I was hoping I could disappear on your mama's stage. I am not looking forward to performing."

"Nonsense, Christina. Your music is perfection. You need not worry. Everyone will love you."

Christina's downcast face had Amanda gathering her skirt and rising from her seat to rush to where Christina stood. "What is it? Has something happened?"

"I do not know, Amanda. I only hope Captain Brentwood attends tonight. I have not heard from him and I am beginning to worry. It is not like him not to call, especially when he is expected."

"He is honorable, Christina. If he said he will come, he will, unless it is beyond his means. It is obvious he cares for you greatly."

"Yes, of course. I do not doubt him, but I fear for him. Do you think he has come to some sort of harm?"

"No, of course not. His family would have heard if he were injured. Besides, he is a captain in His Majesty's Navy, I expect he can take care of himself. He survived Trafalgar after all. Keep your faith and try to enjoy yourself. He would not be pleased to learn your worries about him disrupted your evening. Now make a spin and show me your beautiful gown before we go downstairs. Mama will want to welcome you before all her guests arrive."

Christina left Amanda with her parents to form a receiving line to greet their guests, after which their majordomo would announce them. She had no desire to be formally presented, so she waited in the ballroom for her family to arrive and join her. She stood alone near one of the white columns, watching the string quartet fill the quiet with a sweet melody. The *ton* was fashionably late, so Christina had time to fret over Captain Brentwood's failure to meet with her father. Her mind filled with possible scenarios, from the ridiculous (he hit his head and suffered amnesia), to the tragic (he hit his head and was lost to her). Every explanation seemed to center around his injured head, rather than he had changed his mind and no longer wished to marry her. She did not doubt his love, but he was a thoughtful man. After considering her life as a naval mistress, she worried he decided the life would not suit her, and had simply and quietly "cried off."

Her father's greeting dispersed her sober reflections and seeing him in his formal black attire lifted her spirits. He looked quite distinguished and she was pleased she was able to attend her first ball with her father by her side. His status as a solicitor kept him from being received as a guest in most homes. The noble summoned him for his services, but never socialized with him. She knew he was well respected, but aside from her uncle, she knew no other nobleman who acknowledged him as an acquaintance. Even the Duke of Aubry, who had employed him for over a decade, did not call him friend.

Her father read her earnest face and before she could query him, he shook his head. "There has been no word, Christina. I am sorry."

Christina greeted her aunt and uncle who soon joined them and before long, the men and women fell into separate conversations. Christina and her aunt were remarking on the ballroom decorations when a girl with whom Christina had gone to school, broke into their discourse with a sincere apology for so doing. Surprised at being warmly greeted by someone whose manner had always been condescending to her, Christina reluctantly agreed when the young lady asked the great favor of presenting her parents. Christina saw her aunt's approval of the request. No sooner than the lady and her parents left, than another young debutante approached with her family. The ritual continued, until the music signaling the first dance began to play.

Christina's obvious surprise over the consideration shown her, prompted her aunt to explain. "Your reception by the queen has made its way through every parlour, Christina. The *ton,* in meeting you publicly, is acknowledging and accepting you into their sphere. To be remiss would be an insult to our sovereign, and even they are not foolish enough to do so."

Christina was awestruck. No other word described how she felt. She wondered, "*How is it possible for my life to alter so remarkably in such a short period of time?*" She was about to share her thoughts with her aunt when the room hushed. Amanda's father, the Earl of Larksborough, entered the ballroom with his daughter and walked to the center of the ballroom to open the dancing.

Christina thought Amanda floated like an angel among her clouds. The earl and his daughter took their position for the opening set and soon ladies and gentlemen joined them, taking a place below them in line. Christina smiled when her father requested her first dance. She took his arm and walked onto the dance floor with him, listening to him confess how proud he was of her, and how he knew her mama would be pleased to see her accepted among her peers.

He danced with a lightness of step that bore evidence of a man relieved of the guilt he harbored for casting his daughter from the sphere from which his wife had belonged. If Christina had not known better, she would have thought she was the one being presented to the *ton* and not Amanda. Perhaps, she was, for after dancing her second set with her uncle, she was surprised to find herself overwhelmed with offers. She gave her third set to Lord Matthews and the supper dance to Lord Breckman, knowing if Jason arrived, his lordship would not mind relinquishing his dance.

She was expected to perform after supper, but when His Royal Highness arrived during the third set, she was sure she would be called to play earlier. Prince George liked to make appearances, but he was not one to stay overlong. He was well sought-after; and aside from his intimate crowd, he did not like to be put upon by others.

"I am sorry, my lord," Christina apologized when she saw Amanda's mother hailing her from the perimeter of the dance floor, "but it seems I am called to the podium. You will forgive the interruption to our dance, since it is His Royal Highness who beckons my service."

Lord Matthews smiled. "If you are as proficient as the rumors profess, Miss Rothsborn, then I am as anxious as Prince George to hear you play, and I am glad for the interruption. No apology is needed."

Christina made her way to the stage and saw Monsieur Gervais was already seated at the piano bench ready to perform. They were to play a piece Beethoven composed for the violin and the piano. The Sonata in F major op.24 was composed in 1801 and introduced to her by her aunt, a proficient pianist. Over the years, they learned the music together, and it was a composition Christina could play through rote, should her nerves hinder her at all. It was a beautiful concerto piece that brought visions of Spring, some even called it, "The Spring Sonata."

Timing had been Christina's initial concern playing with Monsieur Gervais. She knew the man was more than proficient with the *piano forte*, but she did not initially know if he played with an ear for his partner. Many duets were ruined when a musician outpaced their associate or overplayed them. A connection needs to exist between partnering musicians. Christina and her aunt had an inherent connection, and until she practiced with Monsieur Gervais, she was not sure if their performance would be a success. Her concerns diminished on their first practice for the man had a keen ear and played with feeling.

Christina took her violin and bow out of its case and looked to her audience. She made her deep curtsy to Prince George, set her violin to her collarbone, readied her bow for her first draw, then alerted Monsieur Gervais with a nod of her head that she was ready to begin. The room immediately quieted. Not even a breath was heard when Christina drew her bow across her strings. And in that moment, Christina closed her eyes and immersed herself in her play. Beethoven had an innate ability to compose music celebrating the beauty of nature and Christina liked this particular piece for its simple and elegant melodies.

It took a resounding applause to break Christina from her cocoon and remind her to open her eyes, the outside world having diminished while she played. As much as it pleased her to be admired by the upper echelons of society, the enjoyment of the accolade was fleeting when she looked around the room and could not find Jason.

Her search had kept her from seeing the large girth of the prince strutting towards her in his ill-fitted clothes. When he came into her view, the sight of him surprised her and she took a step back in defense, though she quickly came to her senses before he took offense. She waited hesitantly to see what he would do and was stunned when he took her hand into his own chubby one, kissed it, and offered his earnest compliments. His approbation did not go unnoticed and the room once loud with applause now resounded with chatter. Christina curtsied again to the Prince of Wales, and like Moses parting the Red Sea, Prince George waved his arm and his subjects opened a lane for him and his entourage's exit.

Within seconds, Christina was surrounded by an overwhelming onslaught of nobles bearing compliments. She was thankful when the quartet retook their position on stage and began plucking their strings to announce the next dance. She knew the next set was the supper dance and could count on Lord Breckman to save her from the crush of people.

Tony was there in seconds and moved her away from the suffocating crowd. He looked at her worried face and knew immediately the cause behind it. He apologized, "I am sorry, Miss Rothsborn. I do not know why he is not here. In all honesty, I have not seen him for days, though I know he planned to attend tonight."

"Could something have happened to him?"

"No," he answered with a smile. "The only thing to keep him from you would be orders from His Majesty's Navy."

"My lord! You are a genius! Why did I not think of it? But why did he not send word?"

"Shall I ask the duke? I had plans to call on him if I did not see Brentwood here tonight. I would be happy to beg a moment of his time this evening if it would assuage your concerns."

"My lord, you are a godsend. I hate to impose, but my fears are overwhelming me."

"It would be my pleasure, Miss Rothsborn, to be of assistance to you." Both he and Christina scanned the ballroom looking for the Duke of Aubry; however, it was Lady Lucinda Marsh's eyes who caught their attention. The smug looking lady was making her way over to them.

"Lady Lucinda," greeted Lord Breckman.

"My lord," she returned.

"What brings you into our company, my lady?"

"I was with my parents and the Duke of Aubry when he received a communication. He was remarkably forthcoming with the news Captain Brentwood has sailed. Apparently, he has not seen his son for days and in concern, queried the Admiralty. His request must have received the highest priority for them to respond and deliver him his answer so quickly."

"But, why, my lady," pressed Tony, "do you seek our company?"

Lucinda took affront to his query. He acted as though her presence was unwelcomed. Ignoring the idea, she said, "I came to offer my regrets to Miss Rothsborn. I know she had hopes in that direction. I thought to be generous and extend my deepest sympathies to her."

Christina was overcome with shock and mortification. She had no counter to the lady's remark and suddenly felt ill. She said to Tony, "You will excuse me, my lord. I fear I have the headache and must retire."

"Of course, you will allow me to call on you tomorrow?" he asked.

Christina nodded her consent and left. Tony and Lucinda watched while she made her way to where Amanda stood. Christina informed her friend she was sorry she could not spend the night for she had the headache and needed to return home. She was glad Amanda did not push her for an explanation. Then, she sought out her father whom she knew would convey her home.

After watching Christina take her leave, Lucinda returned her attention to Lord Breckman. She was surprised to be under his scrutiny and asked, "What are you looking at, my lord?"

"Your eyes."

"Many admirers say they are fine," she laughed.

"They are blazing green, my lady, and unless you take care, they will be your downfall."

"You are most rude and I daresay colorblind, my lord. My eyes are blue and one of my finest attributes."

"Your eyes are full of envy, my lady."

Before she marched off, she fumed, "If we were not in a public forum, I would slap your impudent face."

Chapter Twenty-Four

Christina kicked off her quilted counterpane and swung her legs over the side of her tester bed. Strands of her blond hair stuck to her mouth and she frustratingly batted them away. Her body was weary after enduring a sleepless night. She had felt the fool to think someone of Jason's station would be serious about marrying her and her emotions had run the full spectrum, from shock to sorrow, and now, to anger that she had let Lady Lucinda Marsh make her think less of herself and of Jason. Well, she was done feeling sorry for herself and done doubting Jason.

She quickly rose, pulled on her bell cord, and when her maid arrived, ordered, "Susan, pick me out a walking dress. I have an important errand to run and am pressed for time. Then, go tell Giles to have a hackney ready for me in half an hour." When Susan looked baffled and failed to move, she exclaimed, "Quickly Susan! I have no time to lose."

Less than half an hour later, Christina hurried down the staircase to make her exit when she saw Tony in the foyer. He had just arrived and her butler looked dumbstruck as to what to tell his lordship. The sound of her footsteps had them both turning their heads to see her approach.

"Lord Breckman has called, miss," informed her butler.

"Yes. Thank you, Giles."

"Miss Rothsborn. It seems I have come at an inopportune time."

"I am indeed on my way out, my lord. You will forgive me if I ask you to call on me another day." To Giles, she asked, "Has my hackney arrived?"

"Miss Rothsborn," interjected Tony. "Please allow me the honor of driving you to your appointment. It would please me greatly to be of service and to inquire on your health."

Christina looked at Tony's earnest face. It was obvious the man was concerned for her welfare and she quickly realized her abrupt departure last night from Amanda's Ball must have worried him. She thought it quite admirable he felt compelled to inquire on her health and seriously considered his offer, if for no other reason than to please him. It was during her reflection she realized she could not visit the Duke of Aubry without a chaperone or escort. She needed his help and decided to accept his Providential aid.

"Thank you, my lord. That is most generous of you."

Christina accepted Tony's escort down her front steps and his help into his curricle. She watched him make his way to take his own seat and then once he was settled, declined his offer of a lap blanket. She knew Tony was not obtuse to her anxiety. There was no other reason to explain her uncontrollable trembling other being cold, but she was far from cold.

Tony started his pair of matched bay horses moving down the street before he asked her, "Miss Rothsborn, I have worried about you since your abrupt departure last night. Are you feeling better?"

"You are kind, my lord, to inquire after my health. In truth, I was overwhelmed by the news of Captain Brentwood leaving town. I would not have expected him to depart without word to me. You may have been aware he honored me with his attention."

"The honor was all his, Miss Rothsborn. Do not question his feelings or intentions. I do not know why he left in the manner he did, but I expect it was far from his preference."

"Could he not refuse to leave without sending word to his family? It seems barbaric of His Majesty's Navy to ship their officers off without giving them time to say their goodbyes."

"I do not believe the Admiralty a sentimental lot," he replied. "Have you discovered something more?"

"No," Christina admitted. "I just assumed a duke's son would be granted a boon?"

"Brentwood would never use his connection to gain a favor. If he was ordered to ship immediately, then he would do as commanded."

"Of course, you are right," agreed Christina. "It would make it all more palatable if the captain was unable to send any word of his departure. The alternative, I confess, is rather depressing."

After a significant silence, Tony asked for her direction. He looked moderately surprised when she said Aubry House.

"You must think me bold, my lord, but I must know whatever there is to know. Lady Lucinda suggested the captain escaped my clutches, though in truth, I never held him to me. He wished to be with me."

"I do not doubt he did, Miss Rothsborn."

Christina blushed and looked at her clasped hands in her lap. When she looked up she saw they had nearly arrived at Aubry House. "Will you help me seek an audience with the duke, my lord?"

"Of course. Nothing would please me more than to be of assistance to you, Miss Rothsborn. You need only ask me."

Christina's mouth dropped open in surprise. *Was she reading more into his offer to help or was there a tenderness in his voice suggesting more?* She did not have time to determine Tony's approbation of her. He had stepped down from his curricle and was making his way to help her from her seat.

The door opened at his lordship's drop of the heavy lion-shaped door knocker and he handed his embossed calling card to the stern Aubry butler, requesting in tandem, an audience with the duke. The servant let them into the foyer and asked them to wait until he discovered whether his grace was at home. He returned shortly with instructions for them to follow him to the duke's study. Christina mouthed a silent "thank you" to Tony when she saw him remain behind.

"Miss Rothsborn," the Duke of Aubry greeted. "This is a surprise. I was told Breckman requested an audience with me."

"He is waiting in the foyer, your grace. Lord Breckman was kind to escort me to see you. He thought I would prefer a private moment with you and graciously awaits me."

"I have no idea to what purpose you would wish to speak to me?"

"Truly, that surprises me for I thought you an astute man."

The duke raised one eyebrow and a grin almost broke his face. "Are we to trade insults or shall I tell you what you already know. My son has sailed. I did not know of his departure until I sought an answer from the Admiralty. He was commanded into service and I have no idea when he will return. My guess is at least three years.

An audience with me will gain you nothing, Miss Rothsborn."

"Do you love your wife, your grace?"

The question surprised the duke and he answered without consideration. "I never thought about it."

"If she left you without any word, would you seek answers?"

"Of course I would seek answers, but the circumstances are different."

"How?"

"More than being married, we have an understanding."

"Exactly."

"Am I to understand my son proposed matrimony to you?"

"He did."

"Well, I am sorry, Miss Rothsborn, but without a public declaration, you have no recourse to sue for compensation."

"You misjudge me, your grace."

"Then, why are you here?"

"To determine if your son is deserving of my fidelity."

"He will be gone for years. Are you telling me you will wait to see if his affections hold true?"

"Nay, but I will remain faithful until I know what happened to him, and I will not blame him for leaving me without word, if I learned it was out of his control to communicate with me."

"You have surprised me, Miss Rothsborn. Now what will you do? Take advantage of your popularity to ensnare another nobleman?"

"I will do what I always do, your grace. Live one day at a time and place my trust in God to open my heart and give me the good sense to follow where he will lead me."

"And at one point your heart led you to my son."

"Since the age of eight I have admired him. I doubt that will ever change, but I am a grown woman who desires a fruitful marriage. I am not foolish enough to wait upon an impossible dream; especially one I created for myself at a tender age."

"You will marry then and forget my son."

"I will never forget Jason, your grace, but indeed I hope to marry someday. Thank you for telling me what you know about his departure."

Christina turned and made her way to the door to exit. Before she crossed the threshold, his grace called, "Miss Rothsborn?"

"Yes, your grace."

"I want you to know you have transformed yourself. You are no longer a woman unsure of herself and it would be my pleasure to receive you. I hope you will accept any invitation I send your way."

"Will the invitation include my papa?"

"You are negotiating, Miss Rothsborn?"

Christina smiled and raised an eyebrow in retort.

"Very well, Miss Rothsborn. Mr. Rothsborn will be included."

"Just to clarify, your grace. I attend as a guest only. You see, I have retired from performing my violin publicly, so if you thought to invite me for your musical entertainment, you should reconsider your invitation."

"I fear the only talent of yours I seek, Miss Rothsborn, is a rematch to a chess game."

"Then it would be my pleasure, your grace, to accept any invitation you send me."

Chapter Twenty-Five

Jason stood akimbo on the quarterdeck of his ship looking out to sea. His vision was momentarily blocked when a gust of wind tumbled his blond hair over his forehead. He had been battling with his flying bits of hair ever since the wind picked up and chose to prick at his patience. He shook his blond locks back and refocused on the horizon, breathing in the briny air.

His hair was stiff, his skin dry, and his clothes were weathered from the salty sea carried by the winds that sailed his ship. He was used to living onboard and exposure to the sun and sea did not bother him, though the effects were obvious. His blond hair was several shades lighter, his skin was bronzed and his lips were cracked from the harsh elements. He was a born sailor, his muscles and mind honed from the daily work needed to command his ship and unlike others, who had no stomach for rough waters, Jason did not suffer from *mal de mer*.

He was searching the vast Indian Ocean for threat or danger. He habitually looked out upon the waters for peril, even though he had several watchers stationed around the ship and in the crow's nest at the top of the main mast. His job was to protect Britain's merchant ships from the enemy who wanted their goods, though sailors and civilians were also a valuable commodity who brought a hefty sum when sold into slavery.

His ship was cutting through the waves with elegance and his crew, as only the hum of industry proved, worked without err. Sailors swabbed the deck, others worked to tighten a line or secure a knot, and some sat whistling a ditty while mending a sail. All was well, his ship was sound, the ocean was without intruder, so Jason's thoughts, as they often did, wandered to Christina and whether she ended her Season engaged to a man worthy of her. Perhaps, she was even married, spending her summer in her new country estate, for surely she had made an advantageous marriage with her beauty and popularity. He hoped she did not hate him too much and had come to understand breaking their betrothal was the only gentlemanly thing for him to do.

His mind took him back to that day when he was just about to leave his home to keep his appointment with Mr. Rothsborn when he was intercepted by a messenger from the Admiralty. The letter was an order to report to Whitehall where the new navy board held their offices. His foremost thought was to first meet with Mr. Rothsborn; but he was hindered when the messenger explained he was to escort the captain without delay. His dismay further increased when the marine informed him he was ordered to bring his sea chest, meaning he was likely to sail immediately. Jason quickly scribed a note to Mr. Rothsborn informing him he was unable to make their appointment, but had every intention to meet with him. He decided to write Christina when he learned what lay before him.

Jason knew French corsairs were causing havoc with British merchant ships in the Indian Ocean. He expected his orders would be to patrol the waters once the Apollo became available for him to captain. Once the ship was ready, he figured he had a week maybe two for that ship to be provisioned and manned. Plenty of time for him and Christina to wed. What he did not expect was for Captain Shaw of the HMS Ares to slip and break his leg, making it impossible for Shaw to go to sea.

The Admiralty knew the third rate ship of the line was crewed, stocked, and ready to sail. They would not take the chance of pressed sailors escaping ashore. Only a few captains inspired men to volunteer into service and Captain Shaw was not one of them. Press gangs had been used to fill the five hundred numbered crew needed for his ship. Whether you were a sailor or not, as long as a common man had the strength to pull a line, he was essentially kidnapped to serve in His Majesty's Navy, with nothing to promote his service unless he was an officer and could share in the prize money.

There was little to recommend a sailor's life, unless a man loved the sea and adventure. The crew lived and ate together between the lower deck guns, fitting into a space no larger than one hundred fifty feet long by fifty feet at its widest. Each man was allowed fourteen inches to sling his hammock from the low beams overhead to sleep for four hours before his shift started. The food was bad, the discipline brutal, and the pay menial. To keep sailors from running away the Admiralty kept their salary in arrears for six months. The only thing that made them happy was their daily ration of grog: rum mixed with water and the lemon juice that prevented scurvy.

Before the Admiralty even opened their files to search for a new captain for the Ares, Jason's name was recommended. The urgency to fill the post, Jason's exemplary service record, and his noble connection made it easy for the Admiralty to pick him. Jason's only boon after learning his fate was that his own officer, Lieutenant Croft, was meeting him in Portsmouth and sailing with him.

British intelligence determined the Ile de France, an island under French rule in the Indian Ocean off the southeast coast of Africa had become a base from which privateers were operating under *"lettres de marques,"* written legal authority, from the French Governor of the island. Plundering and pilfering, the privateers were launching successful raids on fully-loaded British cargo ships making their way from India to England. Their assaults were causing great losses for England's investors and they in turn, were putting pressure on the Admiralty to stop the piracy. The Admiralty immediately ordered their British frigates to make their way to guard the ocean lanes England was using to ship their goods. Regardless of England's naval strength and her success at Trafalgar, sea battles with France were still being raged and lives lost.

Jason did not have the opportunity to write a letter to Christina until he reached Portsmouth. At first, he did not know what to say. He could be patrolling the Indian Ocean for years, unless the Admiralty decided to completely eliminate the threat of piracy by launching an attack on the French islands harboring the corsairs. Without a safe harbor it would be nearly impossible for the privateers to operate. The idea of battle got him to thinking about whether he could keep Christina safe. The seventy-four gun frigate he would command was an excellent fighting vessel. Fully-rigged with a long hull, the ship was fast and equipped for combat, but after a thoughtful and soul-searching deliberation he wrote and asked Christina to break their betrothal.

He loved Christina too much to ask her to wait indefinitely for his return, or to place her on a ship destined for warfare. Technically, she need not declare anything, since he never spoke with her father or published an announcement, but his heart had been true when he asked her to be his wife, and in everything that mattered they were betrothed. He only hoped she understood and would eventually forgive him.

The flutter of a sail reminded Jason of his duty. He searched the waters, then bellowed out an order for Lieutenant Croft to have the crew trim the sails and look lively. A ship was on the horizon and only time would tell if it be friend or foe.

Christina looked out her bay window and sighed. The heavy-laden sky would keep her from riding with Lord Breckman to Hyde Park. Tony was expected any moment, no doubt apologizing for the inclement weather. As much as Tony was good company, Christina's mind was not on him. She was thinking about her recent discourse with Lady Irene Caulfield.

Christina was returning some borrowed books to Hookham's, the circulating library on Bond Street, when she literally fell into Irene when she tried to harness the books tumbling from her hold. After a moment of apologies, they recalled meeting each other at the picnic hosted by Captain Brentwood. They were so delighted at their fortuitous meeting, they decided to take tea at Fortnum and Mason. Their spot of tea turned into a light luncheon when they fell into easy conversation and neither of them wished to end their visit. Before long, Irene was encouraged by Christina's warm and friendly manner to confide her troubled heart.

"I am here for the Little Season. My parents were not pleased I did not come up to scratch this past Season. They want me to learn to be more congenial. They believe the Little Season will give me time to improve upon my skills to capture an admirer."

"I was sure you had one in Lieutenant Croft," remarked Christina.

"I do, but my parents will not condone a marriage to a mere lieutenant. In truth, they have been patient with me, but my sister wishes to marry and my parents will not allow it until I have secured a husband. They do not wish to diminish my worth or label me a spinster."

"How can that be, my lady? You are but twenty years old."

"I have had two Seasons and I am sure you realize in the *marriage mart* that means two years where noblemen have found me lacking."

"I don't believe it. I am sure you had offers."

"Well, yes, Miss Rothsborn, but in my heart I am already betrothed."

"Is there no hope?"

"My parents are not heartless, but without a son to inherit my father's title, they fear for their daughters' security. You know better than anyone, how tragedy can befall a family. The properties are entailed and there is little affection between us and my papa's heir. My papa provided each of his daughters with a generous dowry, but he is suspicious of any suitor without his own means to provide for a wife."

"He cannot believe Lieutenant Croft a fortune hunter. His own lineage is impeccable. Why his father is an earl, for heaven's sake!"

"Yes, but William is a fourth son with no prospects other than those he makes for himself. He is hopeful for a captaincy, though in truth, the idea petrifies me."

"How so?"

"His only chance of advancement is to distinguish himself in battle. I fear for his safety."

"You must not think that way. The lieutenant is a capable man. He will not act foolishly. Now tell me, will your parents wait for him to be promoted?"

"He does not know it, Miss Rothsborn, but he has till the end of next Season."

"And if he is unsuccessful?"

"Then, I will agree to a contracted marriage."

"You must refuse, my lady, and be true to your heart."

"I have no choice, Miss Rothsborn. I have no means to declare independency or other family to support me. Plus, I cannot be so greedy to hinder my own sister's chance at happiness. My parents will choose wisely someone I can respect and in time love, though never to the degree of emotion I hold for my dear William. I am sorry to have burdened you with my troubles. You must think me an ill friend."

"Never," replied Christina. "I am honored you found me worthy to share your concerns. I only pray your dreams are realized."

The sound of the heavy rain hitting the window pane abruptly returned Christina's attention to her parlour. She smiled knowing Tony, regardless of the storm brewing, would not send a message with regrets but would present himself in person extolling his apology for the bad weather. He was a gallant man and incredibly attentive ever since she received Jason's letter.

My dearest Christina,

I am sorry we will not have our adventure and I was not able to bid you goodbye in person. My orders came by way of escort and I was taken directly to Portsmouth where I immediately boarded along with Lieutenant Croft the HMS Ares. I do not know how long I will be away and understand how you must break our betrothal, since I can offer you no expectation of when I will return. I wish you every happiness.

Yours faithfully,

Jason

Melancholy had befallen Christina and had it not been for Tony's and his sister's friendship she might never have rallied. Christina was sure it was through Tony's insistence she received an invitation from his sister Claire to sojourn at her country manor for the summer. She was to be one of a party of whom his lordship was also a guest. She was not of a mind to accept, but her family encouraged her to go. She knew they were worried about her, so to relieve them of their distress she agreed to attend Lady Hartwell's party.

It turned out Claire's cheery disposition was the perfect medicine to temper Christina's sadness. Her country manor helped Christina mourn her short betrothal in private. She found much to see in the rolling landscape, ornamental lake, Roman folly, and profuse gardens making up the estate, and she enjoyed walking the trails, designed over the years by generations of Hartwells. Tony often accompanied her on her walks and they conversed, finding similar interests in literature and music. She was surprised to learn he played the *piano forte* and before long they were playing duets for their hosts. The evenings were filled with gaiety. Games were played and since Christina was often paired with Tony, an affection for one another grew out of camaraderie. The joy of friendship in an atmosphere where she could be herself healed Christina's battered spirit. With each day, she felt better and had to credit Tony's company for the reason behind her diminishing melancholy. He made her laugh and she was grateful for his friendship.

"Miss Rothsborn!" laughed Tony as he entered Christina's parlour. "I dare say I caught you *woolgathering*. Where have your thoughts taken you?"

"Hello, my lord. The rain has undoubtedly chilled you. Come make yourself warm by fire."

"I am nothing but refreshed, having laid my eyes on you, Miss Rothsborn; however, if you do not show me the beautiful smile I know you own, I will think myself unwanted. Did you not expect me?"

Christina laughed. "In truth, I would have expected a message of regrets from anyone but you, my lord. You have never failed in your promises to me; though, I would have understood if you did not come. The rain is pummeling the ground as we speak."

"I promised you my company. I only wish it was in my power to offer you a fine day to go with it." He walked towards Christina and proffered her a brown parcel tied with string.

"Another gift, my lord?" inquired Christina as she took the package from his hand. She felt him hold on to the parcel, forcing her to look into his eyes where she saw a clear admiration. She worried it threatened their friendship. She liked him profoundly, but she did not want her feelings misconstrued for something more than what she was ready to give. He was extremely handsome owning thick chestnut brown hair and matching eyes that complimented his rugged face. His body belonged to the Corinthian set, trim and muscled, and being the heir to an earldom made him every debutante's dream. The ennui he displayed when they first met seemed to dissipate as they got to know one another. Had she not met Jason Brentwood at the age of eight and given her heart to him, she was sure she would have given it to Tony.

Tony saw the concern in Christina's eyes and released the package into her care. He felt a fool to develop *tendre* feelings for a woman in love with another man. He tried to convince himself he sought out her good company for no other reason than friendship, for her and for Jason. He surmised the captain would be pleased to know someone befriended Christina, though he doubted the good captain would like to know where his thoughts had recently taken him. He found Christina attractive in all things. There were times when he had to check his impulse to declare himself to her.

"What is this, my lord?" asked Christina as she turned the package in her hands."

"I suggest you open it and find out."

Christina untied the string and unwrapped the brown paper to discover a leather bound book. She read the title and exclaimed, "You have acquired *Lady of the Lake*!"

Walter Scott's epic poem describing the struggle between Scotland's King James V and the Earl of Bothwell, head of the powerful clan Douglas, was breaking all records for the sale of poetry. Published in May, the book was selling out before demand was met, many noblemen were putting their name on a waiting list to assure they received a copy. Critiques gave mixed reviews. The *British Critic* said the story was more interesting than any other of Scott's earlier poems, complimenting his charming ability to paint real manners and interesting people; while the *Monthly Review* found the composition careless and the language barbaric.

"You cannot mean to give me this. I know you have been waiting months for your copy," remarked an astounded Christina.

"If I have been waiting impatiently, it is only because I wished for you to have it sooner rather than later. I have heard you speak of it with your aunt and wanted to gift it to you."

"Well, I dare say many parlours are discussing the epic poem with its plots of love, war, and reconciliation. The young ladies find Ellen Douglas, daughter of the Earl of Bothwell, quite the heroine, with her fidelity to her father and the man she loves."

"I thought we could read one of the cantos, since the rain keeps us from riding through Hyde Park."

Christina smiled. "My lord, you honor me with your company. Nothing would please me more than to spend the afternoon reading aloud with you."

"Then let us make ourselves comfortable before the fire. You will of course, read first."

"If it please you, my lord, I will read until my voice is hoarse," laughed Christina.

Tony listened to her calming voice and then attempted to take the book when she finished reading the first stanza. Christina held tight onto the tome, surprising him with her strength. She raised her eyebrow and remarked how her voice was far from hoarse. Tony laughed and grabbed the book more forcefully saying he would never forgive himself should she prove mute. He confessed he took much delight in hearing her speak, but insisted he take his turn. They continued passing the book back and forth to each other, spending the afternoon in enjoyable leisure. Christina took great pleasure in listening to Tony read for he had a talent for delivering poetry. He knew exactly how to express the verses in proper tempo.

The first canto recalled a deer hunt that had every hunter chasing a fast and enduring stag until one knight's horse dropped dead from exhaustion. Tony recited how the knight found refuge with a young woman named Ellen...

"Fain would the Knight in turn require
The name and state of Ellen's sire.
Well showed the elder lady's mien
That courts and cities she had seen;
Ellen, though more her looks displayed
The simple grace of sylvan maid,
In speech and gesture, form and face,
Showed she was come of gentle race.

...and as he read the verses, the tempo of his recitation decreased until he came to an abrupt stop.

Concerned, Christina asked, "Is something wrong, my lord? Are you tired of reading?"

"No, I am not tired. It is just the poem made me think of you. James is trying to recall this lady who has so much grace. She is familiar to him as you are familiar to me."

"You are sounding forlorn, my lord. I think it is time we stop reading before we both turn pensive."

"Yes, that is a good idea, though I hate to take my leave of you. The time is passing quickly and we will both be leaving for the country before long. I wish you would change your mind and spend Christmas with me and mine."

"First of all, you know my aunt expects me to keep her company and be present at Dewksbury for her lying in. Second, must I remind you, your parents have not extended me an invitation."

"Truth be told, I would rather spend my holiday with you and yours, but you know I am dependent on my allowance which my father threatens to hold since I have been negligent to visit him. I spent the summer with you at my sister's country manor if you recall."

"And I am forever in your debt to you and your sister. I cannot show enough gratitude to the both of you."

"I do not wish for your gratitude, Christina."

"Yet, you have it. I will not chastise you for using my Christian name for you are dear to me, but I caution you, my lord. I do not think it wise. I would despair in the loss of your friendship."

"That would never happen."

"Let my experience guide you, my lord. I once gave my heart to Captain Brentwood and as much as I admire him, I could never again call him friend."

"I fear I turned a pleasant afternoon into a Cheltenham tragedy. I will take my leave and if it pleases you, will bring my curricle at the first break in this dreary weather, hoping you are available."

"That would indeed delight me, as would seeing you at the Somerson Ball. You will come? I am keeping Amanda company and it would be nice to have a dance secured."

"I shall insist on your first, Miss Rothsborn."

Chapter Twenty-Six

Christina descended the staircase and saw Tony shake her father's hand and leave. She waited until the door closed behind him before asking her father, "Why did no one tell me his lordship came to call?"

"Because he came to see me, Christina."

"Why?"

"He leaves for the country and wished to make me a formal farewell. He plans to spend the winter at his parents' estate and then travel, visiting his friends and taking in the local sites. He does not think he will return for the Season."

"That is a shame, Papa. I will miss him dearly."

"He expressed a warm regard for you, Christina, so much he felt compelled to provide me with his itinerary, in case you have need of him. I dare say, he would be happy to call you more than friend, should you desire it. He is completely eligible and more importantly, a man of warmth and integrity. I would not be adverse to calling him 'Son.'"

"Oh, Papa! How I wish I could return his feelings. He is everything you say and more. It is because I do hold him in high regard that I could not marry him without owning an affection equal to what he holds for me."

"Many marriages begin with less than regards for one another and have grown into something satisfying. He would treat you well."

"I do not doubt it. I expect he would do everything in his power to make me happy. He is that sort of man, but until my heart is free of Captain Brentwood, it would be wrong of me to encourage him. I will miss his company, but I understand why he has taken his leave."

Her father grinned. "Of course, you are right, Christina. Come, let us break our fast together. You have not yet eaten?"

"No, it is why I sought your company."

They entered the dining parlour and Mr. Rothsborn looked to see if his butler had ironed his daily newspaper and placed it on the table. Christina saw where his eyes went and waved him to take his seat and read his paper, while she went to the side bar to prepare two plates for their consumption. She began to plate their food and stopped at serving kippers. Unsure, she turned to ask him if he wished for any and immediately saw him pale. "What is it?"

He did not equivocate. "We have sustained a great loss, Christina. The French defeated us in the bay of Grand

Port on the Ile de France. Over a hundred of our countrymen are perished and every British sailor captured in what they are calling Britain's Worst Naval Defeat."

In her panic, Christina felt her mouth turn dry and her throat close as she gasped, "Do they list the ships, the men lost and wounded?" Unable to wait for his answer, she rushed to his side and read the article for herself.

The paper gave a detailed account of the bloody naval battle between Britain and France for the possession of the Grand Port Harbor on the Ile de France. A British landing party seized control of the entrance to the harbor. With control of the fortified Ile de la Passe, the British hoped to blockade the French from using the port. However, when a squadron of French ships were seen on the horizon, Captain Samuel Pym of the HMS Sirius decided to lure them closer by raising a French tricolor and transmitting a message using their French code. He told them the British were cruising at Coin be Mire, a rock off the northern coast of the Ill de France and hoped the French squadron would feel safe to port. Pym's plan was to attack them in the coastal waters before they could take evasive action. Unfortunately, four of the five French ships broke past Pym's blockade and found shelter in the waters protected by a series of reefs and sandbanks where only a pilot with knowledge of the area could maneuver safely. Pym ordered his squadron to follow the ships and attack them, but without a pilot to steer them through the hazardous waters, the British frigates became grounded and trapped, indefensible against the onslaught of cannon fire. Two British ships eventually surrendered and two were set afire to prevent their capture by the French boarding parties. The battle raged for days, filling the sea with bloody carnage and the ships' wreckage. Those surviving were taken prisoner.

"I am sorry, Christina," her father replied with remorse. "There are no names listed."

Outraged, Christina exclaimed after reading the article, "Why this battle occurred two months ago in August! How could they not list the names of the killed and wounded in action. Surely, the Admiralty knows of their losses. I must see the duke. He would have news of his son."

Christina looked at her father beseechingly, "You will escort me, Papa. I am afraid of what I may learn."

"Of course."

The Duke of Aubry was not surprised to learn his prior solicitor, Mr. Rothsborn and his daughter, Miss Christina Rothsborn, requested a private audience with him. The Battle of Grand Port headline had alarmed him into barging his way into the Admiralty earlier this morning to demand news of his son. He expected Miss Rothsborn was driven by a similar concern.

"Thank you for seeing us, your grace," greeted Mr. Rothsborn.

The duke nodded to acknowledge his former solicitor's greeting and then waited for one of them to state the purpose of their visit.

Christina asked, "Is Captain Brentwood safe, your grace? Do you have news of him and his whereabouts?"

"I know little, Miss Rothsborn."

"How can that be, your grace? The battle is two months old, surely there is more current information."

"Miss Rothsborn, it takes time for word to travel from a ship, especially one at a great distance. Only today, the Admiralty received lists of the killed and wounded. I expect news will be reported to the commonwealth in the next few days, though I am happy to tell you my son is not on either list."

Christina sighed in relief, expelling the air from her lungs in a rush. "I am so glad." She breathed in, stood a little taller, a little prouder and requested, "I hope you will keep me informed of Captain Brentwood's whereabouts and health, your grace. I would consider it a great boon if you would do this favor for me."

The duke was not surprised by her request, but he could not let it be known he granted favors just because someone asked it of him. He countered, "Only if you do something for me."

Christina looked at her father unsure what to say. Before he could respond, she turned back to the duke and asked, "What would you wish of me, your grace?"

"A game of chess."

Christina, accompanied by her maid Susan, were being taken to Aubry House in the ducal carriage. The duke had sent his conveyance, so Christina could play the game of chess she bartered to be kept apprised of Jason. Upon arrival, the Aubry butler informed her she was expected and was immediately escorted to the duke, unlike yesterday, when the duke had her waiting.

She removed her pelisse and bonnet and handed them to an attending footman before following the butler to the duke's study where she saw him sitting at his chess table. The duke rose upon her entrance and with a wave of his arm directed her to take the seat across from him. Susan was shown to a chair in the corner of the room where she would become invisible to her betters.

Christina removed her kid gloves, put them in her reticule, and then placed her tote on her lap. She saw the duke had given her the White set, to some the advantage, since White went first. She looked up and saw him raise an eyebrow as though acknowledging his generosity, or perhaps his superiority over her play. The idea goaded her and she moved her king's pawn two spaces. The duke matched her move. Back and forth they went, the duke playing soberly, while Christina's mind began to wander after her first moves.

Her queen was now in jeopardy and she expected the duke to take possession of her and the game shortly after. She was relieved when it came to an end. Her heart was not in the play, though the duke looked pleased with his collection of captured white pieces. With aplomb, he said, "You were not concentrating, Miss Rothsborn. I feel you will need to return for a rematch. This game has hardly been played in earnest, though it would surprise me if it is concern for my son that distracted you, since Lord Breckman has been your companion of late. You are reported to have spent the summer with him at his sister's country home."

Christina did not know whether to feel angry or complimented by the duke's interest in her affairs.

The duke's carriage returned again in three days to transport her and Susan to Aubry House for a rematch. Christina had agreed with the duke that she had not put her best effort forward and consented to play him again. The game seemed to follow a similar pattern as the duke collected a number of Christina's chess pieces. He was preparing to take another one when he said, "You do not have many left, Miss Rothsborn. You will risk your bishop if you settle him there."

"You must risk much to win much, your grace."

"As you wish," he replied and captured Christina's bishop, "but it is a careless loss."

"Perhaps, but if I prevail would you grant me a prize?"

"And what prize do you seek, Miss Rothsborn?"

"Have you any letters you can share when Captain Brentwood first became a midshipman. I would like to hear of his youthful escapades."

"He wrote few letters, Miss Rothsborn, and only at the insistence of his captain." The duke smiled. "However, I believe there may be one or two epistles appropriate for your maidenly ears. If you prevail, I will read them to you. What is my prize, if I win, Miss Rothsborn?"

"Another rematch?"

"I doubt I would want one since you cannot seem to offer me any challenge, Miss Rothsborn."

Christina was dumbstruck for a minute, but then she remembered she had another talent the duke appreciated."

"I will play my violin for you, your grace."

"Ah! We are in agreement, Miss Rothsborn. Make your move."

Christina moved her queen to capture the Black king's pawn and informed the duke he was in check. The duke motioned to take the White queen that threatened his king only to learn Christina's other bishop protected her queen from afar. He realized she had sacrificed one bishop in order to distract him from placing his own queen in a position to protect his king. He acknowledged defeat by toppling his king. Without a word, he rose, went to his desk and retrieved from his bottom drawer a packet of letters bound with a gold ribbon. He brought them back to the chess table, unbound them and made two piles. Christina saw the letters in the small pile had a mark on the corner of each one and were probably the letters he shared with his wife. The duke picked the top letter and she hoped he did not choose the one with which she was familiar. He read,

5 November, 1801

Sir,

I am pleased to report I am now proficient in climbing the shrouds and have been put to task on many occasions to tie off the gaskets, unfurl the sails, and stand lookout on the masthead. You can imagine my determination after the debacle I wrote to you about and I do not mind saying no man can claim to beat me up the ropes. They have tried and put money to back up their assertions. You must not scold me for gambling, sir. As a Brentwood, I was duty-bound to prove my proficiency or else be marked a liar. I am happy to inform you I am not without funds.

Your obedient son,

Jason

Christina laughed wholeheartedly and saw how the duke wished to join in though he only cracked a grin. He placed the letter down and picked up another. He raised an eyebrow at Christina and she realized he would not begin to read until she mastered her emotions. She took a deep breath and remarked, "Please, proceed, your grace."

20 June, 1802

Sir,

The captain says I am sure-footed and witted, among other things, of which he has threatened to write to you about. He is a good man and I have learnt much from him. He was at the wheel and allowed me to hold course while the wind was at our back. It was amazing, controlling so much power, and made me understand the responsibility one owned at the wheel. I was glad the captain stood by me, but someday I know I will feel confident to master a ship of the line. I am forever grateful to you ...

"Well, that is enough of that," remarked the duke. "I shall ring for tea and then see to it you and your maid are returned home."

The duke's embarrassment of his son's gratitude charmed Christina and showed her how he had an uncommon affection for his children. Her grin and bright eyes must have revealed what she thought for he rose rather quickly and walked over to pull the bell cord to summon his butler. The large pile of letters the duke had set aside drew Christina's attention and without thought, she picked the top letter, unfolded it, and began to read,

21 February, 1803

Sir,

I have engaged in my first battle and our captain was victorious, a great feat since we were caught unawares and the French frigate was able to fire off a round at our broadside before we could take evasive action. We did not know the French captured the HMS Defiant. When the ship of the line was spied on the water, our captain saw how she was running fast towards us and raised the flags with a coded message which only our navy can decipher. When the frigate failed to reply, he ordered for all hands to clear the ship for action. The drum and fife quickly beat to order. The sailors knocked away the bulkheads, and released and tied down the cannons. I do not know if it was chaos or discipline swamping the ship, but our sailors reported to their stations and made way for war.

All of us midshipmen helped to store away equipment, placed water buckets in strategic places to fight the fires and cool the cannons. We even helped supply the powder for the cannons. Everyone was doing their duty and after the captain called orders to trim the sails and have the ship come about, he ordered his youngest midshipmen below.

We refused and put ourselves where we thought we would be best used. I have to admit my heart pumped so hard I thought it would jump right out of my mouth. Amazingly, the feeling did not freeze me, but energized me. I don't know what I felt, it seems arrogant to say I was excited, but I do know I felt sure of purpose. The euphoric feeling does not last long once the battle begins. Your senses are overwhelmed. I will not describe the sights, sounds, and smells of battle for they are too much to recall, but they will never be forgotten.

I am sorry to say I lost a fellow midshipman. His name was Archibald and the captain will write his parents how he died valiantly defending his country, but the truth is cannon shot exploded our mast and the wooden spears killed Archibald among others. I will miss him sorely. He was a good mate.

We are scheduled to anchor at Portsmouth for we sustained damages. I hope you will come see me.

Your obedient son,

Jason

Christina saw the duke's hand extended with his palm up, awaiting the letter she just finished reading. She placed it in his palm and then took the square of linen he offered her in his other hand. Not until that moment did she realize tears were streaming down her face.

"You have taken advantage of my trust, Miss Rothsborn," chided the duke. "I would scold you as your father should for trespassing into my private affairs, but it seems you have agonized enough."

Chapter Twenty-Seven

Jason lowered his spy glass and handed it over to his First Lieutenant William Croft. William took the instrument and sought out the merchant ship flying French colors sluggishly making its way across the ocean lane. "She is riding low in the water. Do you think she has seen us?"

"She must be fully-loaded to be moving so slow," responded Jason. "Most likely the ship is heavily-laden with pilfered English goods." He took the spy glass back from William and peered through it once again surveying the water around the merchant ship. He pocketed the scope. "She is not alone. Following behind is a square-rigged vessel. No doubt the reason we have not seen her take evasive action. She is confident in her guard. Have the drums beat to quarters, lieutenant. Clear the ship for action and have the cannons loaded and ready to fire as soon as they are in range. They will be shooting for our masts; but I'll not risk them getting off the first shot. We have the wind and the advantage, so we will fire on their down roll and do damage to their hull. Once we broadside her, lead the boarders. Look alive and for all that is holy, don't go and get yourself killed!"

"Aye, sir." replied an excited Lieutenant Croft who snapped to attention, saluted and left to do his duty.

Christina traveled to Dewksbury Hall with her aunt and uncle and spent the winter months with them and their new son. Her father joined them for Christmas and then returned to Town in the new year. She remained at Dewksbury Hall until her aunt was ready to travel to London for the Season.

Priscilla was thrilled at having finally delivered a healthy heir for her husband. The Most Honorable William of Dewksbury Hall made his entrance with a bellow and like the first Norman King of England conquered all who beheld him. Christina spent as much time as possible with her infant cousin, enjoying the marvel of him, and while the respite from London gave her time to think about her past and her future, she was happy to be back in Town. Forefront in her mind were thoughts of Jason, but equally distracting was remembering her time spent with the Duke of Aubry.

He had surprised her by insisting on a recurring game of chess. Most of the *ton* closed up their townhomes and returned to managing their country estates when

Parliament concluded. Few returned for the Little Season. Christina believed the duke stayed in London because he wanted to be close to the Admiralty to stay abreast of news involving his son. She saw too many dispatches being sent to Aubry to believe he wasn't needed there, nor did she believe their chess matches were being played for fun. It was obvious they were both taking each other's measure.

She came to discern the duke was indeed an arrogant and haughty man, but not unfeeling. By the end of their time together, she came to admire him for his steadfast duty to country and family, and for fulfilling the promise he made to her regarding news of Jason.

"He is reported to have captured five prizes, Miss Rothsborn, two enemy frigates and three merchant vessels all heavily-loaded. He is also highly-regarded for saving the wife and daughter of Admiral Matland who were being held hostage for ransom. He has not shamed the family, so I may still call him 'Son'."

Christina thought she saw a small grin almost break the stoic duke's haughty expression and tried to tease it out of him. "I am glad he prospers, your grace. Any behavior less than heroic and no doubt, you would need to banish him from your sight."

The duke smiled and Christina was amazed at how handsome his features became. "Indeed, but this recent prize money will only make him more independent of me and so in his arrogance, he will most likely continue to do as he pleases. He is a Brentwood, after all."

Christina placed her Sevres cup and saucer down on the carved scalloped mahogany tea table occupying the space between Amanda and herself. She was glad her friend was home to receive her and Amanda's mother allowed them to visit in private. She was feeling rather low after her visit with Lady Hartwell. She had met Claire coming out of Hookham's subscription library and accepted her offer to lunch at Fortnum and Mason. Christina had feared she had done something to Claire for which she now needed to apologize. The lady had looked aggrieved when she first came upon her, but before she could even inquire to her unknown affront, Claire blurted how she was sorry she would not be able to call Christina "Family."

Tony's sister explained she was surprised to learn during her Christmas visit at her parents' home how Christina was adverse to her brother's admiration. After all, she had seen Christina show Tony particular favor last summer. Their obvious congeniality with one another inclined her to believe the banns would be read during the Little Season. After all, what was there not to love about Tony? He was everything a lady could desire in a suitor and she felt Christina had abused him dreadfully, allowing him to believe she welcomed his courtship. Claire's disapprobation pained Christina greatly and she inadequately expressed her sorrow in causing Lord Breckman any injury.

Christina did her best to explain how she was not adverse to him. Indeed, she cared for him greatly, but confessed her heart was still engaged to another. Tony, she had insisted, deserved a lady who could return his feelings equally. Claire uttered a harrumph, scolding Christina for foolishly discarding the love of an honorable man of the realm for someone who had not cared to pay his addresses to her.

Amanda offered her consolation, but argued Christina had done nothing wrong to mislead Lord Breckman. She reminded her how he of all people knew she loved Captain Brentwood. She did her best to lift her friend's mood, suggesting they go shopping on the morrow for some fripperies. She wanted some new ribbons to wear with a new dress her *modiste* just delivered and then she asked Christina if she received an invitation to the Manchester Ball.

Christina left Amanda's company in better spirits, though Lady Hartwell's admonishment of her pining for another hurt her pride. The accusation made her think about whether she was capable, even in the future, of marrying someone other than Jason. She entered her home still deep in thought when she heard her father shout. She ran into the parlour to see what was the matter. Surprisingly, she found him looking ecstatically happy. "What is it, Papa?"

"Well, Christina," replied her father. "You are a true debutante now, for I am able to provide you with a dowry of five thousand pounds."

"What are you talking about?"

"Until recently, your uncle has never allowed me to invest in any of his shipping ventures. He said the trade routes were too risky and he could not in good conscious allow me to risk a great loss through him. But with Britain's capture of the Ill de France, making it a British colony in December, Dewksbury permitted me to invest in one of his coalition enterprises. I have made a substantial gain and it is enough for me to provide you with a dowry. It will give you the respect you deserve and I expect you may have the pick of eligible bachelors this Season."

She did not have the heart to tell him she was not interested in marrying anyone else other than Jason.

There were enough notable peers at Lady Manchester's Ball to mark it a success, though it was far from a crush, where people were pressed against one another like a sandwich. Christina could easily move around the ballroom and breathe through her nose without suffering. Many peers still believed that bathing caused the ague and resorted to cloaking their odors in perfume. Unfortunately, the scents mixed with their unwashed bodies and perspiration, only added to their stench.

Lady Manchester liked to host the first ball of the Season. She was renowned for saying she liked to get her obligation of hosting over and done. Rumored to be tight fisted, most believe she reduced her expenses by holding her affair at a time when most of the peerage were still out of Town.

Priscilla had told Christina she would not attend the ball or any formal gala until her new wardrobe arrived and was quite dismayed to learn Christina was not of the same mind. Christina, unlike most debutantes, had no problem being seen in a gown more than once and was of the opinion a gentleman could hardly remember what was worn last week, much less, last Season. Her aunt disagreed, but offered Dewksbury as escort anyway.

"You do not need to stand attendance on me, Uncle," reminded Christina when they entered the Manchester ballroom and she saw Amanda. "Even if I am not partnered to dance, I will gain much pleasure from keeping company with Amanda and a few others I have come to call friend. Please feel free to make your way to the card room." Her uncle patted her hand, released her unto Lady Larksborough's and Amanda's company, and then took his leave of her.

Christina's popularity from last Season had not diminished and she found her company favored by many. Her dance card filled quickly and between dancing and keeping Amanda company, the evening was more than tolerable. She saw Lady Irene on the arm of a gentleman who was clearly smitten with her, though he was old enough to be her father. She watched him leave her side, most likely to secure refreshments, and made her way to greet her.

"Lady Irene, I am glad to see you."

"And I you, Miss Rothsborn. You are here with Lady Amanda, I see, though she is presently on the dance floor."

"Yes, and you?"

"My parents are present and I am in the company of Lord Barrows, a very eligible and hopeful suitor."

"You are resigned then to a contracted marriage?"

"I am still hopeful. Lieutenant Croft has three months to prove himself to my parents before they consign me to a *marriage of convenience*. Perhaps, Providence will favor me and you will see me happy, Miss Rothsborn, even if with Lord Barrows. He is a widower with three daughters. He is in need of an heir and is seeking my good opinion."

"Lord Barrows returns," said Christina when she saw him making his way to Irene with her refreshment. "I will take my leave of you, my lady, but not before wishing you all the happiness you deserve. Remember, you may always call me friend."

"Thank you, Miss Rothsborn. I hope you know you may call me friend, too!"

Christina waited to be introduced to Lord Barrows and then made her way back to Amanda and her mother. She saw Lord and Lady Hartwell enter the ballroom and momentarily felt a pang of sadness. She wondered where was Tony and how he was doing. Her thoughts were interrupted by Leticia. "Well, look who has arrived."

Amanda asked, "Who, Mama?"

"The Duke of Aubry. How interesting. He rarely shows himself this early in the Season. Lady Manchester will proclaim her ball a success with him and the Almack's Patronesses present. I must say I was astonished to see Lady Jersey and Lady Cowper here."

Christina watched the Duke of Aubry approach Lady Jersey. They spoke for only a moment before he looked about the ballroom as though searching for someone. She held her breath when their eyes met and waited for him to move on in his search. His behavior was remarked upon by all and she thought the room hushed, especially when he advanced towards her.

Christina and the Duke of Aubry had reached a mutual respect for one another last fall over the many games of chess they played. First, their competitions were in earnest, but over time, their mutual joy for playing provided them a foundation to build upon. They engaged in strategic discussions regarding their play. As they grew comfortable with one another, they began to share their views regarding things as trivial as fashion to more serious topics like the war between Britain and France. The duke was amazed Christina read the newspaper and even more surprised she could deliver an elegant address on whatever had drawn her concern. Christina discovered the duke was not always sharp tongued and severe. He grinned on occasion, especially when she recalled some childhood shenanigan or surprised him with an astute remark. His momentary lax from his haughtiness led her to believe he found her amusing and enjoyed her company. If nothing else, their shared concern for Jason's welfare allied them. She had mixed feelings when the time came to leave London. She was excited to be with her aunt when she delivered her baby, but she was also sorry to end her visits with the duke. If their last chess game was any indication, she thought he would miss her too.

She had not spoken with him since and could not imagine a single reason for him to approach her at a ball, unless it was urgent, unless he had news of Jason. Aside from the regular arrogance he bore publicly, she could not decipher any emotion and feared he brought her ill tidings. Her body began to tremble, but when she began to sway, her pride strengthened her. She had no wish to become tomorrow's parlour *on dit.* Besides she reasoned, knowing the duke he would not air family business in public. She curtsied and greeted, "Your grace."

"You will give me the honor of this dance, Miss Rothsborn." The Duke of Aubry raised his hand as though waiting for something. Until that moment, Christina had not noticed the music and dancing had stopped, or how the duke's hand signaled the orchestra to play again.

It was a waltz. Christina knew the waltz was still thought too risqué for young maidens and only those debutantes granted permission by the Almack's Patronesses could dance it. "I am not permitted to waltz, your grace."

"I have secured permission from the Almack's Patroness Lady Jersey, the *ton's* arbiter of decorum, Miss Rothsborn. Permission has been granted." The duke presented his arm to Christina and in her frenzied state, she allowed him to escort her unto the dance floor. She saw her uncle in her periphery vision and assumed someone brought the drama about to unfold to his attention. He looked unhappy. She was sorry to aggrieve him. She recognized his severe expression. She had seen it often enough as a child when he scolded her for either acting unladylike or dirtying her clothes.

The "ahs" and the other murmurings brought her focus back to the duke. He raised his left arm and took her in hold. The music played and he began to lead her gracefully across the floor. She was surprised a man who always appeared stiff could move adroitly and if she was not so worried about Jason, she might have enjoyed the dance. She saw other couples join them. A buzzing of speculation pierced the music and followed them in waves as they traversed the ballroom. Christina was afraid her control on her emotions would break if she spoke, so she waited for the duke to tell her his news.

"You will accept this gesture I am making, Miss Rothsborn, as a public declaration I find you acceptable."

"What?!" shouted Christina. Her fear turned into anger. "I have been frantic with worry something happened to Jason and you speak of nonsense. Do not trifle with me. Is he well?"

"Very much so, Miss Rothsborn. Your exclamation has drawn interest. May I have you remove the outrage from your face and offer me a smile. After all, I am doing you a great honor."

"Until this moment, your grace. I never realized how arrogance is indeed a family trait. Honor? Why you nearly gave me an apoplexy. Would you mind explaining yourself?"

"I received a message from my son requesting a boon from me. His friend Lieutenant Croft made enough of a fortune to pay his addresses to Lady Irene Caulfield. I am, as proxy, to present his offer to her parents, Lord and Lady Chadsworth, and then see if the young lady in question wishes to wed the lieutenant tomorrow morning by special license."

"I am very happy for them, but what concern is it to me?"

"My son will stand witness to Lieutenant Croft and Lady Irene at St. George's Church."

"And this concerns me how?"

"My son asked if you were married?"

Christina's pride prickled. "And did you tell him I have discouraged all suitors and pine for him?"

"My message to him stated you have remained constant, but your wishes for hearth and home will soon persuade you to accept any number of offers."

Christina could not help but smile. "You have exaggerated, your grace, but I do thank you for saving what little pride I have."

"I told no falsehood, Miss Rothsborn. I feel a great responsibility for what transpired between you and my son and wish to make amends. Unknown to Jason I purchased two special licenses; one for Lieutenant Croft and one for him, should he choose to use it. I do not know what my son will do should you arrive at St. George's Church tomorrow, but should you wish to find out and are bold enough to risk your pride for a measure of happiness, then the choice is yours. The wedding is scheduled for eleven o'clock in the morning. Now, I must leave you to speak to Lord Chadsworth and you must decide what you wish to do. Regardless, of what you choose, Miss Rothsborn, I want you to know I was wrong. You would make an admirable duchess if called to serve."

The Duke of Aubry released Christina into the care of a very concerned Dewksbury. Overwhelmed, she asked her uncle to take her home. They made their farewells to Lady Larksborough, Amanda, their hosts, and departed. Her mind whirled with questions. *"Am I bold enough to go to St. George's Church? What if Jason has no wish to see me? What if he doesn't want to marry me? What if he does?"*

Chapter Twenty-Eight

Christina's head hurt from all the chatter prevailing in her parlour. Her uncle had returned her home from the Manchester Ball and then went to collect her aunt, whom he knew would insist on offering her opinion regarding her niece's future. The four of them: her father, aunt, uncle, and Christina, had convened and everything, from Jason's lack of making a formal offer to the difficulties of living away from family and all she knew, was discussed and reiterated. The clock struck four chimes before they all agreed they were exhausted. Their only conclusion was when it was all said and done, it was Christina's decision to make. Her aunt and uncle promised to return in time to travel with Christina and Stephen to St. George's Church if that was her wish.

Susan helped Christina change into her night clothes, asking what would become of her if she married and went to sea. Christina told her maid she had a decision to make by morning on whether she would like to accompany her. Susan left with as many worries as her mistress owned. Christina paced in her room with indecision until her eyes caught sight of the model ship Apollo. She remembered the adventure she shared at eight years of age with Jason and how he pressed her into service. She had followed him because she admired how he knew what he wanted to do and she trusted him to do it. She also recalled why she did not hesitate to respond when Jason asked her to marry him last year. Aside from loving him, she agreed because he knew what he wanted and trusted him when he said he wanted her. Jason had faith in them. He believed they could accomplish anything and she realized she believed them capable as well. She was letting her pride and her fear of rejection create doubts. A feeling of relief overcame her when she decided she knew what she wanted to do. When her head finally hit her pillow, her body fell into a peaceful and deep slumber. The last thing she heard was the long case clock chiming five times.

Christina woke well-rested and excited knowing it might be her wedding day. Her aunt and uncle promised to return in time to escort her and her father to St. George's Church for the eleven o'clock service. She rang the bell cord for Susan to help her dress and was too happy to let her maid's sadness sober her.

"Do not look glum, Susan. Today is my wedding and I will not see anyone unhappy. My aunt will assure your employment if you do not wish to accompany me, but now, you must help me dress and pack."

"But, miss. We thought you did not wish to marry the captain, for you would not rise when I came to wake you. You told me to leave you be."

"No, Susan. That can't be. What time is it?"

"Well, past noon, miss. I am so sorry."

Christina was ready to cry and then rallied. Quick! Susan! Help me ready and then you can pack me some clothes. I have a groom to find and must secure my family's help."

Her aunt thought Christina was out of her mind to race after the captain. Surely, a note could be sent to ask him to call upon her. She looked to her husband and brother-in-law for support.

"You will lend me your carriage, Dewksbury?" asked Stephen.

Christina hugged her father, crying a heartfelt, "Thank you!"

Priscilla was ready to expound on her disbelief when Christina hugged her. "Be happy for me, Aunt!" She then went and thanked her uncle.

"I could never tame your adventurous spirit, Christina," he remarked. "I am not about to check your manner now when it seems only a captain will do in making you happy."

They were so busy offering farewells and good wishes they failed to hear the butler announce their guest.

"Jason," Christina gasped in astonishment when she saw the man she loved resplendent in his naval uniform.

"I hope I have not intruded," he said, "but I beg an interview, Mr. Rothsborn."

"You wish to speak with my papa, Captain Brentwood?"

"Yes, Miss Rothsborn. I am a trifle late for an appointment I requested of him."

"A trifle, Captain?" she teased after noticing the worry lines that marked his forehead. He looked unsure of his welcome and she wanted to remove all doubt from his mind by offering him a bright smile and teasing remark.

Her warm reception smoothed Jason's forehead and sparked him to respond in kind. With a grin, he explained, "Perhaps a bit longer, but you will excuse my tardiness as king and country have kept me away."

Stephen intervened. "There is no need for us to speak privately, Captain Brentwood. Everyone here has an interest in Christina's happiness. State your business."

"I would like permission to pay my addresses to your daughter, sir. I have the means to provide for her and unwavering love to offer her."

"Then, I will leave you to speak with Christina. Her family will await her decision in the hall."

Christina watched her family exit the parlour and close the doors behind them, allowing Jason to ask her to marry him in private. While she was happy he had come for her, she was confused of how it all came to be. She queried, "I understand, Jason, that Lieutenant Croft and Lady Irene are to be congratulated."

"I dearly hope so, Christina."

"You did not stand witness to them?"

"Christina, I do not know why you are asking all these questions, but I am distracted with a question of my own, if you will permit?"

Christina almost laughed out loud. When she spoke no more, Jason took a knee and proclaimed, "I have admired you from the moment I met you. Your beauty, strength, intrepidness, wit, loyalty, these traits and more have enchanted me since I first learned your name. As a child you captured my attention and as a woman my heart. I have thought of no one but you this last year. I love you, Miss Christina Rothsborn. Will you marry me?"

Christina's heart overflowed with love and joy. He had not forsaken her, even when honor and duty encouraged him to do so. He was steadfast, honorable, gallant, and he loved her.

"Yes! A thousand times, yes!" she exclaimed. "Now stand up, seal our betrothal with a proper kiss and explain to me why you did not go to St. George's Church!"

Jason was happy to oblige and eagerly took Christina in his arms, planting more than one kiss on her lips. When she again asked about his absence at Croft's wedding, he complained, "What is it with you and St. George's Church. Have you no words of love to profess to me, Christina. I am felicitous of your thousand yeses, but might you express a modicum of words saying you love me too?"

"You know perfectly well I love you, but I will feed your ego and tell you since the age of eight, I have admired you and from the moment I fell into your arms, I have loved you. You own my heart, Jason. My uncle said it first, but I heartily agree. 'Only a captain will do' for me, provided that captain is you."

Christina knew her family waited impatiently for her to inform them of her decision. Pulling Jason with her, she opened the doors and announced she had accepted Jason's offer of marriage. Her family followed her back into the parlour, offering congratulations to Jason and best wishes to her, before making themselves comfortable on the couch and chairs. Jason pulled Christina down to sit next to him and then asked again of her interest in Lieutenant's Croft marriage.

Christina insisted, "You first, Jason. Why did you not stand witness for the Lieutenant?"

"I have spent the morning trying to secure a special license for us, therefore I was unable to stand witness to Lieutenant Croft's and Lady Irene's wedding."

"But why did you not ask the duke to procure one for you when he purchased the lieutenant's?"

Christina knew when Jason squinted at her that he had discerned she knew more than she was telling. When he told her to "give over," she confessed all she knew.

She astounded Jason by telling him his father had sought her out for a dance at the Manchester Ball. Not just any dance, but a waltz. She explained how in ducal fashion, his father had drawn the attention of Society's highest sticklers by gaining Lady Jersey's permission for her to waltz. Jason laughed when with the wave of her hand, she demonstrated how the duke commanded the orchestra to play. Although, Christina was doing her best to make her recollection humorous, she saw how much the duke's acknowledgment of her affected Jason and how he coughed to mask the emotions overcoming him. Even so, she nor her family were deceived. They knew how much the duke's approval meant to him, especially the special license he purchased for Christina and him to use.

Christina continued her story, recalling what the duke said to her while they danced. "He told me," she said, "in case I failed to understand the honor he did me." Imagine my anger. I had thought he sought me out with devastating news of you. I was relieved to learn you were well, but then my temper spiked. I think I told him his arrogance was a family trait.

After the chuckles subdued, Christina soberly revealed how the duke told her she would make an admirable duchess if she was called to serve. The revelation quieted the room. Her family were overcome with emotion to learn the duke finally recognized Christina as the lady they all knew her to be.

"I told you my father would come around," said a grinning Jason.

His remark garnered him a glare from Christina, but then Stephen laughed and diminished his daughter's temper.

"You know," Jason added, " I would have been here earlier if I had known my father purchased two special licenses. The Archbishop of Canterbury led me on a merry chase this morning while I tried to locate him."

"That reminds me, Captain," queried Priscilla. "You never did answer Christina's question regarding why you didn't ask the duke to purchase two special licenses?"

"I feared he might sabotage my plans to marry Christina," he confessed.

Christina turned to face Jason and explained how she had meant to seek him out at St. George's Church, only to be defeated in her purpose by oversleeping. She was about to journey to Portsmouth when he arrived.

Surprised, he asked, "You would have sought me out, Christina?"

Embarrassed, Christina rebutted, "You sought me out. Is my love no greater than yours? Can I not trust you to welcome me, as you have trusted in me to receive you?"

The revelation she loved him enough to follow him to Portsmouth humbled him. He said to her family, "You will excuse us a moment."

"Of course," they each replied with a smugness that showed they knew what he wished to do.

Jason stood, grabbed Christina by the hand which made her laugh, and pulled her towards the hallway where no prying eyes could censure them. He wrapped her up in his arms and looked into her sparkling eyes. She quieted immediately when she saw his serious nature and asked, "What is it?"

"I love you," he declared and then before she could respond in kind, he kissed her. When he finally broke the kiss, Christina grinned back at him and exclaimed, "I love you too!" And then, Jason kissed her again.

Acknowledgements

I am truly blessed to have a wonderful support team who help me with various facets of publishing. I have a group of friends and family who put aside their busy schedules to read my manuscripts and provide me with their most excellent feedback. Their review is a precious gift when for most people there are not enough hours in the day to get what is needed done.

I am grateful for the sharp wit and expertise of my editor Alicia Floyd. She cuts to the chase and tells me when something is good or has gone astray. Nothing pleases me more than to earn one of her editorial happy faces.

My photographer, Christina Brusaca, has a great eye for capturing my perfect book cover. I cannot thank her enough for her talent and patience in working with me and my models who happen to be my son Lawrence and his fiancée Nicole. It was touching to see the real love and attraction they feel for one another captured for the book cover.

I also want to thank my friend Elizabeth Cooper who scouts rare and used book stores for English history and Regency period books for me. I appreciate her kindness and generosity in helping me grow my knowledge of the Regency period.

Thank you friends and family, especially my loving husband Larry, my amazing children, and my ever-inspiring parents, for their continued support and encouragement.

About the Author

Teresa Sweeney is a wife and mother of four adult children. She dotes on her three grandchildren: Lorenzo, Harrison, and Maria. She loves to read, write, and a myriad of other pursuits where she can use her creativity and imagination. She takes great pleasure penning historical romance novels that focus on the charm, wit, and banter of courtship. Visit her website www.teresa-sweeney.com for the latest information on her novels.

www.ingramcontent.com/pod-product-compliance
Lightning Source LLC
Chambersburg PA
CBHW030525310726
48979CB00010B/1803/J

* 9 7 8 1 9 4 0 3 1 9 0 4 9 *